FINAL
PROJECT

Also by Peter Eisenhut

The Pen Project
(Saigon 1967)
Copyright 2016

Boulder Creek Project
(Colorado 1987-1988)
Copyright 2018

FINAL PROJECT

A NOVEL

PETER EISENHUT

BALBOA.PRESS
A DIVISION OF HAY HOUSE

Balboa Press books may be ordered through booksellers or by contacting:

Balboa Press
A Division of Hay House
1663 Liberty Drive
Bloomington, IN 47403
www.balboapress.com
844-682-1282

Because of the dynamic nature of the Internet, any web addresses or links contained in this book may have changed since publication and may no longer be valid. The views expressed in this work are solely those of the author and do not necessarily reflect the views of the publisher, and the publisher hereby disclaims any responsibility for them.

Final Project is a work of fiction. People, places, organizations, and events not a matter of public record, are the product of the author's imagination. Descriptions of publicly known people, places, organizations, geographies, and events, are the product of the author's memory or interpretation, and may be used fictitiously.

Print information available on the last page.

ISBN: 978-1-9822-6427-7 (sc)
ISBN: 978-1-9822-6429-1 (hc)
ISBN: 978-1-9822-6428-4 (e)

Library of Congress Control Number: 2021903318

Balboa Press rev. date: 03/12/2021

FINAL
PROJECT

1

SETTING THE STAGE

J on Wilson died in his sleep of an apparent heart attack the night after Memorial Day, 1988.

Wilson's death was unexpected and a total shock to his colleagues. He liked to jog and seemed to be physically fit. He had a very congenial and compassionate personality and those who knew him liked him. He was also highly respected. Early in his career, he had served in Vietnam as a special ops officer. At the time of his death, Wilson was a high-level officer in the Central Intelligence Agency. His remains would be interred with honors at Arlington National Cemetery.

In March of 1988, Wilson had received intelligence that the Soviet Union had launched a mission to sabotage the missile defense system of the United States. The CIA, the Department of Defense, and the FBI launched a joint investigation and revealed that Wilson's girlfriend, Mary Lou, was involved. Wilson received this news the weekend he died, and it was noteworthy that Mary Lou was the one who discovered the body and called it in. For this reason, his death was suspicious, and the FBI conducted an extensive autopsy. They ruled Wilson's death a homicide by lethal injection.

The FBI investigation of Mary Lou proved that she was a covert Soviet spy and played a key role in the Soviet's mission to undermine our missile defense. Her real name was Inga Sarnoff. She had used several aliases during her mission, and Jon Wilson was not the first person she had killed. Unfortunately, she managed to escape and leave the country before the FBI could arrest her. The CIA blamed the FBI for allowing that to happen, and took it upon themselves to find her and bring her to justice. Then, almost 15 years later . . .

2

THE ASSASSIN

On Friday April 4, 2003, an agent using the code name DR entered La Copa Máxima, an upscale coffee shop and eatery in Heredia, Costa Rica. The location was convenient. The National University campus was nearby. The international airport was a few miles to the southwest, and the metropolis of San José was a few miles to the southeast. It was still early in the evening and the after-work crowd of business professionals, government workers, and college professors had not yet arrived. A guitarist was setting up his gear on one side of the room. The aroma of freshly ground coffee beans permeated the air. DR paid little attention. He walked directly to a secluded corner in the rear of the coffee shop, and met with a distinguished looking man dressed in business attire.

"Good evening, Sir. I'm DR."

"Please be seated," the man dressed in business attire replied. "May I order you a coffee?"

"I'm sure the coffee here is excellent, but I prefer tea."

It was a prearranged exchange of words for security reasons. Although the two had talked a day and a half earlier, they had never met. The exchange was in English.

"We are pleased that we can work with you, and we agree to protect your identity," the man dressed in business attire said, and motioned for the waitress.

"Likewise. We have a common interest," DR responded.

After the waitress arrived and took the order for tea, the man in business attire continued the conversation.

"I understand that you've been given some preliminary information about this operation. Is that correct?"

"Yes, that's correct."

"As compensation for your help, we have arranged to have 25 thousand US dollars deposited into your overseas account. Are you okay with that?"

"Yes, I'm fine with that." DR smiled, thinking, *the money was unnecessary—the motivation to do the job was there without it.*

The two continued to talk as business associates and enjoyed coffee and tea together while the guitar music played softly in the background.

Before they parted, the man dressed in business attire said, "It's very difficult to bring a gun into Costa Rica. I assume you did not. Am I correct?"

"Yes, that's correct. Have you taken care of that?"

"My position in the government allows me to own a hand gun. I keep my hand gun and carry permit in a case under the seat of my Ford sedan. It's parked in the rear of the building. It's the dark blue one with the tinted windows. The case includes a silencer and an ammo clip. I'll assume it has been stolen. I plan to file a report in the morning, but I don't ever expect to see it again. You'll also find an empty carton on the seat. Take it with you. Your target probably has a desktop computer. It may contain valuable information. Remove the hard drive, insert the drive into the metal sleeve and into the carton. The carton has a name and hotel address on it. Deliver it to the address written on the label before eight tonight. Oh, and one more thing. It's important that you protect your identity. Are you prepared to disguise yourself in the manner we discussed?" DR nodded in the affirmative. "Before you arrive at the target's home you must be wearing it, and you must keep it on until you complete the total mission."

Then he handed DR an envelope and said, "This envelope contains the home address of your target and directions to get there.

I assume you've already been given background information on her, so I won't repeat that. Questions?" he asked, noticing a puzzled expression on DR's face.

"Yes. Have you assessed the security at the address?"

"Like most homes in the area, it has the typical wrought iron security fencing topped with razor wire, a locked pedestrian gate, and a locked garage gate. You can expect that the doors into the house itself will also be locked."

"I see. Do you have keys?" DR quipped.

"Funny! Anything else?"

"Yes. What about an electronic security system?"

"We have determined that no alerts would be sent to a location outside of the house, like to a security service or to the police."

"Does she live alone?"

"Yes, she does. No pets either."

"Should I expect the target to be at home?"

"Our surveillance indicated that on Fridays she usually returns from the National University campus in Heredia after six thirty in the evening. It's only five twenty-five now so you have time," he said glancing at his watch. "However, you will probably need time to put on your disguise and the traffic can be unpredictable. You had best be on your way."

With that, DR, the would-be assassin, stood up, said goodbye to the man dressed in business attire, and exited the rear door of the coffee shop.

DR retrieved the empty carton and the gun-case from the Ford, walked around to the front of the building, and got into a rented late model Toyota.

A shoulder bag on the passenger seat contained the required items of disguise. These came out and the carton went in. DR took a few moments to apply some makeup and don the disguise. The disguise was a ladies' black loose-fitting long-sleeved top, a silky neck-scarf, a ladies' wig, a pair of stylish glasses, and dangling earrings. This complemented the black slacks, and black walking shoes already being worn. *Now I like the way I look*, DR muttered sarcastically. *I never looked better.*

Then DR opened the gun case and removed a Sig 2022 hand gun, a silencer, and a magazine containing twelve 9mm bullets. The gun was small and light weight. It would tuck under the waist band of the pants and be concealed by the loose-fitting top. The silencer would fit into a pants pocket.

Before starting up the engine, DR opened the envelope and read the enclosed note. It had the name and address of the intended target. The target's name was Maria Martin. The address was a home in Rohrmoser, an old neighborhood on the eastern side of Pavas, a district within the Province of San José, west of the city. Rohrmoser was considered an upscale neighborhood. Many high-level government officials and ambassadors lived there and several embassies, including the U.S. embassy, were nearby.

Following the enclosed directions, DR avoided traffic by taking a back road down to Route 1, and then followed Route 1 southeast toward the city of San José. Along the way, Route 1 crossed the *Rio Virilla*, and at this point the river had carved a deep canyon below the bridge. The sun had not yet set, and while crossing the bridge, DR could still make out a blue ribbon of water far below. Seeing it for the first time, normal people would marvel at the scenic view, but DR was not a normal person and remained focused on the mission.

About thirty minutes after leaving the coffee shop, DR arrived at the home of the intended target, and parked the car on the street at a location close to the residence. DR got out of the car and walked toward the residence carrying the shoulder bag containing the empty carton and a small tool kit. The gun was tucked into DR's waist band.

The residence was a small one-story house placed endwise to the street. A short, paved driveway to the right of the house led from the street to a gated garage. As expected, eight-foot-high security fencing topped with razor wire ran along the sidewalk and then up the left side of the driveway all the way to the garage. Two-thirds of the way up the driveway, a pedestrian gate and a path led to the main entrance on the other side of the house. DR walked to the gate and pressed a button on an intercom mounted next to the gate. No one answered. Then DR walked to the gate protecting the garage and peered in between the bars. No car. Clearly the target was not yet home. DR saw no easy way to get past the locked gates, to say nothing of the doors into the house which would also be locked. Looking around, there was no sign of a security camera on this house, and none were visible nearby.

The sun had set and twilight was fading. With the low humidity, the temperatures were cooling quickly. While walking back down the driveway, and following the sidewalk back to the car, DR was thankful for the warmth of the black long-sleeved top. On the way back, a man walking a dog said, "*buenas tardes señora*" as he passed. DR responded with a simple *hola* and nodded politely. *The darkness, the disguise, and the lack of a nearby security camera should protect my identity,* DR thought. Back in the car, DR patiently watched the residence. A lamp came on at the pedestrian gate and then later, another inside the house shined through the security bars covering the two windows facing the street—probably on timers. The only other light would be from sparsely spaced street lamps.

At 6:35 p.m. a car pulled up the driveway and stopped just short of the garage gate. A middle-aged woman got out and used a key to open the two halves of the security gate. She swung them outward, got back in the car and pulled all the way forward into the garage. As she did this, DR donned a pair of latex gloves, readied the gun, grabbed the shoulder bag, and walked quickly up the driveway to the entry of the garage. The woman reached for her purse, got out of her car, and swung the car door shut. As she turned to walk back toward the garage entrance and shut the gate, she was confronted by her assailant.

"*Buenas noches señora.*"

She stopped short and looked up. A look of panic spread across her face as she saw the gun and realized it was too late to respond. Still six feet away, DR fired two bullets from the Sig. The first hit her squarely in the chest, and the other hit her in the throat. Blood-spatter landed on the side of the car and on the garage wall to the left. She fell backwards and landed with a thud on the concrete floor. Her purse spilled next to her. She lay motionless. Her white blouse slowly saturated with blood. It was a ghastly sight, but DR watched, suppressing any signs of emotion, until assured that she was dead!

DR remained calm and cool and retrieved the two bullet casings from the floor being careful not to pick up any trace of blood. Then, DR reached into the woman's purse and pulled out her cluster of keys. To help block any view of the body from the street, DR closed the garage gates and relocated a trash bin between the gate and the body. At the rear of the garage there was an exit door that led toward the house. Rather than risk stumbling over the body, DR walked around the passenger side of the car to the exit door, and then walked from the garage across a covered patio to a sliding glass door that led into the kitchen at the rear of the house. One of the woman's keys worked and the door slid open.

As soon as DR entered the kitchen an ear-splitting beeping pierced the air, loud enough to awaken the soundest of sleepers. *Oh no, a security alarm. Wasn't I told otherwise?* DR looked around, but no security alarm panel was in sight. The cluster of keys were still in DR's hand. *Two remote fobs; only one car.* DR pressed the red buttons on each. The beeping stopped! DR breathed a sigh of relief, but hoped that no one had been alerted by the alarm.

DR passed through the kitchen and a small dining area and began looking for a bedroom or den that might have a personal computer. The house was well-kept with nice furniture, premium woodwork, and tile flooring. Artwork hung from the walls. According to the information that DR was given, friends and associates of the target knew her as Maria Martin. They knew her as a retired teacher and expat from Canada who was in her 50's. She taught English at the National University in Heredia. She also tutored the children of government officials. She did the tutoring in the client's homes. It paid well. Typically, a tutor of her caliber could earn more than 500 U.S. dollars per month, about 150,000 colons in the local currency. In 2003, if you were a resident and not a tourist, you could get by on that much income in Costa Rica. However, DR considered the luxury of the neighborhood, house and furnishings, and knew she was either living rent-free or had more income than what came from teaching and tutoring. If she did retire from a teaching job in Canada, a small pension of only $1,000 per month, would make a big difference, but DR knew the truth.

DR exited the dining area, passed through the living room, and continued down a short hallway. At the end of the hallway, facing the street, was a large master bedroom. The door was open and the light was on. DR took a quick look inside and didn't notice a computer, but did notice suitcases that were almost completely packed, and wondered why she was planning a trip. *Had she been pre-warned of an impending threat?* Then DR exited the bedroom and went back up the hallway. On the left side of the hallway, was a shut door. DR opened the door, flicked on the light switch, and went into a good-sized den. A newspaper lay on a side chair. It was in a foreign language—not English or Spanish—the Cyrillic letters suggested Russian. Then, there it was. A desktop computer sat atop an old wooden desk. As instructed, DR disconnected the power cord, removed the casing of the computer, pulled out the tool kit from the bag, removed the hard drive, and inserted it into the protective sleeve and carton that was provided.

Then DR did something that was unexpected. Feeling the need to make a strong political statement, DR took a sheet of blank paper from the printer, pulled a magic marker from a container on the desk, created a makeshift sign, walked back into the garage, and put the sign next to the body. The sign said:

¡JUSTICIA PARA UN ESPÍA RUSO!

After collecting the tool kit, the gun, the spent shells, and the carton with the hard-drive, DR calmly walked out of the garage, made sure to lock all doors and gates, and went back out to the rental car. The gun was returned to the gun case and put into the shoulder bag with the keys, and everything else.

Now the hard-drive needed to be delivered. The address on the carton was for a Juan Diego, room 299 at the Hotel Grano de Oro. The hotel was two miles east of the residence on the other side of Sabana Park and on the western edge of the city of San José.

DR arrived at the hotel around 7:25 p.m. and parked the car on the street, hoping no local hoods would try to vandalize it. Still wearing the disguise, DR walked quickly into the hotel lobby and approached the manager at the lobby desk.

"Please hold this package for Señor Diego in room 299."

"I would be happy to deliver it to his room, madam," the manager replied.

"No need. He told me he would pick it up after returning from dinner."

"Okay madam. I will hold it for him. Who should I say it's from?"

"DR."

"*Bueno lo haré,*" the manager responded in a friendly tone.

"*Gracias.*"

DR then exited the hotel via a rear door and returned to the rental car in just enough time to dissuade two locals eyeing the car from making their move. *The police should really do more to patrol the neighborhoods.* Back in the car, DR drove to a nearby McDonald's restaurant back in the direction of Rohrmoser, and parked in a space toward the rear of the restaurant that was unlikely to draw attention. A commercial dumpster was only ten yards away. The area around the dumpster was not well lit and did not seem to be in the view of a security cam. *Doesn't matter anyway,* DR thought. *If no one discovers the items that I discard before the dumpster contents go to the landfill, there will be no reason to review the video-cam recordings.*

While still in the car, DR removed the wig, the glasses, and the gloves, and stuffed them into the shoulder bag. Reaching into the back seat, DR grabbed a new pair of shoes. The old shoes went into the shoulder bag and the new ones went on. DR removed the unwanted makeup with wipes and stuffed them into the bag as well.

It seemed a shame to get rid of an expensive weapon. Yet, it needed to be done—but where? DR considered the Rio Virilla that passed under Route 1, but the highway was a dangerous place to be, and conspicuous as well. *Oh, what the hell,* DR thought, *it was in a latched case. The dumpster was as good a place as any.* According to a notice on the dumpster, the next pick up would be on Monday—*not much chance of discovery before then. And besides,* DR reasoned, *if the gun was found, it would be traced back to its owner, who would have reported it stolen.* DR stuffed the gun case and the pull-over top into the shoulder bag, zipped it shut, carried it to the dumpster and threw it in.

Now it was time for a break. DR walked into the McDonald's, used the restroom, and then returned to the car satisfied that the mission had been successful.

3

SHARING INTELLIGENCE

Two days earlier, on Wednesday evening, CIA officer Donna Wolf had flown into Juan Santamaria International Airport near San José, Costa Rica (SJO). It was her first trip outside the United States since her illness, but one she had looked forward to for a long time. After meetings in the morning, she had taken a commercial flight from Baltimore's BWI with a change in Miami. There had been inclement weather, and the plane in Miami had been delayed by almost an hour. She was glad to finally make it to her destination. She passed through border control, retrieved her bag, and then went to the car rental area to pick up her car. Being very observant, she couldn't help but notice that all the full-sized rental cars were Toyota Camrys. She also noticed that one of the tires on the car she was offered was about to go flat. She resolved the matter in a professional manner while suppressing her frustration at being delayed another forty-five minutes. They gave her another Toyota Camry and directions to her hotel.

The InterContinental Hotel in Escazu was on highway 27 just southwest of the city of San José. Following the directions, Officer Wolf headed south. She was tired, and the country roads were not well lit. She strained to keep her eyes opened and focused on the road and the road signs. After she passed two small towns already asleep for the night, and took a wrong turn, she wondered if renting a car had been such a good idea.

The official nature of her mission entitled her to have a limo from the U.S. Embassy pick her up at the airport. She also had the option of staying at the Embassy. However, she did not plan that all her time in Costa Rica would be official business, and she preferred the freedom to come and go as she pleased. She had decided to rent a car and stay at a comfortable top-rated hotel. Officer Wolf had used her official diplomatic passport to enter the country, but as a precaution, she had pre-registered at the hotel under the name Donna M. Rice. The hotel would not know her diplomatic status or who she worked for.

By the time she got to her room, it was almost eleven o'clock—one a.m. back in Baltimore. It had been a long day and she was exhausted. She collapsed on the bed and went right to sleep.

****

The next morning, Officer Wolf drove to the U.S. Embassy for a scheduled nine o'clock meeting. The U.S. Embassy was in Pavas, a district to the west of the city of San José, and to the north of Escazu. As the crow flies, it was not that far from her hotel, but a mountain and a river necessitated going east toward the city and then back the other way to the west. Despite the traffic heading into the city and the bright sun in her face, she arrived in only fifteen minutes. She was expected, so after showing her credentials to several people, she could park her car and be escorted to the office of Eduardo Perez. Ed Perez was the CIA Chief of Station in Costa Rica.

Ed Perez was in his sixties. He had been stationed in San José for more than four years and was in his second year as Chief of Station. Although it had turned silver, he still had most of his hair. He was about six feet tall and had an athletic build. He had retired from the military as a Colonel and now had about 23 years with the CIA.

They greeted each other with a polite hug and a kiss on the cheek, as was the custom in Costa Rica. "How are you Donna?" he asked sincerely, while his hands remained at rest on her shoulders. "When I saw you in Maryland last year you were not doing well. You're looking really good now." Ed and Donna had known each other for a very long time and had become close. Early last year after she was diagnosed with cancer, Ed had made a special trip to Langley as an excuse to visit her.

"Yes, I'm much better now," she replied. "The cancer is in remission. My light brown hair has turned darker and now has some gray in it, but it's good to have it back, and I'm keeping it short," she said as she moved her hand along the side of her head.

"Your hair looks very nice."

"Thank you." She knew that Ed was perceptive enough to realize she was also tinting it. No need to mention that. "When you last saw me, I was wearing a wig. It was hot and itchy—"

"Yes, and glasses."

"I still have them as backup, but I'm wearing contacts now . . . I'm so glad to see you Ed. I missed you."

"I missed you too. Please sit. How was your trip?"

"Grueling," she responded. "Got delayed in Miami, and then when I arrived, I was delayed further because the rental car they offered had a soft tire . . . a negotiation ensued—I need to brush up on my Spanish. The trip took eleven hours door to door. Didn't get in until eleven last night—one a.m. my time. I'm not fully awake yet."

"Sorry . . . where are you staying?"

"At the InterContinental in Escazu off Route 27."

"Oh yea, I live near there you know."

"Yes, I remember," she said, remembering the night she spent at his upscale condominium a couple of years ago.

"Perhaps a second cup of coffee will help to get you going?"

"Sounds good."

"Cream, no sugar?"

"You remembered."

"Make yourself comfortable. I'll be right back."

After a few minutes, Ed returned with the coffee. He sat down and they enjoyed several minutes talking and having coffee together.

He and Donna had worked with each other many times in the past. They were colleagues and friends, but after Donna's husband died eleven years ago, they became more than just friends. The younger generation would call it friends with benefits.

Donna turned 61 years old last month. She had more than 30 years with the CIA, but was not ready to retire. In 1966, after college and two years in the military, she had worked as a CIA field agent in Vietnam. But in 1967 she was forced to kill an important enemy agent. It was the first time she had killed anyone, and it troubled her. Then she unexpectedly became pregnant. She left the CIA and it took six years of counseling and motherhood to get back on track. After that, she rejoined the CIA and her career took off. She loved her work and had received several promotions, but then she learned she had cancer. She considered retiring, but she had treatment and the cancer was now in remission. She felt good now, and despite her age and her recent illness she was still a good-looking woman. She had an attractive face without the need for makeup and she still had a figure. She had resumed visits to her local fitness center, and was regaining her strength. One project kept her going—one she had been working on for 15 years and one she was determined to complete. Ed knew it was the reason she was in Costa Rica.

Their conversation turned to business.

"So, what's on tap for today?" she asked

"Well, the information you shared with me when you were here a year ago has paid off. We discovered that your spy, Inga Sarnoff, entered Costa Rica more than three years ago under an assumed identity. We know where she is and what she's been doing."

"Well, as you know I'm here to start extradition proceedings so we can take her back to the United States for trial."

"Yes. I'm ready to help you with that, but I'm going to warn you, it may be an uphill battle. I have set up a meeting this morning with the Costa Rican *Organismo de Investigación Judicial,* or OIJ. It's the equivalent of our FBI and DOJ in the United States. We need to plead our case for extradition. I expect that the Costa Rican *Dirección de Inteligencia Seguridad Nacional* or DIS will also attend. The DIS is their counterpart to our CIA. By the way, we should get going. The OIJ is on the other side of the city, and traffic is usually heavy. We have a car waiting for us downstairs."

****

The chauffer held the door open for them as they were shown into the back seat of a black Lincoln Town Car. Ed sat on one side of the car, Donna on the other, allowing an appropriate amount of space between them. They moved slowly through heavy morning traffic. Looking out the window, Donna watched motorcycles weave in and out between the cars, buses, and trucks. She wondered how people could put up with this every day. She recalled what the traffic was like around the D.C. area back in the States. Commuting from Maryland to Langley was such an ordeal that she had requested an office closer to home, and she was permitted to work out of an office at the National Security Agency (NSA) nearer to where she lived.

An hour later they sat on one side of a conference table in a secure meeting room at the San José headquarters of the Costa Rican OIJ. Facing them on the other side of the table were Director Jorge Rojas of the OIJ and Director Geraldo Alverez of the DIS. Officer Perez had worked closely with both men in the past. According to protocol, they would address each other by their titles. Each Director also had an Executive Assistant with them. They would remain silent. As was the custom for an important business meeting, all attendees were dressed in business attire. The men wore suits and neckties. Officer Wolf wore a long-sleeved white blouse and a dark skirt that came down just below the knees. Officers Perez and Wolf were here to share intelligence on a matter that would be of interest to both parties with the intent of gaining their support to extradite a Russian spy back to the United States to stand trial. Protocol and decorum were important.

"Officer Perez," Director Rojas began, "I understand you have important information that you want me to know about . . . and I do not believe I have met your associate." It was apparent that Director Rojas was well educated and spoke very proper English.

"Please," Officer Perez replied, "allow me to introduce Officer Wolf. She's an experienced CIA officer and is here on a temporary assignment. We understand that you have concerns about last year's national election, and that you have initiated an investigation into election fraud and meddling by outside parties. The result of that election was that the Socialists gained political power by establishing a new PAC party and electing fourteen members to the legislature. I want to assure you that the CIA was not in any way involved with that election, but with the help of Director Alverez of the DIS, we do have intelligence that you may be interested in. That's why Officer Wolf is here."

"I see," Director Rojas replied and looked at Officer Wolf across the table.

"Director Rojas, may I . . .?" Officer Wolf said as she returned his glance.

"Yes."

"My job is to track individuals that spy on the United States. I have tracked a certain individual for fifteen years. She's known to have orchestrated a plan to destroy our missile defense system and has murdered three people in the U.S. and at least two more in other countries. One of the people she murdered in the States was a high-level CIA officer that I worked with. She has been in your country for at least three years now as a legal expat Canadian resident using the assumed name of Maria Martin. In your country she has tutored the children of government officials, including the daughter of Alejandro Gomez, who I understand you put in charge of the election meddling investigation—"

"Whoa, what are you suggesting?"

"*Nada*. We have no evidence that *Señor* Gomez has done anything wrong, but it's possible that Maria Martin is taking advantage of the relationship in some way. Maria Martin is not who she says she is. She's a Russian national. Her real name is Inga Sarnoff. She's a Russian spy!"

"And you have evidence of all of this, no?"

"Of course, and we will turn it all over to you."

"Uh . . . what are you asking in return?"

Now, Officer Perez got back into the conversation. "We would like you to bring Maria Martin in for questioning, perhaps even an arrest," he said with an air of authority.

"Well, I do not know if we have enough evidence to charge her with a crime in Costa Rica."

Officer Wolf looked puzzled. "Director, isn't it a crime to gain residency using a false identification?" she asked.

"That's just it! We have a very thorough residency application process in Costa Rica. I do not understand how she could have been accepted if she was not who she said she was."

Officer Wolf started to answer but Perez spoke before she could. "Director, I know you don't want to hear this. I'm sorry, but we have proof. All her documents were forged. She assumed the identity of a Canadian citizen that had passed away. She had help from her Russian handlers and may—we don't know for sure—have bribed someone in your immigration department. We do have proof that she lied on her application and we can prove that her documents were forged or stolen."

"I see . . . but you are looking for something in return for this information, are you not?"

"We are!"

"What?"

"Director, we have prepared extradition papers," Officer Wolf replied. "We wish to take Inga Sarnoff back to the United States to stand trial for murder and espionage."

At this point, DIS Director Alverez, who had not said a word until now, finally spoke up. "I thank you for the intelligence you have provided. It would help us with our investigation into possible Russian tampering with our election process—"

"Director Alverez *por favor,*" Director Rojas interjected, "Why do you think the *Russians* are meddling in our elections? And do you think that Maria Martin is part of that?"

"Yes, Director I do. The CIA provided us information about a secret meeting that took place in the fall of the year 2000 at the Russian Embassy in Managua, Nicaragua. The meeting was attended by the Sandinista Party of Nicaragua and the Communist Party of the Russian Federation. This intelligence indicates that the Russians have a long-term plan to regain influence in Central America, including Costa Rica. As you know, they had supported the Sandinistas until 1992 when the Soviet Union dissolved. However, the FSLN party is still strong in Nicaragua and there are rumors that the radical leftist Daniel Ortega may regain the Presidency at some point. At the same time, increasing numbers of Nicaraguans and Russians are coming across our border, many of them illegally. If Costa Rica becomes more socialistic and more sympathetic to Nicaragua, the Russians may increase their influence. Meanwhile, the Nicaraguans are encroaching into the Costa Rican territory of Isla Calero and have plans for a missile base there. They have already established a military base. It's only a matter of time before the Russians resume openly sending arms to Nicaragua. Knowing that we have no military, they may think we will be intimidated and assume that we will not be successful when we take our grievances to the international courts. Our intelligence indicates that they have supported Socialist candidates in our country and that they have paid to have dirt sent to the media regarding more conservative candidates. We believe their objective is to influence relations between our country and Nicaragua to allow them more influence and control over both our countries."

"Director Alverez, do you have proof of any of this?" Director Rojas asked. "We are a country of laws. We cannot take legal action unless there is strong evidence of a crime."

"Unfortunately, not enough to stand up in court," Director Alverez replied. "We only have bits of intelligence that allow us to create a plausible picture of the future. However, we will continue to investigate."

"And what about Maria Martin. Do you have evidence that she had been working to influence our election?"

"We have some Director, but again, not enough to stand up in court. We continue to investigate."

"It seems to me," Director Rojas responded, "if we proceed with extradition proceedings for Inga Sarnoff that will alert the people being investigated and have a negative impact on the outcome of our investigation. Furthermore, Costa Rica does not have the death penalty and if there was an extradition, the death penalty would be off the table, and I am not sure why the USA would want to waste the time and expense to bring this to trial in the United States if the death penalty is off the table. Same with the charges of misrepresenting the residence application. Any arrest would alert the people involved in the election fraud, and by the way, if found guilty by the court of illegal entry, the only penalty would be deportation back to Russia. That's hardly a just punishment in my opinion. Yes, Director Alverez is correct. We need to continue investigating until we get all of the facts about the meddling in our election and the influence that Russia exerts over our elected officials."

Sensing where this was heading, Officer Wolf tried to speak up. "Director Rojas, with all due respect, I don't—," but Officer Perez held up his hand and stopped her before she could say it.

"So, Director, are we at a standoff on this?" Officer Perez asked, directing his question to Director Rojas.

"Perhaps, but we *will* consider your objectives, and if Inga Sarnoff should try to leave our country, we will alert you and she is all yours to do as you wish. We would also welcome your continued help in providing evidence that the Russians have interfered with our election."

They all shook hands and the meeting ended.

****

The limo arrived out front of the OIJ at a few minutes past noon. Officers Wolf and Perez were properly shown into the rear seat. As they rode back to Perez's office, they began discussing the situation.

"You know," he said, "Directors Alverez and Rojas made a good point. It will probably take a while for them to complete their investigations and approve extradition. And, once we have her, it will be a great deal of expense to convict her in the United States. And, with the death penalty off the table, we no longer have a bargaining chip in exchange for useful information—not that she would give us any anyway."

"What do you think we should do Ed?"

"It's already afternoon. Let's have lunch. You hungry?"

"I am."

"We can talk more about our game plan and have lunch at the embassy."

They had lunch and they talked, but by the time they returned to his office, nothing had been resolved.

Finally, Ed said, "Let me make some phone calls this afternoon and see if there is another approach for us to take—" He looked into her eyes. "Donna we don't get to see each other very often. Have dinner with me tonight."

She smiled. "Are you asking me out?"

"I am."

"I'd love to, but I'm very tired. The trip here yesterday and the meeting today took a lot out of me. Could we do it tomorrow night instead?" she asked.

"Yes, for sure. I really want to spend time with you while you're here. How about coming over to the office tomorrow morning? We can talk more when we meet. In the meantime, go back to your hotel and get some rest. Okay?"

"Okay." She got up and turned to leave.

"Oh wait. I almost forgot!" he called out.

She turned back. "What?"

He reached into the top drawer of his desk and pulled out a mobile phone. "Here, take this. Your phone from home is no good here. You can use this to make local calls while you're here. Just keep in mind, it's not secure."

"Thanks Ed. See you in the morning," she said as she tucked the phone into her purse and walked out.

4

JUDI AND JOE

Meanwhile, on that same Thursday morning, Joe Garcia was at his office sitting at his desk and reading his emails and text messages. He and a business partner owned and operated a small but successful security consulting and design business located on the north side of the city of San José.

His office consisted of four rooms in rented office space. He had a receptionist in the outer room, his partner's desk in another, and his desk in a third. The fourth room was a combination storage room and office for a second employee who helped with sales and the installation of security products. Officially, his clients included private individuals, local businesses, and government agencies. He specialized in security surveillance. Although not everything he did was legal, he never had any issues with law enforcement.

It was still early in the morning when the following message popped up on the screen:

> *Joe*
> *Urgent. Must meet with you at once. Please call me.*
> *Judi*

Joe knew Judi as a friend of Maria, who was one of Joe's clients. Unlike Maria, who was middle aged, Judi was in her early thirties.

She worked as a waitress at a nearby chain restaurant. For some reason she put an "*i*" rather than a "*y*" at the end of her first name. She also had tattoos in subtle places. Perhaps it reflected her need to be unique. She said her last name was Smith, but she looked Spanish. Once, when asked, she implied that she was from San Diego. Her slight Spanish accent supported that, so perhaps that was true. Joe had worked with Judi and Maria since 2001 and they had become friends.

Joe called Judi and asked her what could be so urgent.

"So, Judi, either the nice weather has increased your desire for male companionship, or you need my help with something. What's going on?"

"Sorry to disappoint, but it's the latter. I need to talk to you about Maria."

"What's going on with Maria?"

"I can't talk about it on the phone. I need to meet with you. Can you meet me this morning at La Favorita Park?"

"Don't know. Possibly. What time?"

"Ten."

Joe looked at his watch. It was already nine fifteen. "Kind of short notice don't you think?"

"Joe please. This is very urgent. I'll bring coffee."

"Okay," he gave in. "I'll see you there at ten."

Joe was bright and had college degrees in engineering and in computer science. His father had worked for the government as a criminal investigator, and Joe wanted to follow in his father's footsteps. After college, Joe began a career at the OIJ investigating drug and sex trafficking. However, he had felt that he was being stifled every time he got a chance to do something meaningful. He also became disillusioned by the degree of corruption he was finding inside the government. Then, seven years ago his father and his stepmother were killed in a suspicious car accident. So, at the age of 30 he decided to take some risks and start a business with a colleague.

Joe knew that Maria and Judi were Socialists. Joe also knew that the three of them were really working for Vladimir Petrov. Petrov was publicly known as an influential supporter of socialist causes. Petrov was the kingpin that directed them. Joe had worked for them for more than three years and his work had been instrumental in the recent success of the new PAC political party. Maria had hired him to provide surveillance of opposing candidates and supporters—mostly those in power. The intent was to reveal corrupt and illegal activities and use it against them to bring the reformers into office—Socialists. Interestingly, Joe's involvement was not all that bad for the OIJ either. Cleaning up corruption was part of their mission. Yet, Joe was not much of a Socialist himself, and politics was not his thing. The job paid well, but if you asked, he would tell you that he agreed to have Maria as a client because he wanted to uncover corruption in the government, and nothing more.

Joe told his secretary that he needed to go out for a meeting and that he would be taking the car. Although he traveled to work on a motorcycle, he and his business partner leased a late model Toyota Corolla for local travel when working. He had worn a windbreaker over his short-sleeved white shirt earlier when he came to work. No need for that now, the day would be warm and sunny. The thermometer outside his office window had already reached 80 degrees F.

The trip took about twenty minutes. He arrived a few minutes early and parked the car on the road bordering the park. *La Favorita* was a small neighborhood park, nicely landscaped with several benches. As he approached the center of the park, he saw Judi approaching from the other side where she had chained her motorcycle. She was carrying a small picnic bag.

Judi was small framed but fit and trim. She was wearing jeans and a casual tube top. The top engulfed her torso from just above her pieced navel to just above her nipples, exposing her tan arms and shoulders. A black tattoo peaked out from her tube top just above her left breast and complemented her jet-black hair. She had a cute face and was attractive in her own way.

They met at a convenient bench and sat down. She opened the picnic bag, and poured coffee into two paper cups. Joe watched with a smile on his face.

"You really did bring coffee," Joe said gleefully. "Thank you!"

"I'm a woman of my word," she quipped.

"Judi what's so urgent about Maria that you couldn't tell me over the phone? Is she okay?"

"Petrov contacted me in the wee hours of the morning. He thinks Maria may be in danger. He said that intelligence sources tell him that a CIA officer from the United States entered the country last night. Petrov thinks she may be here to arrest or possibly assassinate Maria."

"I think you need to fill me in on some details. Why would Petrov think that's the reason for a CIA officer to be here?"

"Okay, what Petrov told me was that prior to coming here, Maria was a spy in the United States and the U.S. wants her for espionage and murder."

"Oh my, I see!" he said with a display of surprise. "I didn't know this about Maria. Have you warned her?"

"Petrov said he would take care of that, but today she's on a job somewhere, and Petrov said he didn't want to alarm her until we knew more. Petrov told me this CIA officer rented a car at the airport last night and gave me the plate number. Early this morning, I came to the U.S. Embassy and waited for her car to show up. I assume she met with the CIA Station Chief. Then, about two hours ago, a limo came and they left the premises. I followed the limo to the OIJ and I watched them go inside. That's probably where she is now. In any case, her rental car was still at the embassy when I went by on the way back here."

"Where do you think I fit into this?"

"Petrov says you have the expertise to get the information we need. He wants you to find out exactly why she's here and what her intentions are. Petrov says you have sources at the OIJ and you may be able to find out what the meeting is about. He wants you to tail her and pick up where I left off."

"Hmmm, I see. I'm kind of tied up today. I could use your help on this. Will Petrov approve?"

"I think so. How can I help?"

"Do you know what hotel she's staying at?"

"No, I asked that. He said she may be at the InterContinental, but can't be sure. Apparently, she used the name Donna Wolf to get into the country and rent a car, but may have used another name to register at a hotel."

"Judi, here's what I need you to do. Follow her back to her hotel today and find out what room she's in. As soon as you know her hotel and her room number, send it to me in a text message. If she sees you that's okay. You will need to come up with some story as to who you are and why you're at the hotel. If you talk with her, find out everything you can. She may reveal something of value. Okay so far?"

"Yes, but I'm supposed to work today."

"What time?"

"My hours are from four to ten."

"I think you should tell them you can't work today, or at least tell them you'll be a couple of hours late. What I need you to do is find a way to get into her room. I know you're good at improvising so I'm sure you will think of something. If she has a phone or a laptop with her you could steal it, but then she would be suspicious. Better if you could just take a photo of her contact lists or get onto her laptop and email any useful info to yourself, or perhaps you will find something else that's revealing. And once inside her room, if you can plant a bug for me that would be perfect."

"Whoa. You're the expert. How do you expect *me* to do all of that . . . and where would I get a bug?"

"I have the devices you need in my car . . . come."

They went to his car and he opened the trunk exposing an abundance of electronic gear.

He gave her a wireless microphone/transmitter and a receiver/recorder. Then he gave her some suggestions on how to proceed. "This is state of the art stuff," he told her. "Not very heavy and not very big. This is the transmitter, also called a bug. It has Velcro on the back and here are several Velcro strips that can be taped onto a surface. Obviously, you need to place the bug where not only she won't find it, but also where the room maid won't. Don't put it where the sound will be blocked or near the TV or near a fluorescent lamp. The best place might be to tape it to the back of the desk or the chest of drawers, or if possible, the back-side of the headboard of the bed. Okay so far?"

"Where do I put the recorder?"

"You don't. As soon as you tell me her room number, I'll make a reservation for you at the hotel, hopefully a room that's on the same floor as that of Wolf." He noticed her expression. And knew what she was about to protest.

"No, it won't cost you," he added. "I'll prepay the reservation. Think of it as a prepaid vacation. However, you will need to show your ID when you check in so I need to know the name on your ID. Is it Judi Smith, or is that an alias?"

"It's really Judi Smith. I thought I told you I was married once, but I kept the last name after we split."

"Okay . . . When I make the reservation, it will be for two people, you and a husband. His first name should be Joseph if that comes up. I will text you back as soon as the reservation is made, but check in time will not be until four, so you need to be late for work. When you check in, make sure and get a second key for your husband. Text me your room number as soon as you check in. I want you to put the recorder into *your* room. Plug it into the wall socket—no need to run down the batteries."

"What about the batteries in the bug? Won't they run down?"

"Oh . . . hope not. The bug is voice activated. Otherwise it would be even smaller. Let me demonstrate how it works," he said and proceeded to do just that.

"Wow, impressive," she said with only mild enthusiasm.

"Meanwhile this afternoon while you're doing all that, I'll check my sources at the OIJ. Then tonight, we'll meet in your new quarters and we'll see where we are on this."

"So, Joe, were you considering spending the night? I wouldn't mind you know."

"Judi, we've discussed this. You know how I feel about mixing business and pleasure," he told her, despite the temptation.

Judi made no secret of her desire to have sex with Joe. He had allowed this once in what he considered to be a weak moment. She proved to be more sexually experienced and kinkier than he was. Afterwards, she had offered him a joint which he had declined. They were from different social classes and backgrounds, and Joe decided that she was not someone he wanted to have a long-term romantic relationship with, but it did not dissuade her from trying. He often wondered why she found him so desirable. Was it his good looks and his intellect, or was it because his inexperience allowed her to feel more in control than she would with other men?

"Well, you know what they say about all work and no play. I think you should reconsider."

He gave her a hard look.

"Okay," she said with a sincere tone of resignation. "You can't blame a girl for trying. But Joe, there is something else I need from you."

He gave her a questioning look. "What else do you need from me?" he asked.

"Your car."

"What? My car? Why?"

"You want me to follow this woman back to the hotel, strike up a rapport with her, and check in. I need a cover story as to why I'm staying at an expensive hotel. It's not likely I would ride a bike . . . more likely I would be driving a late model rental car, especially if I'm traveling with a husband."

"Okay but the car isn't mine. It belongs to the business. My business partner may need it."

"Take my bike. I keep a larger helmet behind the seat. When you come to my hotel room tonight after I get off from work, bring my bike back. We'll see how things go from there."

He knew she was right. They exchanged keys. Joe walked across the park to the bike and watched Judi get into the car and drive off. Then he wrestled with the adjustments on the bike to accommodate his longer legs, put on the ill-fitting helmet he found behind the seat, and sped off in the opposite direction.

5

CASUAL ENCOUNTER

Donna left the embassy and retrieved her car. As she headed east on Via 104, she sensed that another car was following her. After she turned south toward Route 27, she glanced into her rearview mirror only to see that the same car was still behind her. *Could be coincidence*, she thought. But when she turned onto Route 27 and headed west, the same car was still behind her. Now she began to seriously consider that she was being tailed on purpose. Sure enough, when she pulled onto the side road toward her hotel and into the parking lot, her tail did the same. Although she was a little nervous, she had played this game before and knew enough not to panic. As she walked toward the hotel entrance, she noticed a young woman exit the car and follow her. Donna entered the hotel, walked to the elevators and pushed the up button. As she waited, the woman caught up to her.

"Hello," the woman said with a friendly smile. "I believe I may have been following you all the way from the embassy. I hope I didn't freak you out."

"Yes, I noticed," Donnas replied. "I was wondering why you were following me. Did you have business there?"

"I'm sorry if I made you nervous. Yes, my husband just got

transferred there and they put us up here at the hotel until we find a place to live."

"Oh, I see."

The elevator arrived and they both got in. Without thinking, Donna pushed the button for floor six, her floor, and then she asked, "What floor?"

"Six please," the young woman responded politely.

Still unsure about this woman, Donna scolded herself—*should've asked her first. It's been too long since I was in the field,* she thought. *But perhaps I'm just being paranoid.*

Donna left the elevator first and the young woman followed. They arrived at Donna's door first.

"Have a nice day," the young woman said as she walked by. Donna watched her stop at another door far down the hallway.

****

Once inside her room, Donna locked the door, and set her purse on top of the desk. It was getting heavy. She used the phone that Ed had given her and made a few phone calls. Now she was tired. Time for a nap, she decided. She removed her shoes, her skirt, and her blouse, hung them up carefully in the closet, and threw herself prone on the bed. She quickly fell asleep and woke up two hours later. When she awoke, she felt refreshed. It was only 3:30 p.m. She looked out the window—beautiful day. She felt like a swim, so she put on her swim suit, pulled a cover-up garment over her head, and took the elevator down to the outdoor pool. Although it was Thursday, most of the seats with umbrellas seemed to be occupied, but then she saw someone leave, freeing up an umbrella with two lounge chairs. She went over and plunked down on one of the chairs. No sooner had she settled down than she heard someone to her left trying to get her attention. It was the young woman who had followed her from the embassy earlier. The woman waved and walked over.

"No open seats," she said.

"You're welcomed to join me under this umbrella. The other lounge chair is free," Donna said extending her arm toward the chair.

"Oh, thank you so much. I shouldn't get too much sun. This is perfect. By the way, my name is Judi Smith."

"I'm Donna."

"Donna . . .?"

"Donna Rice."

"Where are you from Donna?"

"Maryland."

"You?"

"New York City."

Donna noticed her accent. It was not quite what one would expect of a New Yorker.

"Your accent seems—"

"More like Spanish? I know. I get that a lot. I grew up in Puerto Rico but moved to New York City where I went to college, and met my husband. I think I mentioned that my husband is in the process of transferring here."

"Have you started your house hunting yet?"

"We plan to start big time this weekend. What about you? You were at the embassy. Are you here on business?"

"No, I'm here on vacation, but I have a friend who works at the embassy and I hope to spend some time with him while I'm here. We had lunch."

"Oh, I see," she responded.

"You said your husband just started working at the embassy. What's his name?"

"Joseph Smith." She knew the lie would eventually be discovered if Donna investigated, but it would take time. "What is *your* friend's name?"

"Edward Gardner," Donna replied, knowing that her lie would probably go undetected or be of no consequence.

The two of them chatted for a spell and then Donna was ready for a swim. She noticed that Judi was not wearing a swim suit and politely asked to be excused.

"It's okay," Judi said, "go ahead."

Donna removed her cover-up, hung it on the back of her lounge chair and jumped into the deep end of the pool. The water was cool and refreshing. Donna relaxed and swam a couple of laps before joining Judi on the pool's edge.

"I need to go and fetch my husband from work," Judi said apologetically. "I'm told that the traffic is bad at this time of day so I need to allow plenty of time. Perhaps I'll see you again tomorrow."

Donna replied, "I look forward to it. Drive carefully," and almost immediately dove back into the pool for another swim.

She stayed in the pool for another 15 minutes or so before coming out of the water and heading back to her lounge chair. She dried off and laid back in the chair. She closed her eyes and dozed off. When she awoke the sun was very low in the sky and she decided it was time to go back to her room. She put her cover-up back on, grabbed her towel, and made it all the way to the elevators, before she realized something was wrong. Her room key was not in her pocket. Thinking it must have dropped out near where she was sitting, she went back to the pool to look for it. Unfortunately, she couldn't find it anywhere. So, she went to the main desk in the lobby. Not having any proof with her of who she was, she had a hard time convincing the lady on duty to give her a new key.

"Buenas tardes," Donna said politely. "I'm Donna Rice in room 603, and I'm locked out of my room."

"Do you have identification?"

"No, I just came from the pool."

"We pride ourselves on keeping our guests secure," the lady stated. "We can't just give out a new key to anyone that asks."

"But my identification is in my room, and I need a key to get it."

"Please wait here for a few minutes, madam. I will have a security guard escort you to your room and you can show him your identification when you get there."

The security guard was a young man who seemed very polite and understanding. He opened the door to her room and held it open for her to enter. He suggested she look around and make sure nothing was missing from the room. She noticed her laptop still atop the desk. She checked her purse. Her phone and wallet were there. No money missing. Everything seemed to be as she left it. And then she noticed it. Her key card was on the floor on the far side of the counter that supported the TV. *Did I really forget to take it with me?* she asked herself. She showed the security guard. "Happens all the time, Madam," he said. Fortunately, he never asked for identification She handed him a five-dollar bill, USD, and thanked him for his troubles. Satisfied, he wished her a good evening and left.

Later that evening, after a light meal and an attempt to watch a TV show in Spanish, Donna got herself ready for bed. As she lay in bed, she recounted the events of the day and scolded herself. *How could I misplace my room key? It's just not like me. Perhaps tomorrow will be a better day.* Then she took a deep breath, let it out slowly, closed her eyes, and fell asleep.

6

EVENING PLANS

The next day on Friday, Donna and Ed met again at the embassy and talked.

"How did you sleep?" he asked.

"Very well, thanks. I'm fully refreshed."

"Donna, I talked with Director Rojas again earlier this morning. He said that the OIJ further considered the situation and agreed to arrest Maria Martin on the illegal entry charge early next week and he will allow us to interview her. He said they will consider allowing us to extradite her if we can guarantee that the death penalty is off the table. He said they are also investigating her for possible espionage within Costa Rica. The OIJ wants to interrogate her, and he wants to have time for a search warrant of her house while she's in their custody. He said it may be a week or two before she could be released into our custody."

"Why the change in heart?"

"I think they realize that other than the possibility of minor charges, their investigation is going nowhere any time soon. I think they want information from her, like the names of those in the government that have been compromised. Otherwise, they probably want her out of the country as soon as possible to prevent her from doing further damage."

"But what's our bargaining chip? Why would she talk to us? And even if she does, what would she give us?"

"Well, one idea is that the OIJ uses our threat of extradition for *their* bargaining chip. They will tell her that if she confesses to a crime here, they will not allow her to be extradited. The penalty here is less than what we would impose, especially if she gives them names."

"You mean that after all the work we did to track her down she will get off on a minor charge?"

"Even if she doesn't confess to anything, the OIJ may have enough to hold her long enough to get more evidence. But, if that falls through, they will just let her go—kick her out of the country. If they deport her, we could try to intercept her before she ends up in Canada or Russia. Then, if we bring her back to the United States, the death penalty would not be off the table. This would be the OIJ's bargaining chip. But let me ask you, after fifteen years, do you still have enough hard evidence to convict her of the murders she committed in the United States? And, you know, if we keep futzing around for too long, she may get wind of our intentions and flee before we can arrest her. If we don't intercept her, and if we don't convict her, won't she just reinvent herself and continue spying and murdering people elsewhere? And, I can't help but wonder if the expense will be worth it?"

Donna gave him a hard look and slowly let out her breath.

"Ed, tell me what you suggest," she demanded.

"Donna, I know you have invested a great deal of your time and energy tracking her down and if you were to take her out, I would look the other way."

"You don't mean that," she said sharply.

"Actually, I do. But in the meantime, I think we should play it by the book, keep our options open, and see how it plays out."

Donna shook her head slowly from side to side. "I suppose you're right," she said with resignation.

Then, after a long pause, "Ed, are we still on for tonight?"

"I don't know. Something has come up. Earlier this morning, before Rojas called, I got a call from Langley. It was your boss,

Brian Matheson. I think he forgot about the two-hour time difference. But anyway, he asked how you were doing and wanted to know the status of our endeavor. I told him you were doing fine and filled him in on our stalemate with the OIJ. Then he asked—directed—that I have you do something for him later today. He wants you to meet with a contact near the city of Heredia. He said that this gentleman is a professor at the National University up there and you should meet him at five thirty this evening. He told me where. It's a coffee shop called La Copa Máxima. Every Friday and Saturday evening from five to eight, they have a classical Spanish guitarist. Many of my associates have gone there and say it's an excellent place to relax after work over a cup of coffee and a pastry. I'm sure you'll enjoy it." Then remembering that Donna only drank coffee in the morning and tea the rest of the day, "They have tea as well," he added.

"Did he say what the purpose of the meeting was?"

"Kind of. He said that the professor has a package that he needs back in Langley, and to save time, he wants you to bring it to me so that I can then send it to Langley via the embassy's secure mail service. Other than that, he said you might find the professor interesting to talk with."

"What's in the package?"

"No idea. He wouldn't tell me. You can ask the professor."

"How will the professor know who I am?"

"Matheson said that he already told the professor your pseudo name. You're still using Donna Rice, aren't you?"

"Yup. How do I get there?"

"I'll give you directions in a minute. But first, regarding dinner, I told Matheson that I was hoping to have dinner with you tonight and we talked about where I was going to be. Originally, I was thinking of us eating at a place called Jurgens, but Matheson also asked me to do something for him and Jurgens would not be convenient for me. However, we can still do Jurgens tomorrow. So, I thought that tonight we could meet at the Hotel Grano de Oro. I can be there by eight, if that's not too late for you. You could give me the package and then we could have dinner. The hotel has a bar and a restaurant. I've been there before and the food is good. You okay with that?"

"Sure. How dressy is it? What should I wear?"

"What you are wearing now is fine," he said as he noticed her dressy white blouse and black slacks. "I really like what you're wearing now."

"Please tell me how I get to the coffee shop and then to the hotel."

"Okay. Let me draw a map and directions for you."

Ed reached for a pencil and tore off a preprinted street map from a pad behind his desk. He turned the page over and began drawing a route and making notations on the backside. After a few minutes he turned back to Donna and showed her what he drew.

"Wow, impressive!"

"Well, the information's there, but I think my drawing skills could be better."

"Looks fine to me."

"Alright, so to orient you, here's your hotel down here," he said and circled the initials IC for InterContinental.

Then he repeated the process for the coffee shop, and circled the initials CM for Copa Máxima. "I'll write the address here."

"And finally, here is the Hotel Grano de Oro," he said as he moved his hand to the lower right of his map and circled the initials GO. Then he turned the sheet over. "This side is a street map of the western side of San José," he said, and showed her where the hotel was on the street map.

"Ah," Donna uttered and pointed to the area marked as Rohrmoser. "Doesn't Maria Martin live in Rohrmoser?"

"Yes, she does. Her residence would be just about here on the street map," he said and added yet another circled set of initials. "I think you already have her address," but then cautioned, "Officially you should not contact her. If she knows we're about to arrest her, she might flee. You know that, right?"

Donna gave him a look making it clear she did not like being talked down to.

He got the message. "Sorry, I didn't need to say that, but I do have a suggestion. The traffic going North from here on Route 39 and Route 3 can be very slow. If you leave from your hotel, I would suggest you head back toward the airport on Route 147 the way you got to your hotel on Wednesday, and then take Route 111 going northeast. I would allow about 45 minutes from your hotel. Anyway, take the map with you."

"Okay, Thanks. It'll help."

"And here, take this," he said and handed her an envelope.

"What's this?"

"It's just more information about tonight. You can look at it later."

"Okay."

"There's really nothing more we can do on the Martin project until we hear back from the OIJ next week, so it's a chance for you to enjoy the rest of the afternoon. I'll see you tonight, and we can talk about spending time together this weekend."

"I look forward to it. See you later." She put the map and the envelope into her purse and left the office.

****

Donna went back to the hotel and used the free time to make a few phone calls. She made one to her daughter Brandy to see how things were at home. She made another to Matheson in Langley to get a better understanding of what he wanted her to do that evening. Then she looked up La Copa Máxima in the phone book and called it to verify the venue and the menu. After that, she went downstairs and had a salad and an iced tea. She explored the InterContinental hotel noting it had a nice lounge with entertainment on Friday and Saturday nights. As she entered one of the shops, she spied Judi who noticed and came over. They chatted for a while.

"Hi Donna. What have you been doing today?"

"Touring the city," she responded. "What about you?"

"Well, I've been hanging out around here. My husband took the car this morning . . . said he might need it, so here I am."

For a moment Judi seemed to be gazing at Donna's body and Donna picked up on this.

"What are you looking at?" Donna asked out of curiosity.

"Sorry, but I was just noticing that you seemed to be dressed up—not like a typical tourist."

"Oh well, I haven't been here long enough to know what is expected, and anyway I plan to go somewhere this evening."

"Do you have dinner plans?" Judi asked. Perhaps you and your friend Ed would like to join Joe and me for dinner?"

"Oh, that would be a wonderful idea, but unfortunately Ed and I already have other plans."

"A romantic evening?"

"I hope so."

"Where is he taking you?"

"Well, he mentioned a nice restaurant in a hotel called the *Grano de Oro* but he said he was taking off from work early and I'm leaving around four to go meet him." She looked at her watch. It was already three. "I wanted to browse through the shops before I went."

"Are you looking for anything special?"

"I'm looking for a birthday present for my daughter Brandy."

"Well, I won't keep you. I hope you have an enjoyable evening."

As soon as they parted, Judi contacted Joe and filled him in on what she learned from Donna. Then she rode her bike to her four o'clock shift at the restaurant where she worked.

7

HOT POTATOES

Donna had a smile on her face as she anticipated a relaxing dinner with Ed at the Hotel Grano de Oro. So far that Friday evening, everything had gone as planned. Donna had been to La Copa Máxima and followed her instructions. She had met with her contact and had the package for Ed. Afterwards, she had stopped at a McDonald's to take a break.

As she exited the McDonald's and walked back to her car, she looked at the map Ed had given her to make sure she followed the best route. Many of the streets were one-way and it was night-time. The map had already proved useful. After leaving La Copa Máxima, she thought a car that looked like the one Judi had driven yesterday was following her. Perhaps it was just a coincidence, but to be sure, she had taken some evasive turns and lost her way. It would not happen again. She would be at the hotel on time.

It was almost eight o'clock when she arrived at the Hotel Grano de Oro. Ed was nowhere in sight. So, she asked the hostess if there was a reservation for dinner under Ed's name. There wasn't. Perhaps he had forgotten, or perhaps he used an alias. The dining room seemed busy, so just to be sure, she requested a table for two at eight fifteen in the name of Donna Rice. She had time to kill, so she went to the bar, ordered a sauvignon blanc and waited for Ed to show up.

Almost immediately, some guy sat down on the bar stool next to her and engaged her in friendly conversation. He told her a joke and they were both laughing when she felt a heavy hand on her shoulder. She turned. It was Ed.

"May I interrupt?" he said with an authoritarian tone. At 61, Donna was still attractive, but she also knew how to handle herself. Ed knew this, and she didn't think Ed had any reason to be jealous, but she began to explain anyway.

"Oh Ed, this gentleman was telling me he comes here frequently and that he works at the U.S. Embassy."

The fellow turned to face Ed, and as soon as he did, the expression on the fellow's face suddenly changed from looking cheerful to looking fearful.

"Hello, Juan," Ed said sternly. Then Ed turned his head toward Donna. "I know this gentleman. I was supposed to meet with him ten minutes ago. Looks like I found him. He and I need to talk about something in private. Donna, please stay put. I'll try not to be long."

Then, Ed looked directly at Juan. "Juan you come with me," he commanded.

Ed and Juan proceeded toward the lobby of the hotel as Juan began to apologize profusely. "I'm sorry, Sir. I was distracted. The time got away from me."

"Are you aware of the time? It's after eight o'clock. And what distracted you more Juan? Was it the drink or was it my lady friend?"

"I didn't know she—"

"**Juan** . . . I went to your room ten minutes ago and you weren't there. Where's the package?"

"It's still at the desk."

"Then go retrieve it and take it to your room. I'll be there in five."

"Yes sir."

A few minutes later, Juan came back to his room. Ed was waiting. They went inside.

"Here sir. I'm sorry I was late. Time got away from me," he said and handed him a small carton that was no more than 8 inches by 6 inches by 3 inches in size. Juan's name and room 299 was handwritten on the front.

Ed grabbed Juan's wrist with his left hand, placed his right hand under Juan's chin, and pressed his right forearm upward against Juan's chest, pinning him against the wall.

"Listen carefully. If you want to keep your job, you need to take your assignments more seriously. You understand?"

"Yes sir."

"Okay, you're still welcome to take advantage of your stay here tonight, but I don't want to see you. Understand?"

"Yes Sir."

With that, Ed released his grip, took the carton, went down the hall to a door leading to the parking lot, and went directly to his car. He hid the carton under the passenger seat, relocked the car, and went back to the restaurant bar.

"Donna I'm sorry for that."

"Ed, you seem agitated. Is everything alright?"

"I'm fine, but I think I could use a scotch."

"Ed, he wasn't bothering me in any way."

"No, I know. That's not it."

"Tell me what's going on then."

"I can't talk about it here. Maybe tomorrow when we go touring."

"Are we going touring tomorrow?"

"Why don't we talk about what we will do tomorrow?"

"Okay, but before we do, the host has informed me that a table is now ready in the name of Donna Rice."

"Oh damn. I screwed up, didn't I? I forgot to make a reservation."

Donna was amused and laughed. "I guess you're not perfect, but I love you anyway," she said and affectionately rubbed the back of his shoulder.

Since it was late, they had light meals, but they had plenty to talk about.

"Donna, before I forget, did you go to the coffee shop and did the professor give you a package for me?"

"Yes, everything went as planned. The professor gave me a small carton. I put it in my shoulder bag, but it was heavy and—I hope you don't mind—I left it in my car. Did you need it now? We can go get it."

"No, just make sure I get it before we leave. Thank you for doing this. How was the professor, by the way? Matheson said you might find him interesting."

"Well, I think creepy might be a more apt description."

"How so?"

"I got there shortly after five, took a small table to myself, and ordered tea and what I believed was a Spanish version of a crumpet. It was very good and the guitar in the background gave it the right ambiance. I was relaxing and enjoying my cup of tea when a slick looking gentleman asked to join me at my table. He said his name was Professor Smythe and he was there to meet a Donna Rice, so I assumed it was the person I was to meet. He seemed to be unnecessarily covert, like he was playing a part in a bad cloak and dagger movie. Unlikely that his real name was Smythe either, considering his complexion. After he introduced himself, we talked about what he does. He said he teaches international politics at the nearby University of Costa Rica. And of course, he wanted to know what I did, and I gave him the usual vague answers. But as the conversation continued, he started getting personal, told me how he enjoyed foreign women and how sexy he thought I was for an embassy courier, etc. I asked him about the package he was supposed to give me and he said he wasn't sure if I really wanted it badly enough. I think he was trying to bargain. At some point he put his hand on my leg and at that point I told him he could either give me the package, or the people I worked for would assure he ended up dead. Then he apologized and said he was only teasing me. Like I said, creepy."

She continued. "After he gave me the carton, I asked what was in it and he said he was not allowed to tell me. However, I had talked to Matheson earlier and I already knew. Matheson told me it was a hard drive and contained information from Maria Martin's workplace at the University. Matheson said he would review it with me after Langley had a chance to analyze it. I was feeling uncomfortable with this guy so I told him I had another appointment and needed to leave. If not for the creep, I would have stayed longer, but. It was around six when I left."

"This place is no more than 40 minutes away from the coffee shop. Did you go somewhere else on the way?"

"Traffic was pretty bad, but I still had plenty of extra time, so I stopped at a pharmacy on Via 104." She paused. "Can we talk about the weekend? What have you got in mind?"

"Of course. The last time you were here, we didn't have much time for touring. I thought I would treat you like a tourist and give you a grand tour of the San José area."

"What is it that attracts tourists to Costa Rica?"

"In addition to the beautiful scenery? Costa Rica is also known for its bananas, coffee, hummingbirds, volcanoes, and its *chicas*."

"*Chicas*? . . . What are *chicas*?"

"*Chicas malas* . . . prostitutes. It's legal down here, or at least it is if they don't advertise or have a pimp. It's becoming part of the tourist industry, especially for male foreigners."

"Ed," she said sternly, "I hope *you're* not sleeping with them."

"Well, *chicas* help—"

"No, never mind. I don't want to know."

He smiled. "What I was about to say is that the *chicas* are an excellent source of intelligence for us. But not to worry, we will skip that part of our tour," he said mockingly.

"Okay, but where are we going and what should I wear?"

"Yes, of course. I thought we could start off with a drive up to the Poás Volcano. They say it's best to see it early in the day before any clouds roll in. The observation deck is a short walk from the visitor center. If you want the exercise there are several hiking trails there as well. The views and scenery are unbelievable. Then I think we should go see hummingbirds."

"Yes, you said that Costa Rica is known for hummingbirds. Why is that?"

"Yup. Costa Rica is famous for its hummingbirds. We have more varieties than anywhere else in the world. You like birds, don't you?"

"Yes, I do, but you never struck me as a hummingbird type of guy," she said with a grin on her face.

"Well, Freddo Fresas is a good place to see hummingbirds—and have lunch. Then after that, I thought you might be interested in touring a coffee *fincá*."

"A *fincá*? That's a farm isn't it? My Spanish is not that good."

"It's a plantation. In this case they grow coffee plants. I scheduled a tour for the afternoon at the Doká Estate. After that we can head back to San José in plenty of time for dinner, certainly by seven. I'd like to take you to Jurgens for dinner and afterward, perhaps we could go dancing. How does that sound?"

"It sounds perfect Ed."

"Okay if I pick you up around nine in the morning?"

"Can you call me from the lobby first?"

"Sure, but there is just one problem. I checked, and there is no one registered at the hotel with your name."

"I'm registered as Donna Rice and I'm in room 603."

8

A WEEKEND TOGETHER

Donna's room phone rang at nine the next morning.

"I hope I'm not too early," Ed greeted her from the house phone in the hotel lobby.

"Good morning Ed. Tell me again what you've planned for today. I'm still not sure what to wear. I heard hiking and I heard Jurgens. Isn't Jurgens a rather upscale place. Will we have time to change before dinner?"

"I suggest dressing for dinner, but not quite that dressy, and bringing a pair of dress shoes with you. Wear walking shoes during the day. Also bring a jacket to wear at Poás. Sometimes it can be chilly up there. I'm planning to wear a jacket for dinner but no necktie if that helps, and as far as shoes are concerned, I'll wear sneakers during the day . . . oh and bring your camera."

"Okay, I'll be down in about fifteen minutes. Please wait for me in the lobby."

Several minutes later, she came down and walked up behind Ed who was gazing out the lobby window.

"Hello stranger," she said, catching him off guard. He turned to face her and smiled. In Ed's mind, she looked like a typical tourist. A white sun hat topped her short brown hair, and a pair of Foster Grants dangled from a lanyard around her neck. She was wearing black slacks and a casual white top that showed off her still shapely figure, and she was sporting white tennis shoes, suitable for light hiking. She clutched a travel bag in her right hand and an outdoor jacket in her left.

"Wow! You look really nice," he said with enthusiasm.

"Not bad yourself."

"Here, let me help you with that bag and jacket," he offered.

"Thank you, sir," she said mockingly.

They walked out together and almost in unison put on their sunshades to protect them from the morning sun. It was a beautiful day, not a cloud in the sky, and temperatures in the mid-seventies. They walked towards a new-looking sand color RAV4. He placed her travel bag and jacket onto the back seat.

****

Once inside and belted in her seat, Donna looked around.

"Ed, is this a new car? I don't remember it from when I was here before."

"I got it after you were here, but it's not new."

"Could have fooled me. Car looks brand new. Totally clean and shiny. And the inside is immaculate. Even has that new car smell."

"Well, I just had it done on Thursday . . .. Just for you Donna."

He said that jokingly, but Donna had known him long enough to know that he may have been serious. He was like a boy scout, always prepared. She liked that about him.

They drove off. Donna watched Ed shift gears as he negotiated his way onto Route 27. She could not help but ask about the vehicle.

"I see you have a manual transmission. Is it also four-wheel drive?"

Yup. It's all-wheel drive, but if I need it, I can lock it into four-wheel drive. The roads, including some we will travel on later today, leave a lot to be desired, so RAV4s with four-wheel drive are very popular in Costa Rica. The fact that they are so popular also means that it's easier and less costly to maintain them. Expect to see quite a few on the road as we drive. And, before you ask, the gas mileage is fairly good . . . about 25 miles to a U.S. gallon."

The ride in the car gave them plenty of time to talk and they were both eager to catch up on personal matters.

"You never told me what you did with your free time yesterday afternoon. Were you able to enjoy the afternoon yesterday after our meeting?" he asked.

"Yes, I did enjoy the afternoon. After I took a nap, I walked around the hotel. As I checked out the gift shop, I ran into a woman that I had met the day before. Her name is Judi. She had said that her husband was transferred to the embassy and they were temporarily staying at the InterContinental. She said they were from New York City, but something about her seemed a bit off. She said her husband's name was Joseph Smith. Do you know him?"

"No, and his name was Joseph Smith? Not ringing any bells."

"I told her I was here on vacation, and that a couple of years ago, I considered bringing my daughter and grandson here on a vacation, but I got sick and it didn't happen so I was glad I could do it now. She asked what I planned to do and see. I told her that I planned to spend time with a friend and do some touring over the weekend. She told me about some interesting places she had heard about. She told me that the more of Costa Rica she saw, the more she loved it, and she was looking forward to living here. I told her I didn't know if I would want to live here, but it seemed like a great place to visit."

"I think you would like it if you did live here," Ed suggested.

Donna reached over and affectionately squeezed his shoulder, but didn't reply to his comment. She knew where he was coming from.

"By the way I noticed that the hotel has live entertainment on Friday and Saturday nights. Would you be interested in doing that?"

"If *you* are. Yes, I would."

From the hotel, Ed headed north-west. Along the way, they passed a McDonald's Restaurant. Donna commented, "I'm surprised to see so many McDonald's in the San José area."

"Like being back home, I guess. Did you know that the first McDonald's in Costa Rica was opened in 1984?"

"Really?"

"Yea, it was in a two-story building in downtown San José. Now they're everywhere."

Donna glanced out the window and looked around.

"Are we headed toward the airport?" she asked.

"Yes, I thought we would go through the city of Alajuela just north of the airport. It's on the way to Poás."

They arrived in Alajuela a few minutes later.

9

THE TOUR

Alajuela was like an old rural town one would find in the U.S. Mostly old buildings, residences now turned into store fronts, nothing taller than three stories.

"Would you like coffee?"

"Oh yes," she said. Just the thought of coffee perked her up.

"Tell you what," he said as he pulled to the curb alongside a small park, "I'll go across the street and get two coffees, and in the meantime, you can check out the park."

"Okay."

She walked into the park and observed a very large pedestal supporting a statue of a man holding a rifle in one hand and a torch in the other. The plaque said it was Juan Santamaria, a national hero.

When they were both back in the SUV, he asked, "So what do you think?"

"I don't know. Juan Santamaria is the name of the airport isn't it? And it says he was a national hero. What did he do to deserve such esteem?"

"Well," Ed began, "the story as I understand it is that in 1855 a military activist from the U.S. by the name of William Walker organized an army of revolutionaries and they successfully took over the government of Nicaragua. The objective was to convert large areas of Nicaragua and Costa Rica into slave states like those in the Southern U.S. The next year he unsuccessfully tried to invade Costa Rica. The Costa Rican army then went north to encounter Walker at a stronghold in Rivas, Nicaragua. After several soldiers lost their lives trying to overtake the stronghold, Juan Santamaria, a poor drummer boy in the Costa Rican army—and I should mention he was born here in Alajuela—took it upon himself to burn down the enemy stronghold under the provision that the Costa Rican government would provide for his mother for the rest of her days. He was successful, but as they never found his body—supposedly burned up in the fire—it's uncertain if he really died. However, his mother lived happily ever after."

"Interesting . . . I suppose every country needs a national hero," she said in a cynical tone.

"You're not impressed?" he said as he smiled and gave her a quick glance. "These stories give hope and build the morale of the common citizens."

"What happened to William Walker?" she asked with a bit more enthusiasm.

"After another major battle in Rivas in which he did not do well against an army from Honduras, he left the country and went back to the States. But then, he returned in 1860 only to be captured by the British who turned him over to the Hondurans. The Hondurans executed him by firing squad."

Can't really respond to that, Donna thought to herself. They sipped their coffees in silence for a few minutes before Ed started up the SUV and they drove off.

They were driving along some very winding and poorly maintained roads when Ed broke the silence.

"Donna, how is your daughter Brandy doing?"

"Fine."

"I only talked to her briefly when I was up your way. We ran into each other at the hospital. I introduced myself and told her I was a long-time friend. She said she already knew who I was. We were both concerned about you then. It seems like perhaps the two of you are closer now than you had been. Is that the case?"

"I think my sickness brought us together. She took care of me the whole time for which I was very grateful."

"Could I ask you something personal?"

She turned her head toward him as he kept his head fixed on the road. "What do you want to know?"

"You told me that you were reluctant to tell Brandy who her birth father was, and I was wondering if you ever told her."

"No. I haven't told anyone. I never told him or Brandy. Neither of them knows."

"Is that a secret that you would take to your grave?"

"Ed, I thought about what you said to me about that. And I understood your need to know who *your* birth mother was, but my situation with Brandy is different. Brandy and her birth father never knew each other whereas you and your birth mother had bonded with each other before she disappeared. You needed to understand why she wasn't there for you anymore."

Ed began to think of his mother and his need to find her. For a few moments he became lost in his own thoughts and began to mentally reflect on his life and the emotions he had growing up.

He remembered growing up near San Diego, California and that when he was almost three, his mother disappeared. She was no longer there to hold him or to read to him, or to scold him when he needed it. He missed her terribly. Then, two years later, Dad remarried. He wondered if his mother abandoned him. How could she do that? Hadn't she loved him?

He recalled his childhood years in California and how devastated he felt when at the age of sixteen, his dad passed away. He remembered hoping that his birth mother would show up at the funeral. She didn't. Then, after the funeral, he remembered how his stepmom explained the situation.

"Ed you're older now and I think you will understand what I'm going to tell you," his step-mom had said. "Your birth mother had been in the United States illegally, and overstayed her visa. She was from Mexico and when she returned to attend her mother's funeral, they would not let her return to the United States. In her absence, your dad hired me to be your nanny, but during the next year, we had an affair. Your birth mother sent a letter to your dad acknowledging there was no way she could ever return to the U.S. or gain custody of you. Your dad filed and was granted a divorce."

Ed was happy with his stepmom. She was from Costa Rica and he remembered how much he enjoyed the time he spent there visiting his stepmom's family or on vacation. She was a loving woman. He was happy with his dad as well. He was a good loving father. His family had money and they were able to provide him with a good home and with a good education. And yet, he always felt a void left by the absence of his birth mother.

He needed to discover the truth about her. If still alive, he wanted to see her, and he finally succeeded in finding her. He was 42 years old then, and this was his first year with the CIA after retiring from the military. He found her in a small town in Mexico. The people there were poor and the crime level was high. She was not well.

His birth mother told him how she was unable to convince the bureaucracy to allow her back into the States. She said she tried to re-enter illegally, but was captured and returned to Mexico, but not before she was raped. When she was told that Dad wanted a divorce, she fell apart mentally and physically. Drugs and prostitution became part of her life after that. She knew she may never see him again, but resigned herself that he would be well taken care of in the States. She cried and asked for his forgiveness. Ed remembered how he hugged her and told her what she wanted to hear, and how sad he felt when she passed away a year later.

"**Ed, watch where you're going!**" Donna shouted.

Ed quickly returned to planet Earth and braked hard, just in time to avoid colliding with another vehicle that had suddenly pulled onto the roadway in front of them.

"I'm sorry, you okay?"

"Yeah. He pulled right out in front of us, didn't he?"

After they regained their composure, Ed resumed the conversation.

"I know Brandy's situation is not the same as mine, but finding my mother and knowing that she loved me turned my life around. It was important to know that I was loved and not abandoned. I would think it would be important for Brandy as well. I think you should reconsider."

"Actually . . . after I thought I might die last year, I did reconsider. I think that Brandy should know, but not while I'm still alive. And of course, once she knows, her father will know."

"Why wait till you're gone?"

"Because I think the negative impact will be less then. The main reason I never told anyone is because I didn't want to ruin his life or anyone else's. He was married and had kids. How would he and his kids react? In addition, I always feared how I would feel towards him if we did reconnect. After all, I was married and I cared about my husband. On more than one occasion, he tried to reconnect with me, but I could not imagine seeing him and talking with him without telling him the truth."

"You're both mature adults and it has been a very long time. His kids are grown up, he's divorced, and your husband passed away many years ago. Why can't you tell Brandy and her father the truth now? Why do I have a feeling there is more to it than what you have said so far?"

"Ed, you and I have been very close, I'm willing to tell you but you must promise that what I say stays between us."

"Of course. You know you can trust me."

"Brandy's birth father was very instrumental in exposing Inga Sarnoff as a spy and later tracking her whereabouts to Central America. The projects he was involved in were highly classified, and yes, he's still alive."

"So, you're protecting him. You must still care about him."

"Ed. I care about a lot of people. I also care about you, probably more than you realize," she said as she placed her hand on his shoulder.

"Yea, I know, I didn't mean to sound jealous. I care about you too, you know."

"The country side is quite beautiful up here," she said changing the subject.

****

Ed and Donna arrived at the Poás visitor center shortly after eleven thirty. They took time to get some information before proceeding up the path to the observation deck. Donna learned that the volcano had erupted three dozen times since 1828 when they started keeping records. She also learned that there were no lava flows since 1952. Rather, these eruptions were explosions caused by high pressure steam and sulfur gas that could spew ash and debris several thousand feet into the sky. There had been big explosions in the 1950's and again in the 1990's. The last significant explosion was in 1996. Many of the explosions damaged nearby property.

Ed and Donna put on their jackets and walked the trail up to the observation deck. The altitude was more than 8,500 feet, and even in late morning it was chilly. They noticed green shrubs and flowers alongside the trail as they walked. Once on the observation deck, they stood at the wooden railing and gazed downward at the expanse of brown ash and rock deposited from prior eruptions. The expanse went for at least a mile in every direction—hard to judge distance without familiar reference points. On the far side of the expanse, they could see a ridge with greenery much like the one they were on. A crater in the center of the brown expanse was perhaps three football fields in diameter with walls that must have been at least 30 feet high. In the crater was a pool of hot water with a greenish blue hue. Wisps of vapor rose from the water and from the edges of the crater where the water met cooler rock and air. Shifts in the breeze gave occasional scents of sulfur. He had his arm over her shoulder. She had her arm around his waist.

"This is truly an amazing view," she said. "Whenever I see something like this it makes me feel small compared to the power and the magnitude of what is before us."

"I know what you mean," he echoed. "The volcano looks calm and peaceful right now, but it can erupt with little notice. And when it does, it can spew boulders and rocks as far as a mile from its center, and that includes where we are standing right now. To me the volcano is a humble reminder of life. Life is uncertain. Things happen to us that are unpredictable and that we have little power to control. It makes me realize that there must be a higher power out there, and my problems are small compared to the universe."

"I can certainly identify with that," she replied, reflecting on events in her own life.

"This is a favorite spot for me," he said as he pulled her close. "I find it inspirational, and I enjoy sharing it with someone."

He said *someone*. She wondered if there had been others.

"And romantic?" she turned her head toward him.

"Yes, that too."

"Have you been here a lot?"

"Not a lot. This is my third time." She seemed to be fishing, so he continued. "The first time I met someone here on official business. The second time I came alone and brought my camera. I took photographs. It's becoming a hobby for me. I hope to really get into it after I retire."

He was about to tell her she was the only woman he wanted to be romantic with, when they both heard something behind them.

They turned to find themselves facing another couple that had just walked onto the deck. The couple asked them if they would take their picture.

"Of course," Donna responded. They were young and probably on their honeymoon. After she took two pictures of the couple and handed back the camera, the couple asked if they would like their pictures taken in return. Ed was about to offer his camera when Donna spoke.

"Oh no, but thank you anyway," Donna said. She knew to avoid having their picture taken together. She was here on official business and her relationship with Ed could not be in the open. She looked at Ed. He seemed to understand.

As they began to walk back to the car hand in hand he asked, "Donna, doesn't it bother you that we can't just be a normal couple like them?"

"No, we aren't like normal people, but we learn to adapt."

****

The next stop was hummingbirds and lunch. Somehow, Ed found his way back to the main road, Route 146, and headed south. They were in the country. Aside from coffee *fincás*, they also passed acres of strawberry patches. Twenty minutes later they drove into the parking lot at the Freddo Fresas Restaurant, a rustic log type structure with red metal and tile roofs. The restaurant was famous for its food and for its *fresas*, or strawberries. Ed talked to the host and was assured a table for thirty minutes later while Donna picked up a brochure about hummingbirds and began to read.

"Ed, did you know that there are fifty different species of hummingbirds in Costa Rica? Two are unique to Costa Rica; others migrated here all the way from Canada. The smallest of the birds can beat their wings up to 80 times per second and hummingbirds are the only birds that can fly backwards."

He smiled at her enthusiasm. "No, I didn't know all that," he replied.

Then they walked across the roadway to the hummingbird park where they meandered along the red clay paths and past a fish pond. Bird feeders filled with sugar water were hanging at strategic spots from the small trees along the way. Ed watched as Donna seemed fascinated by two hummingbirds sharing the same feeder. The one would stick his beak in the food and then the other, alternating in perfect harmony. Although hummingbirds were not so much his thing, it pleased him that she was enjoying it. When she looked at him, his smile reflected her pleasure.

"Ed, I'm really enjoying this and I appreciate your patience."

She took his hand and they continued down the red clay path to a clump of trees.

"Oh look, an oriole," she said excitedly pointing up to the branches. "You would think we would see orioles in Maryland but I rarely see them—a lot of cardinals, but rarely an oriole."

After their walk and a few pictures, they headed back to the restaurant. They had a chicken dish and shared a strawberry and whipped cream dessert.

"Are you ready for the Doká Estate?" he asked.

"Absolutely, let's go."

****

Doká was a medium sized coffee *fincá* in the middle of nowhere. Ed found his way back to the main road and headed south for a short spell before turning off onto an unmarked country road and then another before finally arriving at their destination.

Most of the coffee *fincás* in the area were family owned and operated, usually from generation to generation. *Doká* was no exception. One of the owners named Poncho greeted them.

"Hello Ed, nice to see you again. I see you have brought a lady friend with you." His English was rather good.

"Good to see you as well Poncho. This is my friend Donna. Donna meet Poncho."

"Any friend of Ed is a friend of mine," he said and gave Donna a gentle hug. Poncho explained how they were trying to sell their coffee directly into the United States and how Ed had connected him to the right people. He said he and his brother did most of the work these days but his dad still played a role and they were trying to persuade his son José to work in the business full time. He would be their tour guide.

The tour covered the entire process of making coffee. They joined a tour group of about 12 other people and followed Poncho to a small grove near the main building. Poncho gave everyone a welcome and a short summary of their business and what to see on the farm. In addition to coffee beans, they also grew fruit and flowers, but today they would focus on coffee. Poncho showed them what coffee plants and the "cherries" they produced looked like. He said that researchers were experimenting with different hybrids that would resist disease, and that there were more than a hundred varieties of the Arabica coffee plant. Then they started the tour of the facility.

The group saw the seeding stations and the plantation where the coffee trees were grown. Poncho explained that the "cherries" were harvested over a period of three months, because they ripened at different times and they had to be a certain degree of ripeness when picked. Then they saw the drying fields, the milling and husk removal, the bean grading and sorting, decaffeination, and the roasting machines.

They were shown the difference between light roasted beans and dark roasted beans and explained how temperature and time of roasting was important as both affected the final taste. It was explained that for quality control purposes they periodically tested or "cupped" the finish product to assure that the temperature and length of roasting was optimal. Someone asked about the difference in taste and this led to some interesting facts that were surprising to some. They were told that if measured by volume, the dark roast has less caffeine and less acidity than the light roast. Also, while roasting can make the coffee of a low-quality bean taste more burnt or even bitter, they were told that a high-quality bean like theirs will not suffer such degradation in taste.

Finally, they saw the packaging process and the warehouse where unroasted coffee beans were stored. Since it was already into April, the harvest was completed, the beans had already been processed, and most had been shipped. But they still had a warehouse with an ample number of bags of unroasted beans stored in special sacks, and of course they also had plenty of bags of branded roasted beans and ground coffee in the gift shop. Afterwards they had the opportunity to taste all the coffee they wished to drink. One of the employees showed them how they made coffee "the old fashioned" way, using a *chorreador*. A *chorreador* is a tall wooden tripod stand with a coffee container underneath. A cotton bag is suspended from a hole in the top of the stand and is filled with ground coffee. Boiling water is poured into the bag and seeps through the ground coffee and into the container below. "Interesting," Donna commented privately to Ed. "It's the same process 'Mr. Coffee' built into a compact appliance."

Donna thanked the tour guide for a job well done, and took the time to fill out a survey. She used a fictitious name and left a personal cloud-based email address she used for just such occasions. And of course, before leaving she had to buy a bag of their branded dark roast coffee to take home with her.

Back in the car, Ed asked, "So what did you think of the tour?"

"It was great Ed. I'm glad you planned it. I found it interesting and educational. I never knew how they got the caffeine out of the coffee, and now I know." Then she reached over and gave his arm a friendly squeeze. "Thanks."

Ed took several turns onto unmarked country roads without hesitation which led Donna to ask, "Ed, do you come up here very often?"

"No, why?"

"Because you seem to know exactly where you're going."

He chuckled. "This is only the second time I've been to the *fincá*, but the first time a colleague at work who had been here more than once wrote down very precise directions which I memorized. But just in case I have a senior moment, I put his directions in the glove compartment."

A few more turns and they found themselves heading south to the city of San José via Heredia. Ed was concentrating on driving when he thought some music might be appropriate.

"Donna, if you'd like some music, I have some CDs in the pocket next to you on the door. Are you interested?"

He got no response. "Donna?"

Ed glanced over at her. She had her eyes closed and her mouth agape. She was asleep. He wondered about her stamina and her health. Yet she seemed relaxed and comfortable. He let her sleep.

Donna woke up as they approached the outskirts of San José.

"How long have I been asleep?" she asked.

"The better part of an hour. Have I tired you out?"

"No, I'll be fine," she said as she looked out the window. "Where are we?"

"We're on Route 3 between the city of Heredia and the city of San José, almost to the city line."

"I'm seeing a lot of new residential developments."

"Costa Rica is really starting to boom. We have major manufacturing and technology companies like Bridgestone and Sprint/Nextel that are expanding their presence here. We have a stable government and a low poverty level. It has become a very attractive place to live and to retire to. Many people from the U.S. come here when they retire."

"Ed, you're close to retiring, aren't you?"

"Maybe two more years. I'm seriously considering staying here after that. I really like it here. What about you?"

"Well, I thought about retiring when I was sick, but I wanted to complete this final project and bring Inga Sarnoff to justice."

"The project is very important to you isn't it?"

"Yes! Matheson read me in after Inga Sarnoff escaped in 1988. I've been looking for her ever since. I haven't told you this but not only did she murder Jon Wilson and at least two others, but she also tried twice to kill Brandy's father. I feel like I owed it to them to bring her to justice. Now that the project is about to come to an end, I think I'll retire at the end of this year."

"I think you would like retiring here. We could be together."

"Perhaps."

10

A ROMANTIC EVENING

Jurgens was on the eastern side of the city, not far from the OIJ and the Russian Embassy. Although it was a Saturday, traffic in the city was heavy, and it took another 20 minutes to get there from the northwest side of the city. Parking spaces were also scarce. Fortunately, Ed's position and his contacts provided him with unrestricted parking privileges in San José and he was able to park the RAV4 in a lot, a short distance from the restaurant.

Before they got out of the vehicle, they each grabbed their travel bags from the rear seat. They removed their hats and their shades; they exchanged their athletic foot-wear for dressier shoes; and they covered their tops with jackets suitable for dinner. They completed this transformation simultaneously in no more than five minutes, after which Ed watched patiently as Donna ran a comb through her hair, attached earrings, and put something on her lips. When she was ready, she turned to Ed and smiled; he smiled back. Donna knew that Ed was not a passive person by nature and she appreciated the effort he made to be patient with her. Ed exited the car and walked around to the passenger side to help her out.

"My lady," he said as he offered his arm.

He was putting on airs, but she was enjoying every moment. They walked arm in arm to the entrance of the restaurant.

When they entered the restaurant, Ed and the host greeted each other in Spanish. Then the host addressed Donna.

"*Nos complace tenerte como nuestro invitado.*"

"I'm sorry, *no hablo español*," she replied and smiled.

"He said he was pleased to have you as their guest." Ed offered.

"Ed, have you been here before?" she asked, as they followed the host to their table.

"Many times. They know me. I bring business associates here for lunch . . . sometimes for dinner. The Russian Embassy is nearby . . . and it's amazing what one can overhear," he added in a soft voice."

"I see."

"But . . . tonight is special for you."

They were seated in cushioned chairs at a table for two with a white linen table cloth. The food or *comida* was delicious with a French flair. Donna enjoyed the tilapia with a Dijon mustard sauce and mashed cassava, and Ed enjoyed a curry shrimp dish with rice. Each plate came with carrots, a popular vegetable in Costa Rica.

They complimented their meals with a shared bottle of sauvignon blanc. Donna asked Ed about the cassava.

"This looks and tastes a lot like mashed potatoes, but it's not. Are you familiar with it?"

"Cassava . . . very popular here in Costa Rica. It comes from the root of a cassava tree. The root is shaved down, cut up, and fully cooked to avoid toxicity. Tapioca comes from cassava root."

"Toxicity?"

"Cyanide poisoning. Good way to do away with an enemy agent." he quipped.

"Ed, you're more cynical than I am. Let's talk about something more pleasant."

"Sorry. Too many years in the agency. Like I said. We're not normal people. Not to worry though. The chef here knows what he's doing. You're right, this is a very romantic setting and I'm a very lucky man to be sharing it with such a beautiful lady."

He refilled their glasses with wine and made a toast. "Here's to our friendship and future happiness." He wanted to add the word *together* but knew she was not ready to commit to that.

The dining room was cozy and intimate. A window view of a garden lit with colored lights added to the ambience. The dim lighting, delicious food, excellent service, and the sweet talk between them that ensued, made it a very romantic dinner. The wine helped as well.

After dinner they took a short walk before returning to the car. They had their arms around each other as they turned down a side street. It was dark and there was no one around. Donna was reminded of a time several years ago when they were on assignment in Mexico City.

"Ed, do you remember when we were in Mexico City and two thugs came out of nowhere and tried to rob us?"

"It's okay. No need to worry about that here. Costa Rica is one of the safest countries in Central America—very low crime rate, especially when it comes to violent crimes. But I do remember, I was impressed with the way you handled yourself. You weren't about to give up your purse, passport, and cash. We disarmed them in less than a minute. We could have beat the crap out of them. Hell, we could have killed them. I was about to do just that when you told them they had better run if they wanted to live. I know a lot of operatives that would not have been so compassionate. I had a new admiration for you after that."

She knew it was *discretion* and not *compassion* that motivated her that night, but she did not correct him.

****

They arrived back at the InterContinental around ten that evening. The lobby lounge had a duo, a female vocalist and a male guitar player. The place was busy but they were able to get a small table without a long wait. The music was relaxing and not too loud.

"What would you like to drink madam?" the waitress asked.

"I think I'll have a brandy . . . straight up. The house brand is fine."

"Sounds good. I'll have the same," Ed told the waitress.

"Ed, I really enjoyed today, and as always I enjoyed your company."

"I tried very hard to please you and I was hoping our weekend would continue into tomorrow."

She gave him a hard look. "Ed are you telling me that you did all that so that I would want to sleep with you tonight?" She was giving him a hard time to see how he would react.

"No. No. I didn't mean it like that!"

"I know you didn't. I'm just playing with you. You're welcome to join me in my room tonight, but I want you to tell me something first."

"What's that?"

"I need you to tell me the truth. Are you seeing anyone else right now?"

"No."

"Ed, you're what some women would call a silver fox. You're handsome, in good shape, and you have money. I would think you could have sex with any cute young chick you choose. Why me?"

"I don't think of you as a cute young chick. I think of you as a mature, intelligent, and attractive woman. I trust you and I feel comfortable being with you. You understand me and I can share feelings with you. I think you will agree that in our line of work we can't always do that with other people. Everything is classified and we must always be on guard. If we say the wrong thing to the wrong person, we could put them in danger, put ourselves in danger, or be charged with violating our security agreements. I think you understand that."

"I do understand that. I had a very difficult time trying to be a mom and a wife while at the same time traveling—many times to a secret location where I would become someone else undercover. My husband John accepted that, but it also meant that we were not that involved with each other."

"Donna, think of it. We have risked our lives and we have taken the lives of others. We have experienced things that set us apart and we think differently than others. Very few people are like us. The situation we talked about earlier after dinner is an example of that. If we were like normal people, we would have given them the money they asked for. But it's likely that they still would have killed us so that we would not report them. No, we're not normal people . . . that's why I want to be with you."

"Because we're not normal?"

"Because we're able to share and feel comfortable with each other, something we can't do with others." His tone showed a slight frustration at her response.

"Ed, I'm—" Just then their brandies arrived. "Can we talk more about this later? I don't want anyone to overhear us. For now, let's just enjoy the music and the moment . . . and the brandy." They clinked glasses. "To us and what we have together," she said sincerely. To Ed, her words were reassuring.

****

They walked hand in hand to the elevator. They had the elevator to themselves and once inside, she pulled his head towards hers and kissed him hard on the mouth. "I want you to understand that no matter what, I care about you."

When they entered Donna's hotel room, she immediately took a seat on the edge of the bed.

"Ed, please sit down next to me," she said as she patted the area on the bed next to her. "We need to talk."

"What's wrong?"

"Ed, I want to apologize if I seemed to belittle what you were saying to me earlier. I know you were being serious. I really do like you and enjoy being with you and I can think of no one I would rather retire with than you. Whether it's in Costa Rica or elsewhere wouldn't matter. It's just that I have a problem."

"Tell me."

"I'm scared!"

"Donna, I've never known you to be scared about anything. What's going on with you?"

"If we were together, I'm not sure I would live up to your expectations."

"How so?"

"When I was sick, I went through hell and I thought I would die. As you know, I faced death several times during my career. I thought I was invincible or I just didn't think about it, but when I was sick, I changed and it scared me. Although the doctors tell me that I'm cancer-free now, it could come back and if it does, it would put you through a lot more than I would want. I remember how I felt when my husband John got sick and I know how it was a strain on Brandy when I was sick. I wouldn't want to put you through that."

"You're fortunate to have Brandy as your daughter, but if you were to get sick again, I would stand by you just as she did."

"There's more. You said we were not normal people and that's certainly true. If we were to live together, we would need to share some of those abnormal things with each other. Some of them may turn out to be slightly immoral or illegal. I wonder if we would still love each other after that."

"But this is something I already expect and accept."

"Maybe. But there's more. I don't have the same sex drive that I had when I was last here. I guess my hormones are different now. In fact, I had surgery and don't even have all the same equipment, and I have a scar across my middle. You may not enjoy looking at it. What if you need sex more that I can give you?"

"Don't worry. I'm not going to find the nearest cute young chick if that's what you're suggesting." His tone indicated some annoyance.

"I'm sorry I didn't mean—"

"No, it's okay. I understand where you're coming from. I screwed up my first marriage by sleeping with cute young chicks, but that was a long time ago. Look, my sex drive isn't what it used to be either. But more importantly, it was not meaningful sex with them. There was no sharing of the mind, no sharing of experience, no sharing of dreams. I don't want that. I want to be with you with or without sex."

She gave him a serious look. "Ed, what I need is for you to love me and hold me close."

"I do love you," he said as they embraced, "and no matter what happens between us you won't disappoint me. Please don't be scared."

"Ed, I know you keep a go-bag in your car, so why don't you retrieve it while I use the bathroom."

He left and retrieved his bag, then stopped in the lobby rest room before coming back to the room. While she waited, she washed up and put on a nightshirt. After she let him back into the room, she got into bed and waited for him to undress and join her.

"If you make love to me, I need for you to use one of these," she said and handed him a sealed condom. He laughed.

"Ed, what's so funny?"

He opened his other hand showing her a second condom.

11

SUNDAY

Sundays in Costa Rica were a day of rest and church going. Most of the citizens (*Ticos* as they were called) were Roman Catholic. Local businesses either due to religion or regulation were closed. However, exceptions were made for the booming tourist and business trade. Hotels still booked rooms and still provided food for its guests—although the day was dry with respect to liquor sales.

Donna woke up happy. She looked over at Ed. He was still asleep. He looked relaxed and peaceful. As she listened to the sound of his breathing, she thought about how lucky she was to have him in her life right now. She couldn't resist giving him a gentle kiss on his cheek before heading off to the bathroom. When she returned, Ed was up. He gave her a good morning hug and took his turn in the bathroom.

"Are you hungry?" she shouted so he would hear over the running water. "They have a nice buffet downstairs. You interested?"

"Sounds good, let's do it," he responded.

After breakfast, Donna asked, "What now?"

"Did you bring a swim suit?"

"And if I say no?" she joked.

"I won't ask you to swim in the nude if that's what you're suggesting."

"Ha-ha. I did bring a suit. The hotel here has a pool and I went to the pool and swam Thursday afternoon . . . thought I told you. Anyway, you don't have a suit with *you*, do you?"

"I was thinking we could go over to my place."

"Okay. Let's go back upstairs, get our stuff and we're off."

Donna got into her rental car and followed Ed to his place. Ed lived on the fourth floor of a condo built in 2001. Ed moved in right after it was built. Ed had explained that the U.S. Embassy was the owner of the building and that he and a few other embassy employees—and possibly CIA employees—paid rent to live there. The condo was high end. Ed had two bedrooms—he used one for an office—a common bath, a small washer and dryer, a living room, kitchen, dining area, and hardwood floors, and a bay window that afforded a view of the nearby mountains. The condo was located at the edge of the city of Escazu, not far from the hotel and very convenient to the embassy.

Donna changed into her two-piece swim suit. Despite her ordeal with cancer, she still looked good, and the scar from her recent surgery was too low on her abdomen to be visible. When she met Ed in the hallway, he smiled and told her how great she looked. She returned the compliment. Ed still looked like an athlete. They walked out to the pool together, moved two lounge chairs under an umbrella, and spent the rest of the afternoon enjoying the water and sunshine. Occasionally a neighbor would come down and Ed would say hello and introduce Donna as a business associate. Some may have already known he was the CIA Chief of Station and that Donna was probably a CIA officer, but nothing was ever said. Neighbors were friendly and would engage in small-talk but knew not to ask too many questions.

After a while they went back upstairs. Ed made gin and tonics and then prepared a light supper. While he was busy doing that, Donna made her way down the hallway to the bathroom. On the way she noticed photographs that Ed had framed and mounted on the walls. She did not remember seeing them the last time she was at his place. One of the pictures caught her eye and was of special interest. It was a photo of the Poás volcano. It was awesome, just the way she remembered it the previous morning, and the way it was matted and framed really set it off. When she returned to the kitchen, she walked up behind Ed, put her hand on his shoulder and told him how much she liked the picture.

"I'm glad you like it. Like I said yesterday when we were up there, I'm making an effort to start a hobby and hone my photographic and art skills. I have a long way to go, but I think it's something I'll pursue after I retire."

"Well, I think you're doing a great job of it. Keep it up," she said.

He turned, smiled and handed her a drink.

"Here's to our future," he said.

After supper, it was time to part. The weekend together came to an end and after a hug and a kiss, Donna drove herself back to the InterContinental. She would meet with Ed in his office at nine the next morning.

Later that evening, Ed was about to put a load of dirty clothes into his washing machine when his phone rang.

12

QUANDARY

Ed answered the phone, thinking the call might be from Donna. "Ed, this is Director Rojas of the OIJ. I apologize for calling you at home on a Sunday evening, but there is something you need to know. Are you alone?"

"Yes why?"

"Maria Martin was found dead this morning in her home. She was murdered. It's already on the local news."

This was quite a surprise. Ed's immediate response to the Director was "I didn't expect this. Did the DIS do it?"

"Did you?" the Director threw right back at him.

"No, of course not."

They both laughed.

"What about your associate, Officer Wolf? Can you account for her whereabouts?"

"I don't know. When did the death occur?"

"Our investigators think it occurred on Saturday, but it's possible it could have occurred Friday night. We will know with more certainty tomorrow after the coroner is finished."

"Officer Wolf was with me Friday evening, all day Saturday, and Saturday night."

"There is one more thing I will tell you. Our investigators discovered that Maria Martin's computer hard drive was taken. As you can imagine, her hard drive would have much information on it that would be valuable to your American CIA. Do you know anything about that?"

"No, I don't! I would think the hard drive would also have information that would be valuable to people in your organization and to the DIS as well. There are probably names and information on that hard drive that would incriminate Costa Rican officials."

"If so, I would not cover it up," Rojas responded

Perez understood that Rojas was not about to implicate the OIJ or the DIS. Rojas would need the CIA or even the Russians to take the blame, although Perez didn't think it likely that the Russians would kill their own . . . but then again.

"Look," Rojas continued "I hope you are right about Officer Wolf's whereabouts, but right now the evidence we have points to her, and Russian intelligence also suspects her."

"How would Russian intelligence know why Officer Wolf was here in Costa Rica?"

"My guess is that they were notified when she entered the country. They probably have had their sights on her, know who she is and what she does for the CIA. If they think she did this, and if they think she has the information on the hard drive, she may be a target and the Russians may go after her."

"I'm not convinced."

"*Señora* Martin's body was found with a sheet of paper on her lap with the words '*justicia para un espia ruso*' written on it. Very few people knew that Maria Martin was a Russian spy, and had a motive to kill her. In addition, a neighbor claims to have seen a strange woman leave the Maria Martin's house Friday night. We are still reviewing the security cams."

"Is it possible that the room we met in last week was bugged?"

"I highly doubt it, but I *will* check it out."

"What about Director Alverez? Is it possible that Alverez arranged the assassination? Even if the meeting room was not bugged, he could have anonymously informed the Russians of our mission and placed the blame on the CIA rather than himself. I know Alverez and it's clear to me that he's conservative and doesn't want Socialists to be in power. At our meeting, one of you also made a point about not wasting time with court orders, and most importantly that the OIJ did not want to alert the Russians or the Socialists in the government of the status of your investigation into election tampering. I think the death of Maria Martin accomplished those objectives."

"I talked with Director Alverez. He had an airtight alibi for Friday evening from eight o'clock onward, and on Saturday he was at his kid's football game. And . . . with all due respect, Martin's death would accomplish CIA objectives as well."

"So, do you have enough evidence to arrest anyone?"

"Not yet."

"I see . . . .. Director, if possible, could you send me fingerprints and photos of the body so that I have proof that she is in fact Inga Sarnoff."

"I will, but there's one more thing. Director Alverez thinks that Officer Wolf's life may be in danger. There is mounting evidence that she may have done this and he thinks the Russians may go after her in retaliation. My advice is that she leave the country as soon as possible. I won't have her stopped if she leaves now, but at some point, I may need to question her."

"Gracias. Director, thank you for keeping me informed and for the advice."

****

On Monday morning, officers Wolf and Perez met at the U.S. Embassy to discuss the situation.

"Did you see the newscast this morning," he asked.

"I did. Do you have any details?"

"Yes. I talked to Director Rojas last night. He thinks that the Russians will think that you did it and target you. You didn't do this did you?"

"Surely you can't think that."

"If you did it, I don't need to know. You would have my support. However, there is something you should know. Director Rojas told me, and it was also in the news this morning, that Maria Martin's hard drive from her computer was taken. Friday night I received a hard drive from you and another from Juan. That seems to be more than a coincidence to me."

"Ed, what are you implying?" Her annoyance was evident.

"I'm not accusing you. Please hear me out. Juan has a room at the Hotel Grano de Oro and we often have information from the field delivered to him. Normally he then brings it to me and I review it and have my people analyze it. I told Matheson that we transfer intelligence that way frequently. In this case, Matheson instructed me to go to the hotel, get the package from Juan, and then forward it directly to Langley via our private secure mail service. Matheson said it was for his eyes only. So, on Saturday morning, before I came to pick you up, I took the cartons I received from Juan and from you to the Embassy and arranged for their delivery to Langley. Now that I've heard the news, I think that one of those cartons contained the hard drive stolen from Maria Martin's house. The strong implication is that the hit was orchestrated by the CIA in Langley."

"Ed, I had no part in this!" She was loud and her tone emphatic.

"Okay, calm down. I believe you, but it's beginning to look as if we're being set up. I told Rojas you were with me on Saturday, Saturday night, and Sunday. I hope I did not dishonor you by saying that, but we needed an alibi. But then he said the murder may have occurred Friday night. You said you went to the coffee shop in Heredia and then went to a pharmacy before meeting me at the Grano de Oro. Do you have receipts?"

"Uh . . . no I don't. I've been paying cash for the small stuff because the credit card fees are exorbitant. And anyway, I don't get reimbursed for personal stuff, so I don't need receipts."

"Did you go somewhere else on the way?" As he asked this, he read her expression. "No, you didn't . . ."

"Relax. All I did was drive by. Rohrmoser was on the way to the Hotel Grano de Oro, and as I said, I had plenty of time. I just wanted to see where she lived. I was curious. After I passed by the house, I went to the pharmacy as I told you, and then to the hotel where you met up with me."

He gave her a look and shook his head.

"I'm sorry, I should have mentioned this the other night."

"Tell me what type of passport you used. Was it *personal, official,* or *diplomatic*?"

"To enter the country, I used my *diplomatic* passport, but I also have my *personal* one with me."

"That's good. You were conducting official business, so at least you have diplomatic immunity here. They can't prosecute you but they could still detain you and question you. However, what's worse, someone could kill you. Director Rojas suggested you leave the country as soon as possible . . . yes, I know . . . it's a stretch, but it's better to be safe."

"Who would kill me? The Russians? How would the Russian's know I was here and about my interests in Inga Sarnoff? Only six of us were privy to that . . . weren't we?"

"I asked that question and the Director suggested that the Russians may have been tracking you from the time you entered the country. It wouldn't have taken much to bribe an immigration employee to keep them informed. I also suggested that the Russians could have bugged the meeting room at the OIJ. Of course, he denied that was possible. In any case, here is a newspaper article from this morning's paper. You can take it with you."

"Gracias," she replied and tucked it away to read later.

"The Director also agreed to send me proof that she was Inga Sarnoff. I'll forward it to you when I receive it." Then he looked directly at her. "There is a flight out of SJO at two forty this afternoon. It goes to Charlotte, North Carolina. A connecting flight will get you to Baltimore around midnight. I already alerted my secretary. She can get you on those flights right now if you agree."

"Do you really think—"

"Please say yes."

"Okay."

"Wait right here. I'll have her print out boarding passes."

He returned within five minutes and handed her two boarding passes. "You should leave now. Come here," he said as he pulled her toward him. They hugged as he told her *"Hasta que nos encontremos de nuevo."*

****

Donna Wolf went back to her hotel, packed her things, and checked out using the TV in her room. Her account was settled—no need to go to the front desk in the lobby. She headed down to the lobby and was about to exit the hotel for the parking lot when she saw *la policia* and a tow truck about to tow her rental car. *Oh God*, she said to herself as she remembered the map with the x's. She had left it in the car. She quickly reversed direction and exited via another door. Fortunately, she was able to grab a waiting taxi and go directly to the airport. At the airport counter, she presented her official government passport and her boarding pass, but instead of returning her documents, she was asked to step aside. Her heart began to thump. Were they going to stop her? She watched as the guard that took her passport talked on the phone. It seemed like a year before he came back, returned her passport, and returned her boarding pass.

"Sorry for the delay," he said. "You are free to proceed." She breathed a sigh of relief.

Once seated on the plane, she pulled out the article that Ed Perez had given her and began to read it in Spanish. *La Extra* was known to be the most widely read newspaper in Costa Rica. It also had a reputation for being the seediest.

> *Diario Extra—Monday April 7, 2003*
> *By Carman Diaz, reporter*
> 　*Maria Martin was found murdered in her home Sunday*
> *morning when two of her neighbors went to take her to Sunday*

Mass. Señora *Martin was known by her neighbors to be a Canadian expat who tutored children. She was 51 years old.*

Interviews with people on the scene revealed some interesting facts. A neighbor reported that he witnessed an unknown woman sitting in her car across the street just after sundown. Another neighbor claims to have seen a woman get into a rental car parked nearby sometime after 7 p.m. An anonymous source tells us that the hard drive from the woman's computer was missing and that evidence found in the home included a passport in the name of Inga Sarnoff, a Russian spy wanted by the United States for murdering a high-level U.S. CIA official 15 years ago. Another anonymous source told us that a female using an official U.S. government passport is known to have entered Costa Rica last Wednesday and met with someone at the U.S. Embassy the next day. Speculation is that this could have been an assassination orchestrated by the American CIA.

The San José police and the OIJ are investigating.

Next to the article was a picture of Inga Sarnoff lying dead on the garage floor with her blouse covered with blood and a sign on her lap that said *'¡JUSTICIA PARA UN ESPÍA RUSO!'* *Oh my God,* Donna thought. How could they print this stuff? Was there no crime scene security? The release of this information would certainly not help a legitimate investigation. She shook her head and stuffed the article back into her pocket.

Then she began to muse over the events of the past several days. The outcome was not what she expected, but she had no regrets that Inga Sarnoff was dead. She was responsible for tracking Soviet spies but tracking this spy had become almost personal for her. Sarnoff was evil. The woman had killed multiple times. In 1988 she had assassinated Jon Wilson, her friend and a high-level CIA official, and then escaped arrest and fled to Moscow. She had spent the last 15 years tracking Sarnoff down. Two years ago, she had provided Ed Perez with intelligence that Sarnoff may be part of an undercover operation in Costa Rica. She was elated when he notified her that the information had paid off.

The demise of Inga Sarnoff was even more rewarding for Donna because when she was diagnosed with cancer, her future became very uncertain. Life could be so uncertain she thought, and she was glad she had a chance to avenge Jon's death before the cancer ended her own life. She had surgery and chemo—she was better now. She felt good and for the moment at least was cancer-free. She felt at peace and was glad to be on her way back home. She relaxed, put her head back against the head rest, and fell asleep to the drone of the engines.

13

HOME

It was late Monday night—early Tuesday morning actually—when Donna arrived home to her townhouse in Guilford, Maryland. As soon as she stepped into the hallway and set her luggage down, she was greeted by Tabby. Tabby was her cat—very friendly. She reached down and petted him as he rubbed against her leg and purred, happy to see her. Donna's daughter Brandy had come over every day while she was gone to feed him and clean out his litter box.

Donna felt so grateful to have Brandy as a daughter, but the relationship had been strained for many years. Donna's frequent travel away from home and her often covert operations with the CIA didn't help. The early years living with her mother who did not look favorably upon out of wedlock affairs, including that of Donna's father, was not helpful either. Brandy needed a father so when Brandy was six, Donna married John whose wife had died. He had a son a year older than Brandy. John was a good father and it was a good relationship for all four of them until Brandy got married and moved to Ellicott City. When John passed away about ten years ago due to a bad heart, Donna sold the house they were in, moved to a garden apartment complex in Jessup, and then to her current townhouse in Guilford. Although she still reported to the CIA in Langley, Donna was able to work out of an office at the National Security Agency at nearby Fort Meade.

The relationship with Brandy got better with time. Then, when Donna was diagnosed with ovarian cancer, they became even closer. Brandy was very attentive and took care of her when she needed it. Brandy scheduled her appointments and went with her to each one. While Donna was in the hospital, Brandy took care of Tabby, her housekeeping, her mail, and so on. Donna and Brandy had become close.

From the age of four, Brandy wanted to know who her birth father was, and Donna had kept it a secret. But circumstances had changed. Brandy was in her mid-thirties and more mature now. She was divorced and shared custody of her teenaged son Brian. Brandy could understand now, Donna reasoned. And then there was the conversation she had with Ed. He had told her how important it was for him to learn about his birth mother. With her recent illness, Donna had come to realize that she would not be on this earth forever. After her death, there would be fewer reasons for keeping the secret about Brandy's birth father. Donna reconsidered her decision. She typed a letter to Brandy explaining the circumstances and reasons for the secret, and secured the letter in her safe deposit box at the bank. Donna also left a letter for Brandy's birth father. No one would see these letters until after she passed.

She felt good that she had completed her project to track down Inga Sarnoff. Tomorrow she would contact her boss and talk about retiring by the end of the year. She would have more time for Brandy and her grandson. Tonight however, she was only thinking about how grateful she was to have Brandy as her daughter and how tired she was from her trip to Costa Rica. She collapsed on the bed, happy to be home as Tabby cuddled up next to her.

****

On several occasions over the next few weeks, Donna met with Matheson at Langley, to discuss the aftermath of the Inga Sarnoff Assassination. Matheson made it clear what he wanted.

"I am disappointed about the bad publicity we are getting," he said. "The Russians have spread the word that you and the CIA are responsible for the death of Maria Martin, aka Inga Sarnoff. It looks bad for you and for the CIA. But to the Russians it also looks bad. To lose one of their own makes them look weak. I am receiving intelligence that the Russians are planning revenge. They now are aware of who you are and what you have been doing to them for the past fifteen years. They may try to tap into your files and steal classified information. I must also warn you that your life may be in danger."

"What do you want me to do? Should I retire now?"

"No. I am putting together a plan that will turn lemons into lemonade, to use a cliché."

"What is it?"

"I can't tell you everything."

"I'd like to know my role, and how it fits into the bigger picture," Donna demanded.

"Okay, over the next few months, I'd like you to help the technical staff set up some bogus files and documents that might attract the Russian's interest. But other than that, I would like you to continue as normal, doing everything you're already doing."

"You said my life could be in danger. Will they come after me?"

"They may, but we'll have eyes on you. You'll be protected."

"No names. I can't give you any more details at this time. I need to avoid leaks and assure plausible deniability. Look, I know you have invested years into this project. Many of the spies you have been tracking, including Sarnoff, report directly to Ivan Markov, one of Russia's top spies. We believe that Markov will be running the operation to take you down. This is our chance to take him down first. I need your support."

His answers to her questions implied that the operation may be off the books. Yet, she had worked with him for years and felt he could be trusted. She wanted very badly to see the completion of the project she started 15 years ago, and she wanted to see it soon. Her eagerness was partly because she wanted to retire, but it was much more than that. She had strong personal reasons that she kept to herself.

"Okay, whatever the plan is, I'm on board," she finally said.

14

GARCIA'S OFFER

T hree weeks after the death of Maria Martin, Joe Garcia received a message at his security company office in San José.

25/4/03
POR FAVOR, REÚNETE CONMIGO - 2 P.M.
MAÑANA EN LA HABITACIÓN 305 DEL
INTERCONTINENTAL... VP

It was written in Spanish, but basically it was a request from Vladimir Petrov to meet him in room 305 at the InterContinental Hotel tomorrow at 2:00 p.m. It was not publicly known that in addition to being a supporter of socialist causes, Petrov was also the chief intelligence officer at the Costa Rican office for the SVR-RF. The SVR was the international intelligence service for the Russian Federation. Petrov's position was the equivalent of the CIA's Chief of Station, Eduardo Perez.

Joe knew who Petrov was, but wondered why such a meeting would be required. He and Judi had already provided Petrov with reports of their surveillance activity regarding Maria Martin. On the other hand, after three weeks, the Costa Rican OIJ did not have enough evidence to arrest anyone for her murder. The Russians had reason to believe that the CIA was responsible, and were doing their own investigation. They would need to know what he knew.

****

Tomorrow came. Joe went into the office that morning and did some homework in preparation for his meeting. He needed to make sure that he had his details straight.

The seasons were changing early this year, more typical of the month of May than April, and by noon it was starting to rain. When it was time to leave for his meeting with Petrov, Joe put on his rain slicker and made his way to the garage and got into the Toyota Corolla that he shared with his business partner. Traffic was terrible, but he arrived at the InterContinental with a few minutes to spare. He made his way up to room 305 and knocked on the door.

Petrov opened the door, let him in, and glanced up and down the hallway before closing the door. As Garcia passed through the foyer and entered the main room, he was surprised to see another man rise from the sofa to greet him.

"Joseph Garcia, please meet Ivan Markov," Petrov said politely. "Markov is a comrade who is here from Moscow."

"Pleased to meet you Señor Garcia. I hear good things about you," Markov said in Russian.

"Uh, pleased to meet you as well," Garcia responded, doing his best to pronounce clearly in Russian.

Markov smiled. "Russian is not your native language?" he said in broken Spanish.

"No sir," Garcia responded switching to English. "My native language is Spanish. I speak fluent Spanish and English, but I'm still learning Russian."

The rest of the conversation was in English.

"Señor Garcia, I am here to talk about the death of Maria Martin. The SVR is investigating her death and we intend to hold her killer responsible. We believe the killer is Donna Wolf, an agent with the American CIA. We have had eyes on Wolf for some time now. We believe she's responsible for the exposure of several of our agents. Some have turned up dead and others have had their missions compromised. We knew that she was here last year prior to the elections and then we learned that she may be coming to Costa Rica again. I alerted Petrov. We were suspicious about the purpose of her trip. Petrov tells me that he asked you to investigate her arrival and do surveillance of her activities while she was here. He also told me that you had worked with Martin. We thought you may have additional insight as to what happened. I would like to ask you some questions."

"What would you like to know?"

"When did you first learn that Maria Martin had at one time been a covert Russian agent wanted by the United States?"

"Not until two days before she was killed," Garcia replied.

"How did you find out?"

"Judi told me."

"Judi?"

"One of my agents," Petrov interjected.

"Was it you that killed Martin?" Markov asked.

"What! . . . Look—"

"Relax. I joke," Markov said with a grin.

Then Markov got serious. "Señor, please tell me what information you have. I need to know how she died and who did it," he said sternly.

"Okay, I gave a summary to Petrov after she was killed and I gave him my written report on the eleventh of April. I wish I had more, but I'll tell you what I know. On Thursday more than three weeks ago, the third of April to be exact, Petrov's agent, Judi, met with me. Judi informed me that a CIA officer named Donna Wolf had entered the country Wednesday evening using a U.S. government passport. Judi told me that Petrov wanted me to track Wolf and find out why she was here. I had a listening device and an informant in the Director of the OIJ's office. I learned that CIA Officer Donna Wolf and the CIA Chief of Station, Ed Perez, had a meeting that morning with the OIJ Director. The purpose of the meeting was to discuss extradition of Maria Martin on the grounds that she was a Soviet spy wanted by the CIA for murders fifteen years ago. I know that the Costa Rican DIS also came to the meeting. I didn't have ears inside the secure facility in which they met, but it's almost certain that someone in that meeting ordered the hit. According to the coroner, Maria was murdered the next evening, Friday evening."

"The newspapers blamed the CIA. Do you not agree?" asked Markov.

"It's entirely possible and consistent with the evidence, and it was probably Wolf that did it. I know that she was at Martin's residence that Friday evening around the time of the murder. I also know that before she was in Martin's neighborhood, she met with an unknown man at La Copa Máxima in Heredia, and I know that after she was in Martin's neighborhood, she delivered a package to someone at the Hotel Grano de Oro."

"What do you think was in the package?"

"I don't know for sure, but the package delivered to the hotel could have been the stolen hard drive from Martin's house."

"How did you learn this?"

"I was tailing her on Friday evening."

"Why—"

"I had asked them to track Wolf," Petrov interjected.

Joe continued. "Judi and I were working together to find out what Wolf was up to. It was prudent to tail her. Judi had determined that Wolf was staying at the InterContinental Hotel. Then, Judi posed as the wife of a newly hired employee of the U.S. Embassy and struck up friendly conversations with her at the hotel. That was on Thursday afternoon and again on Friday afternoon. On Friday they talked about things to do and places to eat. Wolf mentioned places that included Hotel Grano de Oro, and Jurgens. I knew from my experience working with Maria, that these places were favorite places for having business meetings and sharing intelligence. On Friday afternoon, according to Judi, Wolf mentioned that she was having dinner that night with a friend who worked at the U.S. Embassy. Wolf didn't say what time the dinner was, but she said she was leaving the hotel around four o'clock to meet that person somewhere. It seemed too early for dinner and we surmised that something may be going down. We had planted a bug in Wolf's hotel room, and on Friday afternoon we heard her talking on the phone with a place called La Copa Máxima in Heredia. Judi had another commitment that evening and I had the car, so I was the one that tailed Wolf when she left the InterContinental at around four o'clock. I followed Wolf from the InterContinental to the coffee shop."

"What happened there?"

"Wolf arrived at La Copa Máxima between five and five thirty. I observed that she met with a gentleman who I did not know, and that he gave her a small package. I don't know what was in the package. It could have been money, could have been directions, could have been a weapon, or it could have been empty. When she left, I followed her to Rohrmoser. I was a few cars behind her when she made a left turn from Via 104 and headed into the Rohrmoser neighborhood. Unfortunately, traffic was very heavy and a car had stalled in the intersection, and I didn't make the light. When I got into the neighborhood, her car was no longer in my sights. However, I assumed she may be heading towards Maria Martin's house. I had been there when I worked with her, so I knew the address. I passed by the house and found Wolf's car parked on the street near the house. I kept a safe distance, and waited until she returned to the car about thirty minutes later."

"Then you did not actually see her enter residence?"

"No, but I saw her walk down the driveway and return later."

"While you waited, were you not concerned that Martin might be in danger?"

"I didn't believe that a female CIA officer would also be an assassin, but things did seem off."

"Did you intervene? What did you do?"

"I called Maria's cell phone in the hope that she may still be on the way home from work. No answer. I left a warning message. Then I took a chance and walked up the driveway and peered into the garage using my flashlight. I could see a bare leg on the floor. I knew

I was too late, so I returned to my car." As he said this, he knew that these actions had not been described in his written report.

"So, you sure that Officer Wolf did this?"

"Wolf was there and Maria was dead. But there was additional evidence. One of my sources in the OIJ said that a security camera showed a woman leaving Maria Martin's residence on Friday evening but the video was grainy, and while they couldn't say with certainty that it was Wolf, they couldn't rule it out either. My source also told me that a man walking his dog said he passed by a woman on the sidewalk coming from the direction of Martin's house around six fifteen that night. His description matched that of Wolf. And then what about the sign that was left on her body? Who else would have been emotional enough to leave a sign, accusing her of being a spy that was brought to justice?"

"Yes, some women can be that way," Markov stated in a matter-of-fact manner. "Did you follow her after that?"

"I did. I followed her to the Hotel Grano de Oro. She carried a package into the hotel and left it with the desk clerk. It may have been Maria's hard drive. I later saw her have dinner with a man I thought was CIA. Again, my sources say that both are on security cameras in the area of the hotel." Garcia knew that his account of events was not precisely true, but it was what he needed them to believe and it could not be disproven.

"So, it sounds like you are quite certain that the CIA is involved and that Officer Wolf is the assassin. Is that correct?"

"Yes sir. That's correct! I informed Petrov of everything I saw later that evening and gave him a written report on April eleven."

Then, changing the subject, Garcia continued. "May I ask a question? Earlier, you said that over the years Wolf has caused you great harm . . .. Are you planning to take her out?"

"We're considering it. She has exposed many of our operatives and it needs to stop."

"If you want to go after Maria's killer, I want to help you do that. You probably know I was a friend of Maria. We worked together for three years. We exposed the corruption in the Costa Rican government and helped to form the new Citizens Action Party. I liked her. She even gave me private lessons to help me learn Russian. If anyone wants to retaliate it would be me."

"How would you help?"

"Agent Markov, I have special skills—security, computer hacking, reconnaissance, and communications. While Wolf was here, I learned some things about her. I learned that she's a cancer survivor. I also learned that she's divorced and has a daughter—"

"How did you learn these things?" Petrov interjected.

"On Thursday, Judi was able to lift Wolf's room-key and entered her room while she was at the swimming pool. This allowed her to transfer information from Wolf's personal mobile phone and to bug the room with a listening device that I provided. Then when Wolf talked with Judi on Friday, Wolf had said that she planned to go sightseeing the next day with her friend. The next morning, Judi saw Wolf in the lobby of the InterContinental with her friend. I believe he was the same man I saw at the hotel the night before. That night she and her friend slept together—spent the entire night. I later learned that her friend was Ed Perez, the CIA Chief of Station here in Costa Rica. They never said anything incriminating and never mentioned Maria Martin, but they did talk about personal stuff."

"They were well trained," Markov commented.

Garcia continued. "After Wolf left the country, I did additional research using the Internet. I discovered that Officer Wolf lives in the Washington D.C. area. The daughter's name is Brandy. She's divorced and lives alone. Addresses and phone numbers are available. I could set up the kill scene for you."

"Don't know if we need more help. You have already helped by providing this information. The SVR also has special training you know."

"Sir, may I suggest something that you may want to consider?"

"Okay, feel free."

"Wolf has access to highly classified information that may be of interest to you. Rather than taking her out right away you may want to access her files. I have the skills needed to hijack her IDs, security keys, and passwords. I could set it up so that the CIA computers think it is her every time you access a file. This could go on for a long period of time before it's detected. In the meantime, you would learn things like what the CIA has learned from Maria's computer, except that now we're talking a bigger picture with information on more tactics, contacts and agents. Once you have all the information you want, or they change the access codes, or Wolf leaves the CIA, then you can take her out if you still desire, but you may not want to do it publicly."

"How do you mean when you say not publicly?"

"Maria's murder here was made public. The idea that she was a Soviet spy was leaked to the media. I don't know if you want to kill Officer Wolf in retaliation and make it publicly known that your SVR did it. It may be viewed as an escalation of tensions between the United States and Russia. Perhaps you want to make it look like Wolf dies from an accident or natural causes? If you have the right poison it could be made to look like a return of cancer. It would be a long time before the public finds out that it was murder, if ever. Then you could get back to Moscow before anyone is the wiser. Of course, the CIA would still get your message but it just wouldn't be made public. Either way, I can help set it up for you. It's what I'm trained to do."

"If I choose to go that way, do you have a specific plan?"

"I do. I could use the daughter to get close to Wolf . . . initial reconnaissance, information on her habits, access to her files and her house. I travel to the Washington D.C. area at least once per year. I'm a marketing rep for a company in the D.C. area that sells security products internationally. I learn about their new products and how to market them. My next trip is planned for early September."

"Don't know if—"

"I'm about the same age as the daughter and I don't like to boast, but I still pride myself on my ability to attract women. The daughter is also in the security business. That gives us something in common to talk about and maybe develop friendship and trust. My research indicates that she works for the U.S. National Security Agency. By the way, that may be a connection that you may consider worth developing as well. Anyway, this year I also plan to attend a security conference in D.C. in September. Perhaps I could encourage Miss Brandy to attend and hook up with her at that time."

"I appreciate the offer, but I need to think about it."

"That's all I ask. If you decide to use my help, perhaps we could meet when I'm in D.C. and nail down the specifics of our plan?"

"I will let you know."

"When you decide you want my help, get ahold of Petrov and he will contact me. May I please leave now?" Garcia asked, looking at Markov and then Petrov.

They both nodded in the affirmative and Joseph Garcia left, knowing exactly what he would need to do next.

Markov looked at Petrov and asked, "Can we trust him?"

"Absolutely," Petrov replied.

Back in his office, Joseph Garcia was pleased with what he just accomplished. He sent off a secure text message to another one of his clients. It was short and to the point.

Wheels set in motion. Will meet in D.C. – JGM

15

THE RUSSIAN PLAN

In early September, Joe Garcia flew to Dulles Airport and took a van to the hotel in downtown Washington D.C. where he would stay. He normally came to the D.C. area around this time each year to meet with vendors of security hardware. There was also an expo that he would attend. It was an opportunity to become familiar with all the latest equipment and how to employ it. It was a legitimate business trip that his company would pay for. However, this year he would also meet with potential Russian clients to discuss his possible role in an operation that was clearly illegal.

He checked into his hotel, and then went to the hotel lounge for a late afternoon refreshment while he waited for his contact to show. He was halfway finished with a ginger ale when a gentleman sat down beside him and introduced himself.

"My name is Aleksei Chaban," he said with a heavy Russian accent, "but just call me Aleksei or Alex. I work for Markov."

"Nice to meet you Alex. Have a seat. I'll buy you a beer."

"Markov wants to see us in his room."

Joe looked at Alex quizzically.

"He wants to see us right now!"

Not to be intimidated, Garcia slowly finished his ginger ale, and put a $5 bill on the bar top before sliding off his bar stool. He stood before Aleksei for a moment, looked him in the eye, and said, "Okay, let's go."

Then the two of them took the elevator up to Markov's room.

"Hello Garcia. You have good trip?"

"It was fine but tiring. I didn't expect meeting with you until tomorrow."

"I'm eager to get started. I want you to tell me how you plan to accomplish my objectives."

"Uh . . . Please tell me specifically what you decided you want to accomplish."

"First, I want access to Donna Wolf's classified emails and documents, and then I want you to take her out. How will you go about that?"

"Okay, my plan is to gain access to Donna Wolf's residence. I've already made an initial assessment of what is required. There will be door keys and a security code. Then to access her computer, I'll need multiple passwords. I'll develop a relationship with her daughter because she'll help me get what I need. My plan is to essentially clone Wolf's laptop and give you the clone to use—"

Aleksei interrupted. "Why a clone? Why not just steal her laptop and bring it to us?"

"Because, as soon as her laptop goes missing, she will report it stolen, and as soon as it's reported stolen, the CIA will deauthorize its use. We're talking a matter of only a few hours. And it's not likely that the laptop has anything on it that's classified, so it would become useless to you. If I give you a clone, you can continue to access her accounts indefinitely. The network will think you are her."

Markov looked at his subordinate and smiled. "Our new comrade knows what he's doing. I think we should let him continue."

"The next thing you said was that you wanted to take her out. Are you leaving it up to me to decide how to do that, or do you have something in mind?"

"We have used many techniques in the past—radioactive isotopes, cyanide, heavy metals, antifreeze, nerve gas, various chemical injections, and so on. They all have their limitations." His tone and demeanor were even and calm as he spoke. "I want it to be low key. Make it look like a natural death—no publicity, no investigation. This time we try something new."

"Like—"

"Like cancer," he replied with an increased display of enthusiasm. Our labs back home developed a new chemical that can be ingested. They say it causes a form of blood cancer. That's what we use," he said with conviction.

"Okay, you let me know how I can help with that, and I will do my part."

"I have asked Aleksei to work with you. He will let you know, and keep me informed of your progress."

"This plan will take time to develop," Garcia said addressing Aleksei. "I'll need to establish a residence near where the mom and daughter live, and establish my cover. I will also need some financial help to get started and cover my expenses," Garcia said as he turned toward Markov. "As my client, this would be expected. I'll open a bank account here in Maryland in the name of my company, JR Seguridad, Srl. My company is asking for eight-grand a week for my services."

"Make it four," Markov quickly replied.

"$200 per hour for my time and expense is not unreasonable for this type of work. If I put in a 40-hour week, that's $8,000 a week. We should make this look legit. Don't you agree?"

"Let's split the difference."

"Okay then let's shake on six-grand per week." They shook hands.

16

GETTING STARTED

Joe Garcia had already determined the addresses of Brandy Evans and her mother Donna Wolf. The next step would be to find himself a place to live that would be convenient to both addresses. He found a three-bedroom townhouse on the south side of Columbia, Maryland in the Kings Contrivance section. He agreed on a six-month lease. Donna's address was about three miles to the east of Joe's townhouse off Guilford Road. NSA at Fort Meade was another five miles to the east where both she and Brandy had offices. Brandy's address was in Ellicott City, north of Columbia, and about twelve miles to the north of Joe's place. Joe's next step was to put eyes on them and find out when and where they went each day.

He started with Brandy. Brandy lived in an older house on a half-acre of land. She left her house each day around seven fifteen and headed to her office at Fort Meade. She returned between six and six thirty each day except on Tuesday and Thursday. On these days she returned home around eight thirty. Joe needed to find out what she did on the evenings she came home late. He made note of her car make, model, and plate number.

Meanwhile, Joe watched Donna leave her two-bedroom townhouse around seven thirty in the morning and drive the short distance to her office at Fort Meade. He couldn't help but notice that she had her laptop with her. He would need to access it in order to clone it. He hoped for a time when she would leave it home, otherwise the job would take longer than he first thought. Joe observed that Donna returned home between five thirty and six each evening, except on Thursday. On Thursday she stopped home and went right back out. Joe followed her to a Lifetime Fitness Center in Columbia not far from her townhouse. When he got there, he also found Brandy's car in the parking lot. On that day, Joe kept his distance. He did not want to arouse suspicion, but he knew exactly what he would do next. He joined the fitness club. His membership would begin the Tuesday after Labor Day.

Joe was at the fitness center that Tuesday evening and he reasoned that in addition to Thursdays, Brandy would be there on Tuesdays as well. He was right. She was there. She was using a stationary bike. He positioned himself on a treadmill just across the aisle from the stationary bikes. He watched her as she pedaled energetically, hardly breaking a sweat. She was trim and her body well proportioned. She had black hair tied in a short pony tail above her neck, and a pretty face with a clear complexion. He couldn't help but stare.

Brandy noticed and returned his stare with a few glances of her own. When she finished her required time on the bike, she dismounted and walked across the aisle to confront him.

"You were staring at me. Did you like what you saw?" she said mockingly.

Joe stepped off his treadmill and faced her directly. "I apologize if I creeped you out, but you are a very attractive lady . . . and I think you were also looking at me. Were you not?"

There was a pause, and Joe was not sure which way this conversation would go.

Brandy had noticed his well chiseled body and six-foot frame, his tanned skin, and his full head of short black hair. He was eye candy and she had noticed. However, she decided to ignore his question, and finally said, "I haven't seen you here before. Are you new?"

"I'm afraid so. This is my first visit. My name is Joe. Pleased to meet you," he said and extended his hand.

She was impressed by his slight accent and formality.

"My name is Brandy," she said as they shook hands.

Joe was impressed by her assertiveness, but knew that winning her over would not be easy.

Over the next two weeks, Joe frequented the fitness center at the times that he expected Brandy and her mom to be there. He told her that he was on temporary assignment as a security system consultant and designer. Brandy told him that she managed an IT organization, and worked at Fort Meade. On Thursday the following week, he met Brandy's mother, Donna, for the first time. Joe was entering the locker room area and he encountered Brandy and her mom on their way out. Joe said hello and engaged them in conversation for a few moments before they left. But while Joe's relationship with Brandy was friendly, it was still superficial and it wasn't getting him any closer to Donna Wolf's classified files. The relationship needed to move to the next level. So far, Joe's attempts to do this were politely rebuffed. Brandy seemed reluctant to become involved.

****

Sometime during the last week of September, Joe got a call from Aleksei. "We must meet," he said. "Meet me tomorrow at nine at the sports bar in the plaza near the Metro stop for Glenmont, Maryland." Glenmont was the last stop on the Red line from the District of Columbia. The trip was easy for Aleksei. All he had to do was hop on the Metro from wherever he was staying in the city. On the other hand, Joe had to drive down from his townhouse in Columbia. When he arrived, Aleksei was already seated in a small booth that offered some privacy to the conversation that ensued. Aleksei was already nursing a vodka. Joe ordered a ginger ale.

"What's wrong? You don't drink?"

"No, I don't. Don't take it personally," Joe replied.

"But it reflects your hesitation to take risk."

"What are you saying?"

"Markov thinks things are moving too slow. In Russia we know how to get our women in bed."

"The objective is to compromise Donna Wolf's computers, not to have sex with her daughter. Tell Markov to be patient."

"He wants me to help you."

"How would you do that?"

"If opportunity happens, I hope you would be smart enough to take advantage of it."

"What are you suggesting?"

"I'm told you have high IQ. No? When opportunity happens, you will know."

"I don't want Brandy to get hurt."

"She won't."

"Okay."

"I go now. Must catch Metro back to city before they stop running," he said as he put a ten spot on the table.

As Aleksei got up and left, Joe's ginger ale arrived. *Nice talking with you too*, Joe said to himself.

****

On Tuesday of the first week in October, Joe was already heading out of the locker room toward the exercise equipment when Brandy entered the building. They waved to each other but continued along their respective ways. Two hours later, after completing his workout, Joe waited around, hoping to catch Brandy before she left. He really did need to move things along. He waited near the entrance but someone engaged him in a conversation and he was talking as Brandy passed by. He waved, and she acknowledged, but he chided himself for missing another opportunity.

After a few minutes he headed out to the parking lot, where he saw Brandy standing in front of her car and on the phone. She seemed distraught. As he approached, it became evident what the problem was. Both front tires on Brandy's car were flat. As he looked at her, she held up a finger to indicate she would soon be off the phone. While he waited, he stooped down and looked at one of the tires. It was totally flat, but did not appear slashed or punctured. Sure enough, when he removed the cap on the tire stem, it was evident that someone had loosened the valve stems and let out all the air. He stood up just as Brandy was finishing her call.

"Brandy, who would do this?"

"Good question. Whoever it is, is sending me a message. None of the other cars are affected. Maybe my ex-husband. We just had a legal dispute over money set aside for my son's college education and he lost. He can be a real asshole at times."

"You were just on the phone, were you calling a road service?"

"Yes, but they said they don't do tire repair and they don't have air compressors on their trucks, so the car must be towed."

"How long?"

"Not till tomorrow."

"Oh, that's not good. Can I give you a ride somewhere?"

"Thanks for the offer, but I don't know, I tried to call my mom, but I get a message that says her home phone is unavailable and she's not picking up on her cell. I left a message but she may not get it."

"Okay look, let me drive you home. You can continue to try and reach your mother, and hopefully she'll be able to help you in the morning."

"I don't know . . . I don't want you to—"

"Brandy, it will be okay. I don't mind helping you."

Brandy locked up her car and followed Joe back to his. Joe could tell she was nervous as they pulled out of the parking lot. She was wringing her hands and he could see the stress in her face.

"Who would do this to me?"

"Brandy you need to relax. Everything will be okay . . . .. Which way?"

"Take Snowden River to Broken Land, then head west to Route 29 and go north to Route 100. It's about eleven miles."

"Okay."

"I don't understand why I can't reach Mom."

"Does she live nearby?"

"She lives in a townhouse off of Guilford Road."

"That's interesting. I live off Guilford Road also," he responded to get her talking.

"Where on Guilford Road?"

"Eden Brook."

"Oh okay, Mom lives further to the east closer to Route 1"

"Isn't that kind of out of her way to come here to help you in the morning?"

"Yes, but she owes me a few favors. She was very sick a year and a half ago and I spent a lot of time with her, and when she goes somewhere, I water her plants and tend to her cat. I was thinking she could come stay with me tonight and come back here with me in the morning, and then if my car isn't available, we would continue onto work together. We both work at Fort Meade—different buildings—but I can walk from one to the other."

"Are you and your mom close?"

"We weren't for many years, but three years ago after I got divorced, Mom helped me to deal with it, and then later when she got sick, it was clear that she needed me, so we've grown much closer now."

"You're lucky to have your mom around. My dad and my stepmom were killed in a car crash about five years ago. That's when I started my consulting business."

"I'm sorry to hear that your parents passed away," she said with sincerity. "Here get off at this exit. My house is on the opposite side of the highway but there is no exit so we need to loop around and cross over to the other side."

"Okay."

By the time they pulled into her driveway it had become dark, but there was some light from her porch lamp and a street lamp. "So, here you are—safe and sound . . .. Nice-looking house. Well landscaped too."

"It looks better in the daylight," she quipped. "Thank you for your help," she said and reached for the door handle.

"Brandy, before you go, I'd like to ask you something."

She sat back in the seat and looked at him. "Yes?"

"I would like to ask you to have dinner with me."

After a moment of silence, she replied. "Joe, I like you enough, but I'm not sure I'm ready to date anyone."

"Why? You've been divorced for three years. You need to have a life, don't you?"

"That's just it. I have a life and I'm happy with it. I don't need to get involved in a romantic relationship. You're a very attractive man. If you're looking for sex, you can do better than me."

"Brandy, that's not what I'm looking for, and if I were, I don't think I could do better than you."

"When we first met, it seemed that way. You were looking at me that way. So, what are you looking for?"

"I'm looking for a friend that will enjoy my companionship and vice versa. I don't expect sex. Just go to dinner with me. We don't have to call it a date . . .. Think of me as you would a girlfriend if you want."

The way he said it made her smile.

"Joe if I say yes, I need to know something first, I need to know if you're married."

"No! I'm not married, never have been, and I have no children. And if you say yes, I promise to respect you."

"Okay."

"Okay yes?"

"Yes."

"Here take this." He gave her one of his business cards. "My local mobile number is on the back."

"I don't have a business card to give you," she said.

"Not a problem, just tell me. I'll remember it." She told him the number and he repeated it back.

That Friday evening, they had a very enjoyable dinner together and afterwards they took a leisurely walk around the nearby lake. They learned a lot about each other—everything except Joe's actual mission in the States. By all accounts it was the start of a romantic relationship—but without sex. Joe was keeping his word out of respect—or was it out of necessity.

17

A CLONE JOB

Joe's relationship with Brandy developed, but it was not until late October that Joe had the first opportunity to accompany Brandy to Donna's townhouse.

The two had a date for Saturday evening, Brandy called early that afternoon to request a change in their plans.

"Joe, would it be okay if I pick you up rather than you driving all the way up here?"

"Sure, why?"

"Well," she said. "Yesterday, Mom decided to spend the weekend in D.C. with an old friend, and she asked me if I could go over to her house to feed her cat and water her plants. I could pick you up early and then you could go with me to Mom's before we go on our date. Do you mind?"

"Not a problem," he said, as he recognized this was the opportunity that he had been waiting for.

Brandy drove them to Mom's townhouse and they parked right out front. As they walked to the front door, Brandy asked Joe to wait on the porch. Joe watched as she went to the edge of the townhouse and retrieved a key from the downspout. *How convenient*, Joe thought to himself. She unlocked the door and they entered the foyer. As Joe followed her in, he could hear the beep-beep-beep of the security alarm. Brandy went to the alarm box mounted on a nearby wall, opened the door and began to punch the buttons. Joe watched intently as she punched in the code '0-0-2-9-6'.

Then they walked down a hallway and into the kitchen. Joe looked around and spied the empty food dish for the cat. "Where's the cat?" he asked.

"Tabby's a little shy with strangers. But if we put some food into his dish he may come," she said. "Would you mind getting his food bag from inside the utility closet over there?" She pointed to a door along the side of the kitchen wall near the back entrance-way. "I'll be watering plants in the living room."

Joe went inside the closet and saw the bag in a corner. He also saw the panel for the security system, and noticed the key in the key slot. He couldn't resist. He opened the panel and looked inside. He noticed the AC power connection that came from a transformer plugged into the wall socket below. He also noticed the black brick that served as backup power supply, and he also noticed the phone line circuit that communicated with the security company's monitoring service. All of this could be useful information in the future. He picked up the bag of food, walked out of the closet and over to Tabby's dish and poured a small amount of the dried food into the dish, but Tabby didn't come.

"He's probably upstairs in the bonus room," Brandy said. "Come up with me. I need to clean his litter box."

On the second level was a small extra room called the bonus room. It was at the rear of the house just past the laundry room. In addition to Tabby's litter box there was a bed for him to sleep in, and another food and water dish. Cleaning supplies, extra cat food, and miscellaneous who knows what were on a shelf on a side wall.

"Wow! You mean Tabby has his own room? One lucky cat!" Joe exclaimed. Brandy laughed. "But I still don't see him."

After they took care of the litter box, they came back to the kitchen. Sure enough, Tabby was at his bowl eating. Joe slowly approached. Tabby looked up, but decided he was no threat and dipped his head back into his bowl. "Where do you suppose he was?"

"Probably upstairs in Mom's office. He likes to sit on the window sill on a sunny day."

"This is a nice place. How long has your mom lived here?"

"About three years now."

"She's lucky to have you nearby to take care of things when she's not here . . . Where did she go this weekend?"

"Well, she has a long-time friend. His name is Ed Perez. He lives in Costa Rica, but every now and then he comes to the States on business. Maybe you know him."

He smiled. "It's a big country. Lots of people."

"Well, anyway they see each other once or twice a year. And when they do, they make the most of it."

"You don't mind?"

"No, my dad has been gone for about ten years now, and Mom needs a life outside of her work. I'm happy for her."

"She coming back tomorrow?" Joe asked.

"No, not till Monday, and that reminds me, Mom said she forgot to water her plant and wanted me to check on it. It's upstairs in her office. Come on up with me."

While Brandy put water onto a palm in a large pot to the left, Joe looked around. Straight ahead was a double size window overlooking the parking lot. Venetian blinds had been pulled up and the sun beamed in. Under the window was a shelving unit, the top of which was covered with a cloth upon which Tabby like to sit in the sun. The lower shelves contained books, manuals, CD ROMS, and a locked box. A file cabinet was in one corner to the left of the door and, a wooden desk with a swivel-chair was up against the wall to the right. Sitting atop the desk was Donna's laptop. He observed that it was a powerful Lenovo, not an Apple.

As they left, Joe watched Brandy reset the alarm. This time it was '1-0-2-9-6.' Brandy returned the key to the downspout and then they went back to the car and drove to a nearby pub where they met two of Brandy's friends for drinks, supper, and conversation. Brandy introduced Joe as a friend from the fitness club. Afterwards she drove

Joe back to his place and dropped him off. They both said how much they enjoyed the evening. Joe was tempted to ask her in but held back.

****

The next morning, Joe was up early, He had a job to do. After a quick breakfast, he gathered up his laptop and his gear, and drove over to Donna's townhouse. He let himself in but did not return the door key to the downspout. Instead, he slipped it into his pocket, then he entered '0-0-2-9-6' into the key pad on the wall and headed upstairs to the office. He powered up Donna's laptop and verified that it required a password just to be able to use it. He tried a couple of obvious possibilities like '*password*' and like '*Tabby*' but as expected they didn't work. He reasoned that multiple passwords would be required to access the CIA network, her email, and the various files and programs that she used. There would be too many to remember. She probably used a password manager program. In any case, he reasoned that she probably had all her passwords and user IDs documented somewhere. He began to search the office. He remembered the locked box on the shelf under the window. He pulled it out and set it atop the desk. It had a simple key lock. No key. No problem. He picked the lock and opened the box. Inside he found several USB memory-sticks. A label on one of them said '*pw mgr*'—just what he was looking for. It would have all the passwords and a backed-up version of the password manager program. He inserted the memory stick into his laptop and copied the contents bit by bit onto his laptop. He now had the password needed to log onto Donna's computer and the master password and user ID required by the password manager program. He returned to Donna's computer and entered the password to log onto the computer itself. It was '*TabbyCat1.*' Once on her computer, he was able to use the master password and access everything. However, that would not meet the Russian's requirements. They wanted to access the CIA network from their own computer at a different location.

He didn't know Donna's Wi-Fi password so he plugged a cable directly into her cable modem and attempted to access the CIA network from his laptop. As expected, it didn't work. Access to the CIA network required a unique access protocol program and a unique identifier for Donna's computer. Perhaps the MAC address or a cookie—which would uniquely identify that computer—was communicated during the connection process, or there may have been other reasons why it didn't work. He would need to analyze it. It would take a few days, but for now, he copied her MAC address and all her cookies onto his laptop. He copied the registry information and he copied the network access protocol. Then, he made sure everything was back in its original place, and before he left the townhouse, he took time to say hello to Tabby. Tabby was becoming his friend.

On the way home he stopped at a hardware store and had the key duplicated. He would return it to the downspout later that evening. It took another two weeks and another secret trip back to the townhouse before he had a working system he could turn over to Markov. Essentially, when all was said and done, he had cloned Donna's laptop onto another computer.

18

FALLING IN LOVE

It was mid-November and the three of them had driven to Philadelphia to attend a three-day computer security conference. After the second day of sessions, Joe, Brandy, and Brandy's friend Jill joined several colleagues and went to the Travelers Lounge in their hotel for drinks and conversation. The sessions had ended late that evening and dinner consisted of bar food. Joe, Brandy, Jill and a guy named John sat at a table for four. Jill had met John at one of the sessions and they seemed to hit it off. An entertainer sang and played dance music in one corner of the lounge while one or two couples danced.

Joe took the opportunity to dance with Brandy. He was an excellent dancer especially to Latin music, and Brandy loved it. Meanwhile, John seemed to be sweet-talking Jill. At some point, John went to the bar to get himself another beer and Jill another Pina Colada. Joe just happened to glance over to the bar from the dance floor and couldn't believe what he saw. He whispered something into Brandy's ear and they walked back to the table.

"Would you care to dance?" he politely asked Jill.

She hesitated and looked to Brandy and then to John, as if to seek approval.

"Go ahead," Brandy said as John remained silent.

She got up from her seat, and took a quick gulp of her drink before walking off with Joe.

Once on the dance floor, Joe momentarily put a hand on each shoulder, pulled her close, put his mouth down to the side of her cheek, and spoke.

"Jill, I saw John put a roofie into your drink."

"Hah, hah, funny," she replied.

"Jill I'm not joking. Don't drink that drink."

"I don't believe you . . . Let's dance," she said in a matter-of-fact manner.

When they returned to the table and sat down, Brandy and John were talking. John was still unaware that his secret was out.

Jill reached for her drink, and was about to take another sip. Brandy interjected just in time. "Jill would you mind coming to the ladies' room with me?"

After they left, Joe looked hard at John and spoke sternly but calmly. "John, I saw you put a roofie into Jill's drink. But why? She already likes you. If you asked her to have sex with you, she probably would have said yes anyway."

"I wanted to help things along."

"Look, Jill and Brandy are friends of mine. I can't let you do it."

"Did you already tell her?"

"I did."

"Did she believe you?"

"Do you want to be here when they return? We'll find out."

Before John could respond, the ladies returned.

"Jill says she's not feeling well. We're going to go up to the room."

John waited for them to leave and then stood up and addressed Joe with hostility. "Thanks for messing up my evening. I'll get you back for this."

"Don't waste your time John."

Joe watched John go to the bar and made sure that he was not going to follow the ladies. Then after a few minutes, he got up and headed toward the elevators.

****

Joe took the elevator up to the fourth floor. He was relieved that John did not follow. Brandy and Jill were sharing a room. He knocked on the door.

"Who's there?" It was Brandy's voice.

"It's Joe . . .. May I come in?"

"Of course," she said. "C'mon in."

"Is Jill okay? Where is she?"

"She's in the bathroom. I think she's okay. She didn't have very much of the drink. I think she's mostly embarrassed. Joe, she didn't believe you. She thought they were really hitting it off. Are you absolutely sure that John did what you said?"

"Yes. He admitted it to me after you guys went to the ladies' room. I asked him why he did it, and he said he wanted to help things along. I'd like to tell Jill I'm sorry this happened, but she shouldn't be embarrassed. Will she speak to me?"

"Have a seat, I'll see how she's doing."

A few minutes later she entered the room.

"Joe, I should have believed you. I'm embarrassed that I allowed him to deceive me, but the fact is you saved me from being raped. I owe you."

"You have nothing to be embarrassed about. You had no way of knowing. Things happen. I'm glad you're okay."

"Look, Brandy, you don't need to stay with me. I mean if you two want to be together, it's fine. Perhaps you have things you need to talk about in private?"

Brandy looked at Jill. "Are you sure?"

"I'll be fine . . . Go."

Brandy and Joe walked down the hall and around a corner to Joe's room. Once inside, Joe took a seat on the edge of the bed. She remained standing. "What is it that Jill thinks we need to talk about in private?" he asked.

"Joe, I think we should talk about our relationship. I—"

He started to interrupt but she cut him off before he could say anything.

"No, hear me out. I like you. We have known each other for two months now. We've had several dates. We've had dinners; we've gone hiking; we've been to concerts; we've gone out for ice cream; we've gone swimming. We even dressed up and went to a Halloween party. We've enjoyed each other's company. Last week we went dancing and tonight we danced. You've been to my house. You've been to my mom's house and you've met her. My mom likes you. She's happy that I have a male friend. We've been able to discuss topics that range from trivial to matters of national interests. We've shared personal information about ourselves. You've shown me that you're a caring and considerate person, and I really like you—"

"Okay, I like you too. I like you a lot. Aren't we good friends? What's the problem?"

She shook her head. "Joe that's the problem right there. We're good friends and I know that's my own doing. I told you I was afraid of getting involved sexually and you promised to respect that . . . and you have, but I know it's been hard on you to do that, and it's been hard on me as well—"

"Are you about to tell me you don't want to be friends anymore?"

"No, I'm telling you that I don't want it to end, and I want to be more than just friends, but I need to know how you really feel about me. How is it possible for you to show so much restraint?"

"You said you didn't want to have sex, and I kept my promise not to pressure you."

"I know, and that was unfair of me, but you don't need to keep your promise anymore."

Joe sat there looking bewildered. She went over to him, pulled his head toward hers, and kissed him hard on the mouth. He hesitated.

"Joe, what's holding you back? You told me you don't have a wife or a girlfriend back home. Please tell me if you do. And you said you weren't gay. Is there something wrong with *me*? Don't you desire me?"

"Oh, God, no! There's nothing wrong with you. I think you're a wonderful person and I care deeply for you."

Emotionally, Joe briefly wished he could tell her everything, but he knew he couldn't do that. He had to complete the mission. Until a few days ago he thought that Brandy's part in his mission could be completed soon. He had access to Wolf's house, and he had provided Markov access to Wolf's on-line accounts, and he was ready for whenever Markov gave the word to deliver the poison. After that, he could just disappear. It would be so much easier if he and Brandy were not sexually involved—at least that was his thinking. But then when he met with Aleksei just a few days ago, he realized that the mission would require much more time, and that meant more time with Brandy. Apparently, there was an issue with the email access process, and Aleksei said that there were other items on the network that he wanted to access. Perhaps Wolf had reset passwords. Perhaps something else. He would need to go back to Wolf's townhouse and find out. And then, when was the next part of the mission supposed to take place? He would need to know when Wolf would not be there and he would need to assure that the same key code was being used for the townhouse security system. The poisoning would probably require multiple visits. If there were any suspicions, or perhaps as a matter of routine, Wolf may change the keycode or the passwords. The problem was, he was conflicted. He thought he might be falling in love with Brandy, while at the same time he knew he was taking advantage of her to complete his mission, and he didn't like that. So, he told her what he could.

"Brandy, when I first saw you, I thought that you were attractive and my desire was to have a fling, a sexual one to be sure. But I quickly got to know you and realized how wonderful a person you are. I've never met a woman like you before, and I've never felt this way about a woman before . . .. But that's the reason for my hesitation. My assignment here is short term. I have no idea where I'll be four months from now. It's possible we won't see each other after my assignment is complete, and I don't want to hurt you."

She turned toward him and reached for his hand. "Joe, if you leave in four months without having made love to me, it will hurt me even more."

"Are you sure?"

"Yes."

He pulled her to him and they hugged tightly. Then they slowly undressed each other, exploring each other's bodies for the first time. He told her how much he cared about her.

19

THANKSGIVING

Brandy invited Joe to come to Thanksgiving dinner at her mother's house, and naturally he had to accept. Brandy said her son Brian would be there, and Joe asked if anyone else would be there.

"No. Just us," Brandy replied. "Mom saw Ed less than two weeks ago, and so he can't make it, but he might come around Christmas."

Joe felt relieved that Ed Perez would not be there, but still felt uneasy about what he was getting himself deeper and deeper into. He had previously met both Brandy's mom Donna, and her son Brian, but only briefly. Now he would be having a long visit. They would ask questions. He didn't want his mission known, and if Donna knew, she would be very upset that he was romancing her daughter. And that was becoming more and more of a dilemma for him. He was beginning to have strong feelings for Brandy. He didn't know how much longer he could carry out the charade, and Markov was not yet ready for part two of his plan.

"Brandy, how much do we tell them about our relationship? Does your mom already know we have slept together? How does she feel about that?"

"Joe, relax. She's very happy for me and I'm sure she expects that we've slept together. And besides, this is the year 2003 and we're both in our mid-thirties. She's not going to judge us. And, I'm sure she has been sleeping with her friend Ed, and I don't judge her. So, like I said, relax. Just be yourself."

****

On Thanksgiving, Joe drove the short distance from his place to Donna's house. He was told that dinner would be at three o'clock but to come early around two. He arrived on schedule and brought two bottles with him. He had a bottle of Sauvignon blanc for Donna and Brandy, and he had a bottle of cider for Brian and himself. Brandy and Brian were already there when he arrived. Brandy was in the kitchen helping with the food, and Brian was in the living room playing a game on the TV screen. As he came in, he could smell the pleasant aroma of the turkey and what he thought to be baked bread. He greeted everyone and offered to help. They immediately put him in charge of setting the table. It had been many years since Joe had celebrated holidays with family. His head now filled with pleasant memories of when he was young and he and his dad and stepmom had holidays together. He snapped out of it when he felt a tug on his arm. Brandy gave him a kiss on the cheek and asked if he would please say hello to Brian and tell him his mom would like him to wash up for dinner and come to the table.

They sat down to dinner and Joe poured the wine and the cider. Donna said a short grace, a thank you to God. Then Joe raised his glass:

"I want to thank all of you for inviting me to join you."

After they each took a sip, Brian asked, "Joe how come you aren't drinking wine?"

Brandy started to say something, but Joe held up his hand. "It's okay. It's a personal choice I made. My mother's brother was an alcoholic and I found his behavior to be obnoxious, and at a young age my mother was run down and killed by a drunk driver. I tried drinking in college but it made me sick. I decided I didn't want to be like my uncle, and I didn't want to harm anyone. I haven't had a drink since."

Donna then asked, "Joe, would you be willing to carve the turkey for us?"

"It would be my honor."

"I'm sorry about your mom," Donna said. "Brandy says you're from Costa Rica. Where about?"

"The San José area. Have you ever been to San José?"

Joe poured more wine into Donna's glass.

"Yes, I have. I have a friend that lives there."

"And where does he live?"

"Escazu."

"That's a rather upscale place to live. What does he do?"

"He has a high-level government job. And where do *you* work?"

"I work to the northeast of Sabana Park on Route 2, and I live several kilometers south of there. Brandy has my business card."

"Do you like living there?"

"I do, but I also liked living in the States. Don't know if Brandy told you, but I was born in Texas, and I lived there until my dad got a good job in Costa Rica and we moved. I was about six. I also went to graduate school in the U.S."

"So, wait a minute, aren't you a citizen of Costa Rica?"

"Yes, my dad was, so I have dual citizenship."

"How did your dad and mom meet?"

"He was in graduate school at the University of Texas and she worked at the school."

"You mentioned that your mom passed away. What about your dad? Is he still alive?"

"No, unfortunately he and my stepmom died in a car crash about seven years ago . . .. So, Donna tell me," Joe said changing the subject, "What did you think of Costa Rica when *you* were there?"

"Well, my friend would like me to retire there—with him of course. I think it's a beautiful country, but I'm not sure I would want to live or work in the city. The traffic in the morning and evening seemed almost intolerable. I remember hardly moving in traffic while motorcycles whizzed in and out between the vehicles."

"I'm afraid to tell you this, but on most days I'm one of those motorcyclists. And you're right, the traffic is terrible, but the bike allows me to cut significant time off my commute, and the gas mileage is a lot better than the car I share with my business partner."

"What model bike do you have?" Donna asked.

"It's a Yamaha 2000 XV635. five-speed manual. Do you know bikes?"

"Actually, I had a bike once," she responded . . .. "It was a small Suzuki, a souped-up moped really. I had it for the same reasons, traffic and gas mileage . . . and parking," she added.

Now Brandy started to show an interest and looked at her mom with a degree of disbelief. "Really Mom?"

"I loved that bike," she said excitedly. "It was nicknamed little Susie. Your father and I, we . . ." Her voice tapered off as she realized the impact of what she was about to say.

"My father? Tell me about him."

"Brandy, we've been through this. I can't do that yet. Please be patient with me."

"Sorry Mom."

"Anyway, it was a long time ago—before you were born."

"I can't imagine you riding a motor bike Grandma," Brian added.

"And I never saw you on a bike," Brandy added. "Why did you stop?"

"I had a very scary accident. I was lucky I wasn't killed. And soon after that, I got pregnant with you, so I decided it just wasn't worth the risk and I haven't been on a bike since."

Joe, who was paying close attention to this exchange, decided to change the subject.

"Donna, did you say you were thinking of retiring?"

"Yes, I had originally planned to retire by the end of this year, but now it has slipped to the end of January. I'm counting the days," she responded.

"Grandma, how come you delayed it?"

"My boss wants me to help finish a project I've been involved with."

Joe thought about the significance of that. *Did the delay have anything to do with his mission? Markov only has another two months to get what he wants using her access codes, and if part two of his plan is for a slow death by poisoning, it would need to start very soon.*

"Here's to your future retirement," he said and held up his cider glass.

After the dinner they agreed to take a break and come back later for pumpkin pie and coffee. Joe helped to clear the table. When he walked into the kitchen, he was surprised to see Tabby at his bowl off in the corner. He walked over and noticed the bowl was empty. Tabby looked up and meowed. Joe crouched down to pet him. Donna, who had just entered the kitchen, watched as Tabby rubbed up against Joe's leg and started purring.

"Wow!" she exclaimed. "Tabby usually doesn't warm up to strangers that fast."

Then Joe went to use the rest room near the kitchen, but apparently Brian was in there. He heard Donna telling him he could use the one upstairs if he wished. He thanked her and headed off upstairs. On the way back, he encountered Brandy. She was in Tabby's room looking out the window. He walked up behind her and put his arm around her shoulder.

"What are you looking at?"

"I was just thinking about Mom. You probably noticed how she reacted when she started to say something about my birth-father."

"Yes, I did, and I was wondering what that was about."

"All my life I've wanted her to talk about him, and she just won't do it. Until tonight, I had the impression he was still alive, and it was always my hope to meet him someday. I thought maybe Mom needed to protect his identity for some reason, like maybe he was a secret operative or something. But what she said tonight implied that maybe he was killed in her motor bike accident, and I remember when I was a child, my grandma told me he was killed in the war in Vietnam, so maybe that's true. Anyway, that's what I was thinking about."

"I see. I always wanted to know more about my birth mother, so I understand. I hope she tells you about him."

After everyone had used the restroom, they returned to the dining room. The table was cleared and reset, and after the coffee was ready, they were ready for dessert. Donna brought out a home-baked pie, and Joe poured the coffee. More talk ensued. Joe made a point of complimenting Donna on how good the pie was. At some point Brian excused himself but after a few minutes he returned. A flash of light seemed to come out of nowhere.

"Brian, what are you doing?" Joe exclaimed in horror.

"I wanted a picture of you and my mom. Aren't you and Mom like boyfriend and girlfriend?"

"We're good friends Brian," Joe responded showing some annoyance.

"Do you really like her and care about her?"

"I do."

"You have been seeing each other quite a bit over the past two months. Are you sleeping together?"

Donna spoke up. "Brian, you don't ask something like that."

"I just want Mom to know that if they like each other, I'm okay with it. Dad says he doesn't want her back, and I want her to be with someone who cares about her."

"Well, we do care about each other, but we're taking things slowly. Joe is only here on a temporary assignment and we don't know yet how it will play out. Okay?"

"Okay."

It was about ten in the evening when Joe excused himself. He thanked Donna again and gave her a goodbye hug. Then he kissed Brandy and gave Brian a man-hug. On his drive home he concluded that the evening had gone quite well.

20

THE POISONED WELL

In early December, Markov gave the order to initiate part two of his plan. Aleksei met Joe at their meeting place in Glenmont. The day was chilly and it was natural that they both wore gloves. This time their meeting was brief. Aleksei reached into his coat pocket and pulled out a small package which he handed to Joe. The package contained a small liquid-filled bottle with an eye dropper top.

"Here is your weapon," he said. "Do a dropper full, five times over next two months and she is dead. If not, *you* are dead."

Joe gave him a look.

"I joke. Markov wishes you good luck."

Joe put the bottle in his pocket. The two shook hands and they parted.

The next day, Joe parked in front of Donna's townhouse, walked up to the front door and entered with the key he had copied from the one in the downspout. As he entered, he heard the low beeping sound from the home security system. He went to the wall mounted box and entered '0-0-2-9-6'. He was pleased that it hadn't been changed. The beeping stopped. As he went into the kitchen, he saw Tabby cowering under a chair. He offered a treat and was pleased that Tabby acknowledged him by coming out, sniffing the treat he held in his hand, and rubbing up against the leg of his pants. He placed the treat in Tabby's dish and proceeded to the refrigerator. Inside the refrigerator he found a pitcher of iced tea sitting on the top shelf next to the milk and orange juice. As he pulled the small bottle of clear liquid from his pocket, he knew exactly what he had to do.

Two weeks later he went back to Donna's place to apply dose number two. He kept Aleksei informed. As before, he knew exactly what he needed to do. And once again, he took the time to play with his new friend Tabby.

****

It was a short week. New Year's Eve was on a Wednesday, and Brandy had decided to have a small gathering of friends and neighbors at her house that evening to celebrate. Joe learned that neither Brandy nor her mom would go to work that day, and the two of them would spend most of the day at Brandy's house helping with preparations. Joe saw Donna's expected absence from her townhouse as an opportunity. He informed Aleksei of his intention on Tuesday evening.

"Markov wants to know if Officer Wolf has shown any sign of becoming sick."

"No, I was wondering about that. How long is this supposed to take?"

"Markov is getting impatient. He wants me to go with you for the remaining three doses."

"Sounds like you don't trust me."

"Just following orders."

Early the next morning, Joe met Aleksei at the Metro's Greenbelt station and they drove from there to Donna's townhouse.

Joe unlocked the door and they walked in to be greeted by the expected beep, beep, beep.

"What is the key code?" Aleksei asked as he went directly to the key pad on the wall.

"Press '0-0-2-9-6'," Joe said, as he set the small bottle of poison on the counter top.

"It don't work!" Aleksei responded.

"What? What do you mean? Do it again."

"I did!"

"Oh crap! Keep trying," Joe yelled as he ran down the hallway to the utility closet. He opened the door on the panel and quickly disconnected the phone line to the security company with only five seconds to spare. He was about to go back to the kitchen when he heard the alarm go off upstairs, as well as on the panel itself. *Oh damn*, he said to himself. He pulled off the wire for the back-up battery and then using the small screwdriver he kept in his pocket he removed the AC connection. The alarms stopped. He hoped that no one outside the house had heard it. He closed the panel door and headed back to the kitchen where he noticed that a red flashing light on the key pad unit had replaced the beeping.

"I think I got it in time," he said to Aleksei who already had the container of orange juice on the counter and was adding a dropper full of the poison, "but as soon as you're done, I suggest we hightail it out of here, just in case."

They locked the front door as they left, got back in Joe's car and drove off.

"What happened? Why code don't work?"

"Could be Donna changed it. When she gets back, she will know someone was here."

"We come back two more times, no?"

"Yeah, I'll figure it out." Joe drove Aleksei back to the Metro station and dropped him off.

Later that evening, Joe joined Brandy, Donna, and their friends at Brandy's house and celebrated the new year.

****

Two and a half weeks later, it was Martin Luther King's Day, Monday the 19th of January, 2004. Donna and Brandy had the day off and decided to have mother and daughter time by spending the day shopping. This afforded Joe another opportunity. There was still no indication that Donna was getting sick. As Joe and Aleksei entered the townhouse, they saw Tabby scurry away and hide. This time Joe went directly to the utility room and disarmed the system all within 20 seconds. When he exited the utility room, he encountered Tabby peeking at him from under a shelf. Joe couldn't resist saying hello. When he returned to the kitchen, Aleksei had already opened the refrigerator and was looking at the orange juice. The orange juice container was low. It appeared that Donna had been drinking it. Joe watched as Aleksei returned the orange juice container to its position and pulled out the iced tea container. He watched as Aleksei squirted what seemed to be less than a full dropper of the liquid poison into the tea. "That should do it. Let's go," he said.

"I need ten minutes," Joe told him. Joe had researched the alarm system and was able to reset it back to the way it was before they entered without knowing the keycode. It took ten minutes, but when he powered it back up, there were no alarms going off. After walking out the front door he paused, no beeping, and no alarm. Then they left.

****

The well was poisoned again two weeks later, on February first, Super Bowl Sunday. In the morning, Donna was with Brandy. They may have gone to church and then afterwards Donna helped Brandy with preparation for a Super Bowl party that would take place at Brandy's house that evening. Many of the same friends that had attended the New Year's Eve party would be there including Joe. Up to this point, Donna had not displayed any noticeable effects of having been poisoned, and once again Markov assigned Aleksei to accompany Joe to Donna's townhouse that morning.

"It appears Donna has been drinking orange juice—there's a brand-new container on the shelf. Looks like it could use some of this," Aleksei said as he inserted the dropper into the bottle of liquid poison. Meanwhile Joe went into the other room and befriended Tabby.

"Did you put it into the orange juice?" Joe asked when he returned.

"I put a dropper full in the juice but some poison left in the bottle, so I add it the tea."

Donna came home later in the afternoon to clean up and change for the party that evening. Joe did not know if she drank any tea or orange juice before she left for the party. However, after the party that night, Donna said she was feeling sick and rather than return home she stayed over at Brandy's house. Brian was at his father's house that night and Joe had planned to stay over, but realized that under the circumstances, the right thing to do would be to return to his place after the party and sleep alone.

21

MISDIRECTION

During the months of December through January, Ivan Markov had reaped a great deal of intelligence by tapping into Donna Wolf's CIA email account. As a result, he had uncovered the identities of several Russian officials, some within the FSB and the SVR, who had passed information off to the CIA. Arrests had been made. Of course, they all pleaded their innocence, but the emails spoke for themselves, and Markov was quite pleased with the cyber access that Joe Garcia had set up for him.

Now, in early February 2004, Ivan Markov sat in an easy chair in his make-shift office with a laptop computer spanning his thighs. He had just come across an email from the CIA in Russia. It was addressed to Brian Matheson with Donna Wolf on copy. The classification was Top Secret.

> *Agents uncovered evidence that Putin worked with KGB and SVR to suppress and eliminate opposition leaders, especially in the Liberal Russia Party and took further action to prevent or hinder opposition voting in the Parliamentary elections in December. Evidence includes photos and recording of Putin and associates. I put Officer Wolf on copy because one of the SVR participants is identified as Ivan Markov, who I believe is a person of interest to Officer Wolf.*

The full dossier is in the referenced file. The code word is "United."

This information could have an impact on April's presidential election in Russia. Please advise if further action required.

Reply to Chief of Station, St Petersburg.

Markov accessed the dossier and read with astonishment the extent to which he, Putin, and others were incriminated. He couldn't help but ask himself questions. Who was spying on them? Who was leaking secrets? How did this stuff get revealed?

A week later, Markov saw the following response from Matheson:

I will leak this dossier to the Washington Post. My agent will deliver thumb drive to WP rep at the coffee shop on 15th and K on Saturday mid-morn. President Bush gave go-ahead. Your sources will be protected.

****

Twenty-five-year-old Daisy Clark was called into her manager's office at the Washington Post. Daisy was a recent hire at the paper and was still learning the ropes. She was also eager to take on any assignment that might help her get ahead.

"Daisy I have a field assignment for you."

"Yes sir . . . A field assignment. That sounds interesting."

"This assignment is very important because I want you to receive a digital file from one of our secret sources. Secrecy is very important. The information will result in a big exclusive story for the Post."

"Okay. Exactly what do you want me to do?"

"I want you to go to the coffee house on the corner of *15th and K* around ten in the morning. Buy yourself a latte or whatever, take a seat and wait for a man to arrive and introduced himself as Mr. Jay Smith. Allow him to initiate the conversation. You will respond with your name, and say 'pleased to meet you.' He will ask if you have been waiting long and you will answer 'yes, actually I have.' Then he will apologize and shake your hand and say he appreciates you waiting.

The hand shake will deliver a USB thumb drive from his hand to yours. Don't fumble it. Put it directly into your purse. Stay seated for about five minutes and talk about the weather or whatever small talk you can think of. Then excuse yourself and leave the restaurant. Come directly back here and give me the thumb drive. Got it?"

"Yes sir."

Daisy performed her assignment as planned. She arrived at 9:50, enjoyed a double mocha latte, and met Jay Smith at 10:05. At 10:15, with the thumb drive secured in her shoulder purse, she left the coffee house and walked down the sidewalk toward her car. Before she got to her car, a man came up behind her, put his arm around her, and told her he had a gun and if she wanted to stay alive, she had better cooperate. She was scared out of her wits.

"Please don't hurt me. I'll do whatever you want," she whimpered.

"Good. You get idea," he said with his mouth up against her ear. Then he grabbed hold of her arm and forcefully led her to the rear door of a waiting limo. "Get in," he said gruffly.

"Please, you're hurting my arm. What do you want?" She was in tears as she was forced into the rear seat of the limo. The man slid in behind her. Once inside the limo, she found herself sitting between two beefy men, the one on her right who had accosted her and another on her left. The limo began to move forward.

"Where are you taking me? What do you want?" she pleaded.

"We want the thumb drive," the man on her left said as he grabbed her purse and began to rummage through it. "Ah, here it is," he finally said and held it up in the air as if to declare victory. She sensed a slight accent. "Now, tell me young lady, what were you planning to do with this? Did you think you would write a masterpiece article that would make you famous?"

"I don't even know what's on there," she pleaded.

The two men turned and looked at each other. "Really?" one of them said. "Can we believe that?"

"Please I'm telling you the truth. This is my first assignment. I was just told to deliver the thumb drive to my boss. I have no idea what's on it."

"What we do with her boss?" the man on the right asked.

"I think—"

Just then they were interrupted by two vehicles that cut them off and forced them to come to a complete stop. Within seconds they were surrounded by FBI agents with guns drawn. The doors to the car were opened and they were ordered out.

The man on Daisy's left objected. "We have diplomatic immunity," he calmly protested.

"Doesn't matter," the agent said. "The lady next to you needs to exit. You need to let her out."

"Okay fine," he said reluctantly and stepped into the street, allowing Daisy to slide out of the limo.

As soon as Daisy was out of the car, she was escorted away by a female FBI agent. At the same time, the man who preceded her out of the limo was forced face first against the roof of the limo and handcuffed. He got a pat-down and the thumb drive was recovered.

"You can't do this. I've done nothing wrong and I have diplomatic immunity," he calmly proclaimed.

"Ivan Markov, I am charging you with stealing classified documents, kidnaping, and conspiracy to commit murder." Then he was read his Miranda Rights.

"So, you know who I am? Then you know you cannot arrest me."

"You need to brush up on the law. We caught you in the act of putting someone's life in imminent danger. We can arrest you, charge you, and hold you regardless of your possible immunity from prosecution. And, as far as your diplomatic immunity is concerned, I don't think you have any. I think you're in this country illegally, and I think your passport is phony, but we'll deal with that later."

The Feds took Markov, his bodyguard, and the limo driver into custody, and impounded the car. They entered the thumb drive into evidence. It never made it to The Washington Post.

22

ESCAPE PLAN

Aleksei Chaban was not with Markov when Markov was arrested, but Aleksei soon got word, and now he was on the lam. On February 20, Joe received a message on his smart phone.

> *Urgent. Markov arrested. We are at risk. Need your help. Call me on 999-555-4321. Identify yourself using your initials.*

Joe did not recognize the number—probably a burner phone and not likely being tapped into, he decided. So, he made the call using *his* burner phone.

"Hello, who is this?" the voice answered.

"JG. Who is this?"

"This is Aleksei. I need your help."

"Where are you?"

"Can't tell you. I'm safe now but think Feds may be on to me."

"Why would they be on to you? Would Markov give you up?"

"No, but his bodyguard might."

"What do you need help with?"

"I want to leave country and return to Moscow before they find me."

"Why me?"

"You friend. I trust you."

"Tell me what I can do."

"I want you to make plane reservation for me to Moscow."

Joe wondered why he couldn't do that for himself unless he thought his phone was tapped, but he played along. "Okay, he responded, but you need to give me some details."

"Tell me what you need."

"What airport do you want to leave from? Does BWI work for you?"

"Fine."

"I don't think there are any direct flights. One would normally be routed via Kennedy or Heathrow, but this is last minute. You may not have a choice. That OK?"

"Do your best. Get me out fast."

"Okay, I will. Tell me what name you want on the reservation. I assume it won't be Chaban."

"No, not Chaban. Make the name Alexander P. Sarnoff."

"What does the P stand for?"

"Doesn't matter. Just initial is fine."

"Okay. Now I'm sure you realize they will want a passport number with that name on it. Can you read the number to me?"

"Of course. The number is 45 02 987654."

"Issue date and expiration date?"

"16 June 2001 and 15 June 2006."

"And the nationality?"

"Russian."

"How soon?"

"As soon as possible."

"How do you intend to pay for this?"

"You friend. You help me. Put on your business card. We paid you enough—no?"

"Anything else?"

"Yes. I need ride to airport. You pick me up at our pizza place in Glenmont. Bring tickets and small suitcase with three days of clothes and toiletries."

"Alex, you know you're asking for an awful lot from me."

"Look at it this way Joe. It's in your best interest to get me out of country. If I get captured, I don't know what the Feds might force me to say."

It sounded a little bit like a veiled threat, but Joe let it pass.

"Okay. I'll call you back and let you know the day and time that I'll pick you up in Glenmont."

"It must be soon. *Spasibo*."

Joe made the reservations for Alex as requested. As he did so, he had a fleeting thought. *Supposedly, Inga Sarnoff was Maria Martin's real name. Could Aleksei be related?* Then, Joe gave some thought to his own safety. His plan had been that at the end of his assignment he would disappear and return to Costa Rica. No one would know of his true mission. And could he trust Aleksei to not see him as a loose end that had to be dealt with. He also needed to consider the possibility that both he and Aleksei could be arrested by the Feds. And there were other complications, like his involvement with Brandy. Could he ever see her again after this?

He decided on a course of action. After making the reservations for Alex, he made reservations for himself to fly to Toronto. His flight would leave after Alex's flight, also from BWI. He explained to Brandy that he had to leave on business, and made up a story as to where he would be and why. She came to his townhouse the evening before he was to leave and they spent the night together. She was still at his house when he left to pick up Alex in Glenmont the next day, Monday, February 23.

When he arrived at the Glenmont Pizzeria, Alex was already standing outside in the cold waiting for him. Before getting into the car, Alex peered into the back seat, as if to assure that it was safe to do so. He noticed that Joe had brought more than one bag with him.

"Joe, I only need one bag. Why you have two bags?" he asked as he opened the door and slid onto the passenger seat.

"Because I'm leaving the country too. Fasten your seat belt."

"What about Brandy?"

"I'll have to live with that. I can't take the chance that Markov or his muscle man will rat us out."

The two drove directly to the car rental facility, turned in the car, and took the shuttle to the terminal building. Then they went to their respective airline counters to show their passports and check in. Alex waited for Joe, who seemed to take longer than expected. Then they followed each other through security to Concourse D. They stopped at the junction of two corridors. The flights to Canada were down one; the flights to JFK and Moscow down the other. This is where they said goodbye. Alex surprised Joe with a bear hug. "You good friend. I wish you well," he said. Then, Alex continued down the corridor to his gate. He would board shortly.

Joe looked around. He saw no sign of the Feds. Before heading down the corridor to his gate, he went to the men's room, made one final call on his burner phone and dumped it into the trash. When he came out of the men's room, he saw them, two well-built gentlemen wearing suits and wing-tipped shoes. The Feds had arrived. He watched them head toward the gate for JFK. It was about to board, but the flight to Toronto would not board for another hour. Joe wondered if the Feds would nab Alex and then come back for him. Joe had already considered this. He had spent extra time at the check-in counter, changing his flight to go to Quebec. It would board in 10 minutes, and he planned to be on it. He went to a neutral place until he heard the boarding for his flight to Quebec was called. After boarding, he half expected to be dragged off the plane, but it never happened. His deception had worked. He breathed a sigh of relief. He had escaped. He doubted that Alex would have had the same luck.

23

HER FINAL YEAR

Donna lay on her back staring at the ceiling waiting for the next interruption from the hospital staff. She had had one medical test after another and they still couldn't tell her if she had been poisoned or if she had some rare form of lymphatic cancer. Her condition was getting worse and she knew it. At least the medication had dimmed the pain and she still had clarity of mind. As she lay there with nothing else to do, she began to reflect upon all that had happened since returning from Costa Rica ten months ago in April of 2003.

During the time following her return, Donna had worked hard to bring closure to all her projects. Her plan was to retire early in the spring of 2004, and with that in mind she began training someone to take over her job. Together they even exposed two more Russian operatives before September. She considered the possibility of retiring with Ed Perez in Costa Rica, but her priority was to have more time to spend with Brandy and with her grandson. Perhaps she could make up for all the time she had not been there for them. Perhaps she could begin to give back to Brandy. Would Ed be willing to retire in Maryland, she wondered. She received a letter from Ed telling her it was safe to come back to Costa Rica. No charges would be filed. However, she politely declined. Before any of this could happen, there were things she had to complete.

Inga Sarnoff, the Russian spy she knew as Mary Lou, was dead. That was not the original plan. The original plan was to interrogate her and gain valuable information about her colleagues, other agents she worked with, her superiors, and actions they were planning. Now that she was dead, they only had Mary Lou's computer hard drive. However, the hard drive was enough to get started. The DIS in Costa Rica had a copy as did the CIA. The DIS and the OIJ in Costa Rica would begin an investigation into the corrupted Costa Rican authorities who were helping the socialist causes.

Meanwhile, the CIA would focus on the higher-ups that Mary Lou reported to in the Russian Federation's SVR. Matheson said he had a plan and Donna had agreed to it. She knew it was a sting operation, and she had helped to create phony documents and files that would serve as bait. Other than that, she had known very few details.

In the early fall of 2003, Donna had a follow-up medical exam. Her doctor had told her that while there was no visible cancer now, her blood test indicated the possibility that the cancer could return. He had recommended another round of chemo to be sure. After giving this much thought, she made the decision not to go through that again. The chemo sessions were too painful and she would have no quality of life during that time. She decided to enjoy the quality of life she had now, use it to accomplish something important for her country, and let nature take its course. She did not mind being a target of the Russians. If they managed to kill her, she would die for her country. If they didn't kill her, she would likely die anyway. Over the next several months, she traveled very little. She was home for holidays like the Fourth of July, Thanksgiving, Christmas, New Years, and Super Bowl Sunday the following year. She was happy to spend a great deal of her free time with her grandson, her daughter, and with her daughter's new boyfriend, Joe.

By the end of the year 2003, however, Donna began to get suspicious of Joe. Brandy seemed to be getting serious with this guy and he had come to Thanksgiving dinner. She had met him briefly before, but this was the first time they had a chance to really talk. He said he was from Costa Rica which seemed a bit coincidental to her. He said he was working for a large client here in this country but wouldn't say who. He seemed to travel a lot. His Costa Rican driver's license said Joseph Garcia but he told Brandy his name was Joe Martinez. When they saw him for dinner the week before Christmas, she noticed he had what looked like cat fur on his pant leg, and one day when she was talking with a neighbor, the neighbor mentioned that she saw a young man enter her townhouse during the day on more than one occasion. Each of these observations could possibly be explained individually, but taken as a whole, they aroused her suspicions. This was especially true, considering that she had already been informed that she was a possible target. As she became more concerned about her daughter's boyfriend, she began to wonder if he was working for the Russians.

She had gone to Matheson, and discussed her concerns, but got no help from him. "You promised me protection," she had said, "and I want to know what it is."

"I can't tell you. Just trust me," he had replied.

On the one hand, she wondered if Joe was the protection. If so, she did not like the idea of Brandy's involvement with him. On the other hand, if he was the one stealing information or the one sent to kill her, that was even worse. Either way, if Brandy found out, she would be upset. Her instinct was to protect her daughter.

She recalled that at the Thanksgiving dinner, her grandson had taken a photo of them at the dinner table which Joe was not happy about. Sometime in December, she had pulled out the picture that her grandson had taken, and thought hard. Had she seen Joe before? Was it in Costa Rica? Was Joe the man standing at the coffee bar in La Copa Máxima?

So, she had contacted Ed Perez for help and sent him a copy of her grandson's photo. Perhaps Ed knew who he was. She also told Ed that she was concerned for Brandy's safety. She seemed to be falling for this guy, and she was quite certain that they were sleeping with each other. She had told Ed she was not sure that Joe was who he claimed to be, and she wanted to know who he really was. He had replied to Donna that he would investigate the matter and get back to her. Only he hadn't gotten back to her. *Why hasn't he responded*? she asked herself.

During the month of January, 2004, Donna's anxiety had increased. Someone had broken into her house on New Year's Eve and had disarmed the security system, and the next day she saw a text message on her phone from an unknown source that said:

DO NOT DRINK THE ORANGE JUICE. IT IS POISONED!

Naturally she reported this to Matheson, and he claimed credit for the warning message. They agreed that it must be the Russians trying to poison her, but she wanted to know who specifically was doing it. She wondered if Joe was an assassin. Ed had not yet replied to her request and she had become more anxious. It was right after this that she started having days when she was not feeling so well. She wondered if it was stress and anxiety, or if she was being poisoned? And then on Martin Luther King's Birthday she received another text message from an unknown source. It said:

DO NOT DRINK THE TEA!

Two weeks later, on Super Bowl Sunday, she helped Brandy prepare for a Super Bowl party. Brandy had invited her, Joe, and several friends to her house to watch the game on her large plasma TV. Everyone enjoyed the food, the drinks, and the hospitality. The fourth quarter was exciting. The Patriots edged out the Panthers 32 to 19. After the game, Donna did not feel well at all. Brandy convinced her to stay the night, much to the apparent chagrin of Joe who told them it would be best if he went home.

Then on Monday, the day after the Super Bowl, she received another text message:

DO NOT DRINK THE ORANGE JUICE OR
THE TEA. THEY ARE POISONED!

A few days after the Super Bowl, she became sick enough that she sought medical attention. Again, she wondered if she had been poisoned. She thought she had heeded the warning messages and had been careful. Yet she couldn't be sure. Her condition deteriorated rapidly. Two weeks later she was hospitalized full-time.

Now as she lay there, she realized that there was so much she wanted to understand, and she looked forward to Ed's visit later in the day. Perhaps he would explain why she had not heard from him until now, and perhaps he could give her answers about Brandy's boyfriend.

Her face lit up immediately when Ed entered her room. No sooner had he kissed her, than she asked, "Ed, where have you been?"

He apologized profusely. "Donna I wanted you to know everything, but Matheson never read me in to the operation and I didn't know that you weren't fully aware of Matheson's plan."

"Ed, I may be dying. Please tell me what is happening," she pleaded.

"Okay, but I'm not authorized to tell you everything, and you can tell no one what I'm about to say. It's highly classified."

"I understand," she said.

Matheson had told her that the Russian spies were in custody, but Ed also told her everything he knew about Joe, and reassured her that Brandy would be safe. Donna was dying. It was the right thing to do, he thought.

"Thank you," she said to Ed. "I'm pleased that my final project with the agency has been successful, but even more important to me is setting things right with Brandy. Her welfare and happiness are my number one priority. Perhaps you could help her get past her relationship with Joe."

"I will . . .. You also said she wants to know about her birth father. Were you going to tell her?"

"Yes, I left a letter for her. It will be up to her if she wants to pursue it."

"I think you've done the right thing."

A week later, with Brandy and her grandson at her side, Donna passed away. She died peacefully in the hospital knowing that she had left matters in the best of hands.

24

DONNA'S FUNERAL

Donna was interred in mid-March of 2004. The day was dreary— cloudy and breezy with temperatures in the forties. The cemetery was just north of Bethesda, Maryland, the same one where Donna's parents and her husband John were buried. The ceremony was short but respectful. Donna's casket arrived in a hearse escorted by armed plainclothesmen—probably FBI. Several of Donna's local friends and colleagues attended. Donna's boss, Brian Matheson, and several colleagues, drove up from Virginia. Matheson said a few prepared words. Brandy, Brandy's son, and Brandy's half-brother, rode together from Ellicott City. Brandy said a few heart-felt words and became overwhelmed with tears. Matheson had never met Brandy, but he took the time to offer his condolences and support.

Ed Perez flew back up from Costa Rica. He came alone. After the ceremony, he walked over to Brandy.

"I'm Ed Perez. Don't know if you remember me. We met briefly a couple of years ago when your mom was sick. I was a colleague and a close friend of your Mom, and I feel your sorrow," he said sincerely.

"Yes, I remember you. Mom has talked highly of you, but I wondered why we didn't see you more often."

"I live and work in Costa Rica. It's a long way and your Mom and I didn't see each other very often, but she always talked proudly of you."

"Were you and Mom close?" Brandy asked, even though she knew the answer.

"We worked together for many years, became close friends after your Dad passed away, and I think you already know that we've been intimate more recently."

"Yes, she said she spent time with you a few months ago."

"I'm going to miss her. We talked of retiring together. She also told me about your boyfriend Joe. She was concerned about him. Wondered if he was taking advantage of you in some way."

"Well, I assume she was just being my mom—always looking out for me."

"Where is he? Is he here?" he asked as he looked around.

"No, he is not! He left three weeks ago and I have not heard from him since."

"Sorry . . . any idea where he is?"

"He said he was on a business trip to Toronto, but I followed up on that. The company has never heard of him. Perhaps he went back to Costa Rica, but now, I don't even know if Joe Garcia is his real name. I'm angry! Mom was right. He took advantage of me!" She paused and looked Ed in the eyes. "Joe said he had a business in San José. That's where you're from right? Did you know him?"

Ed felt for her but all he could say was "Brandy, I'll look into it when I get back and I'll let you know what I find out."

"I would really appreciate that. Thanks."

"Brandy, there's something I want to ask you . . ."

"Yes?"

"Did your mom say anything to you about your birth father?"

"Why do you ask?"

"I encouraged her to tell you. She said she would leave you a letter telling you about him, and leave it up to you as to whether you wanted to contact him."

"Yes, she left me items in her safety deposit box, but with the funeral and all, I haven't had time to look at them . . . Wait! You mean he's still alive?" she said excitedly.

"Yes. You didn't know that?"

"No. All my life I was led to believe that he died in Vietnam. Ed do you by any chance know who he is . . .? Is it you?"

"Huh, no. I've never met him, but I would like to. Your mom had good things to say about him."

"I never understood why she would never tell me about him."

"She had very good reasons. You need to read the letter she left for you. It will explain a lot. Look, I would like to talk more but my ride is calling for me to leave," he said, motioning to a large gentleman standing by a black limousine on the road nearby.

"Ed, I hope I will see you again."

"Likewise," he responded. "Please take this. It has my contact information on it. Feel free to contact me any time."

****

That evening at home, Brandy began to think about the conversation she had at the cemetery with Mom's friend Ed. He told her that her birth-father was still alive, and did not know she was his daughter. A letter would be in Mom's safety deposit box he had said. Brandy had gone to the bank last week and now everything was in a shoe box on the top shelf of her bedroom closet. She pulled it down and thumbed through the contents until she found two sealed envelopes, one with her name, the other with the words "For Brandy's birth father."

Brandy opened the envelope addressed to her. In the enclosed letter, Mom provided the contact information for her birth father. His name was Peter Troutman and he lived nearby. Mom said she had met him in Saigon where they had an affair. She said he worked with the Agency over the years, but she never told him that she was pregnant and that he had a daughter. Mom's explanation was that she married John who provided them with a happy home, and that Peter had a family too. "No need to destroy families and careers, but now things were different," she said in the letter. The letter ended by saying that if she decided to contact Peter, she should give him the other envelope addressed to him.

Brandy pondered whether to contact Peter. What would the impact on him be? Should she just leave things as they were? Mom had said that things were different now. Were they? She had many unanswered questions about the relationship that he and Mom had. She wondered how she would react to the answers. On the other hand, her curiosity was overwhelming, and she had an unexplained innate desire to know him. It was not an easy decision for her to make. Three weeks went by before she decided.

25

AN UNEXPECTED
PHONE CALL

It was a Saturday morning in April of 2004. Peter Troutman was alone in his townhouse. He and his wife Carol already had breakfast, and she had just left for her community garden. Peter was sitting at the kitchen table having a final cup of coffee and working the morning's crossword puzzle. It was his quiet time and he was not yet ready to start work on a long list of Saturday chores. He was thinking of an eight-letter crossword meaning peace and quiet when RING . . . RING . . . RING ended his thoughts of *serenity*. It was still very early in the morning, and he wondered who would be calling. Could it be Carol? Did she have car trouble? Hoping for the best, he answered with a simple "Hello."

"Hello, my name is Brandy Evans and I would like to speak to Peter Troutman please."

He was relieved that the call was not from Carol, but now expected it might be an annoying marketing call. "This is he. How may I help you?" he said. He always tried to be polite but perhaps there was a hint of annoyance in his voice.

"Mr. Troutman, I hope I haven't caught you at a bad time. I believe you may have known my mother, Donna Wolf."

"I'm sorry but I don't think I knew her," he lied. The name was familiar but he was wary and suspicious of the caller's intent.

Ms. Evans responded right away. "Mr. Troutman, you may have known her in nineteen sixty-seven as Donna Cinelli."

The mention of the date and the name was enough to provide some credence to the caller.

"Yes . . . I did know her. Why are you calling?"

"My mother recently passed away from cancer. Before she died, she specifically requested that I contact you. I'm honoring her wish."

"Thank you for notifying me. I'm so sorry to hear that your mother passed away, but more than thirty-six years have passed by since I was last with her. I'm not sure I fully understand."

Peter had tried several times over the years to reestablish contact with Donna, but had given up 15 years ago when it became apparent that she did not want to see him. And now she had passed away and someone claiming to be her daughter wants to notify him. He was suspicious, but he was also curious.

Ms. Evans then explained, "Before my mother died, she had determined your whereabouts, and she gave me something she wanted you to have. Mom was very insistent that I deliver it to you in person. I would like to set a time to meet with you and talk about my mother. Would that be okay?"

Peter's curiosity was really stimulated at this point.

"Yes, that would be fine. I live in Columbia. Do you live or work in the area? Where can we meet?"

"I live in nearby Ellicott City so we could meet somewhere in Columbia."

"Okay, there's a coffee shop called Lakeside down by Lake Kittamaqundi. Do you know where it is? Would that work for you?"

"Yes, I know where it is. Could we meet next Saturday morning at ten?"

"Yes," he agreed. "Please let me have your phone number in case something changes."

Ms. Evans gave him her number. The number had not shown up on his caller ID and he wanted to check it out.

For most of his career, Peter had worked as an analyst, and was quite good at what he did. Peter and his wife Carol were now in their early sixties. After Peter retired from the IBM Corporation, and after Carol retired from the FBI, they started a small consulting business. They advised business and government organizations on how to make smart business decisions regarding telecommunications technology. They also did what they called audits, or investigations. Carol had an office upstairs on the top level, and Peter had an office downstairs on the basement level.

Immediately after he got off the phone with Ms. Evans, Peter headed downstairs to his home office and logged onto his computer He wanted to know more about the caller. He entered the phone number into one of his computer applications. Within minutes, he knew the phone number was registered to a James Evans. He also knew Mr. Evan's address in Ellicott City, Maryland. There was more information if he wanted it, but that was enough. He was satisfied that the call was legitimate and probably not a scam. He put a note on his calendar and began attending to his Saturday chores.

****

As he ran the vacuum cleaner, a mindless job, Peter began to recall the intense experience that he and Donna had in Saigon in 1967. Peter was in his mid-twenties then, technically very smart and creative, but socially naïve. In 1967 he had gone to Saigon as a private contractor to implement an intelligence analysis program called the PEN that he had developed in graduate school. In 1967, the war was getting closer to Saigon, and many enemy bombings and killings were taking place in and around Saigon. The PEN Project was intended to predict attacks so that preventative actions could be taken. Saigon is where Peter had first met Donna.

Donna Rice, as he knew her then, was an operative or agent with the CIA. Donna was about the same age as Peter. She had had military training and had only recently become a field operative for the CIA. She was assigned by the CIA to work with him. Perhaps a more apt description would have been baby sitter. He was an asset and she was his handler. Saigon was also where Peter had first met Jon Wilson, Donna's CIA boss. Both Jon and Donna had legitimate cover jobs, but in fact they were covert CIA operatives.

Initially Donna's job was to escort Peter, to introduce him to the military people he worked with, and to keep him out of trouble. However, before they left Saigon in 1967, her assignment, and his involvement, had evolved into much more. Peter and Donna had an affair during that assignment. But then, after four assassinations Peter and Donna were sent out of country for their protection. Before parting, they had promised each other to remember this experience and to stay in touch. Although Peter tried to keep the promise, Donna had not been responsive to his attempts, and they had not spoken since they said goodbye at an airport in South East Asia more than thirty-six years ago. If Donna had continued in the same line of work, locating him would have been a cinch, but this was the first time she had initiated contact, and she was dead. Peter did not know why Donna would want her daughter, Brandy, to contact him after all this time, especially when she had avoided his efforts to reconnect with her. He could only speculate.

Later that afternoon, Peter's foot was on the frame of his upside-down lawnmower and both hands grasped the end of a socket wrench. He pushed downward on the handle of the wrench with all the force he could muster. He was trying to replace the blade on the lawnmower, but the damn nut was frozen tight. He set the wrench down and stood up to contemplate a new tactic. At that moment, it dawned on him that he would need to explain to Carol why he was meeting with a Brandy Evans next Saturday.

This was a second marriage for both Peter and Carol. They often referred to events in their first marriages as occurring in their "prior lives." Their prior lives belonged to their private space and they had learned from their first marriages to respect each other's private space. Carol knew almost nothing about Peter's experience in Saigon and absolutely nothing about his affair with Donna Wolf. She did, however, know of his contacts with the CIA. After all, that was how they met seventeen years ago, and then after they were married, they jointly participated in another CIA project as part of their consulting business. But in the sixteen years they had been together, Donna Wolf was never mentioned and Peter had hoped to keep it that way. Now however, Peter realized that things would change. He would need to have a long discussion with Carol and he wasn't sure how it would go.

****

For the remainder of Saturday and for most of Sunday, Peter and Carol were busy with chores and social activities. Perhaps he was just using their activities as an excuse, but it was late Sunday evening before he broached the subject of his planned meeting with Brandy Evans. He told Carol about the phone call and why he needed to meet Ms. Evans. He told Carol that he had known Ms. Evan's mother, Donna, in Vietnam and that Donna had passed away. Carol and Peter communicated openly on most things and he hoped she would understand. Of course, she was initially suspicious and asked many questions.

"Peter, how did you know Brandy's mother? Why did you never mention her before? Did you say her name was Donna? Had you been in touch over the years? Why would her daughter Brandy need to see you? Did you say she wants to give you something? Have you ever met Brandy before?" and so on.

Carol and Peter talked about Saigon and about Donna Wolf for an hour Sunday night, but there was only enough time to scratch the surface. Carol wanted to know the whole story—everything. Clearly, the whole story would take a while. As they both worked in their business during the day, they agreed to talk each night prior to Peter's meeting with Brandy the following Saturday.

By Friday evening, he had described his entire Vietnam experience to Carol, including the affair. Of course he omitted a few intimate details out of consideration. Peter was relieved when Carol said she was okay with what he was telling her, "so long as it was not on her watch." He reaffirmed that he had been, and always would be, faithful to her.

Yet, he still did not have answers for two questions. Why, was he notified of Donna's death, and what did Brandy need to give him? Peter would meet with Brandy the next morning.

26

MEETING PETER

On Saturday morning, Brandy walked into the Lakeside Coffee Shop in Columbia. It was five minutes after ten. She was only five minutes late.

The Lakeside was located on the bottom floor of an office building, and shared a parking lot with the Rouse Headquarters next door. Large windows afforded a view of a small park and a partial view of Lake Kittamaqundi. The lake was only about fifty yards down the stairs and across a grassy area where they held concerts in the summer. Inside the shop were tables with comfortable chairs and in one corner a sofa and three large cushioned chairs. Just outside the main door was a patio with tables. When the weather was warm, you could eat outside and enjoy the view, or the music.

Although she knew of the place, she had never been there before. She had pondered what she would say to Peter. A part of her was angry at him and her mom for keeping the secret for so long. She needed to keep those feelings in check. She was also unsure how her revelation would affect him. She wondered how he would react. She was nervous. Nevertheless, it was a week ago when she had arranged to meet him. There was no turning back now. She was committed.

As soon as she entered the shop, she looked around for someone that looked like he could be Peter. She spied an older man who rose from a small table on the far side of room. It looked like it would be him, and he seemed to recognize her as well. She came over to the table and they greeted each other.

"Hello, are you Peter Troutman?"

"Yes, are you Brandy Evans?"

"I am," she said and smiled. "I hope I haven't kept you waiting too long."

"Please have a seat," he said motioning to the empty chair. "Brandy you look remarkably like I remember your mother." Although she looked to be in her mid-thirties and probably married with kids, she looked like the way he remembered Donna. Like her mother, she was tall and trim. But, unlike her mother, her hair was black, like his. Somehow, he knew it was her right away. It was uncanny. "As you came in, you seemed to know who I was," he added. "How is that?"

She chuckled. "My mother had a picture of you from nineteen-sixty-seven."

"Surely, I no longer look like that do I?"

She chuckled. "You also have a business website with your picture on it."

"Oh, I forgot about that. Would you like a coffee, and perhaps something to go with it?"

"Just a regular coffee," she answered. "No cream or sugar. Thanks."

"I'll be right back."

Peter went to the counter, ordered two house coffees, and to save time brought them back to the table himself.

"Brandy, did you have any problem finding this place?"

"No, not at all."

"Have you been here before?"

"Not to the coffee shop, but I often stop here in Columbia on my way home from work. I work over at Fort Meade."

"Oh, may I ask what you do over there?"

"Nothing like what my mother did. I'm just an Administrator."

"Nothing wrong with that," he responded. Then he changed the subject. "I was sorry to hear that your mother passed away. Did you say she had cancer?"

"Yes, ovarian, but it was in remission, and then more recently, the cancer came back quickly in a different form. She only had a few months to get her affairs in order."

"Where did your mother live?"

"Well, after my dad died, she was reassigned to an office at Fort Meade, and she moved from Potomac to a townhouse complex nearby."

"When was that?"

"Dad died in nineteen ninety-two, and she moved in nineteen ninety-four after selling the house I grew up in."

Her tone and the expression on her face as she answered his questions made it clear that she was eager to get to the point of their meeting. Peter sensed this and said, "I'm sorry if I'm asking too many questions. I was surprised that I was notified of your mother's passing, after all these years. Why did your mother want us to meet?"

"Well, Mom left a letter for me. In the letter, Mom said she knew you a long time ago in Saigon. I had always thought she was in the military but she told me more recently that she worked for the CIA and that she knew you then. When I was younger, I tried to get her to tell me who my father was, but she would not say much. She and my grandmother said that my biological father died in the war."

Brandy sounded angry as she continued. "However, when I was little, I overheard them argue about something in which I thought they said my biological father was still alive. After Mom married, her husband adopted me and I always thought of him as my father. Mom was not home very much, but Dad and Grandma spent a lot of time with me. When I asked where Mom was, I did not get answers, although sometimes I would receive postcards from strange places. However, several years ago, I came across some memorabilia and I found proof that she was lying to me about my biological father. It made me angry and we fought over this. Then after Dad died, she told me she was a CIA operative and that she worked with you in Vietnam. To hear that she was a CIA operative made me even angrier. Another secret she kept from me, but it explained why she was never home. I want to know if you're my biological father, and I want to know if you and my mother were seeing each other behind my father's back."

Peter had to let this sink in before he could respond. "Brandy, if I'm your biological father, I never knew it. Your mother and I have not seen each other since nineteen sixty-seven. I tried to contact her in sixty-eight and again in eighty-seven and eighty-eight, but we never connected. Tell me your birth date."

"It's May the tenth, nineteen sixty-eight. I'll be thirty-six," she responded.

Peter did the quick math in his head and it hit him that she really could be his biological daughter. "Wow! I could be—" was about all I could get out before she interjected.

"Really? You never knew?"

"No. I did not!"

"Why would Mom not tell you?"

He shrugged and held up my hands. "I do not know."

In the back of his mind, Peter had thought that this news was possible. Yet he found it to be shocking nonetheless. He was feeling strong emotions and he was trying not to show it in front of Brandy. The problem was that he was feeling a mix of emotions that he needed to understand and come to terms with. He was sad that Donna had passed away. He was disappointed that he was unable to see her again, yet he was pleased and happy that she remembered him. He wondered if Donna and Brandy had a happy life together. Brandy sounded angry with her mother and with him. He felt guilty that he was not there for her, and at the same time he felt slighted that he was not told he had a daughter. He was anxious, perhaps fearful, as to what was going to happen next. Who needed to know about this? How would they react? Was Brandy here to serve her mother's interests, or her own? Did she want something from him? Peter tried to collect himself and appear in control, but inside he was shaken.

"Brandy, when you called last week, you said your mother had something she wanted me to have. What is it?"

"She wanted me to give you this envelope."

27

DONNA'S LETTER

Brandy handed Peter a sealed envelope with his full name neatly printed on the front. She then answered the question he was about to ask. "Mom's letter to me said you should open it now in my presence."

"Okay, I will," he said as he began to unseal the envelope. They were both nervous with anticipation. He removed the letter and began to read in silence. Brandy could only sit and watch his facial expressions as he did so.

> *Dear Peter,*
>
> *I asked Brandy to be sure you received this letter. I told her that I hoped she would deliver it in person so she could also meet you and talk with you, but it was her choice. Although I have addressed this letter to you, I wanted her to see it as well.*
>
> *If Brandy is there with you now, you already know that I have passed away. I have been fighting cancer for more than two years now. However, there is no longer any hope and the end is near.*
>
> *I am writing this to you because I owe you an explanation about why I was not responsive to your attempts to see me over the years. After I returned home, I learned that I was pregnant.*

When I exchanged Christmas cards with you that December, I knew, but had not accepted the reality of it until I saw a doctor after the holidays. Your card and note told me you were happy, your wife had given birth, and you were going to finish your MBA and start a wonderful career. I also learned that you turned down an offer a year later that the CIA made to you, and went with IBM instead. In retrospect, I think you did the correct thing for yourself and your family.

Let me get right to the point. Brandy is your daughter. I made a conscious decision not to tell you and to keep that from you. I wanted to protect you and your family. You seemed so happy and that was all I wished for you; I did not want to destroy what you had.

My mom helped me take care of Brandy until she was five, so that I could do what I did. She knew about my USAID job but not about what I did for the CIA. During those five years, I thought of you often. I remembered how you comforted me after what I had done on that Friday. I have had to re-live that experience a few times, and I want you to know that I never stopped feeling something afterwards. Unfortunately, the only people I had to talk with afterwards were jaded CIA operatives. I could not confide or get emotional support from my mother. However, I was able to take comfort when I thought of you and what you said to me that night, and later that weekend.

Brandy was five when I married John Wolf. She probably remembers being the flower girl at the wedding. Just so you know, your name was never on the original birth certificate, and when I married John, we legally adopted Brandy and changed her name to Wolf. John's wife had died and he had a son, Daniel. Daniel was a couple of years older than Brandy. He left home to go to college and then he moved to California. John was tolerant of my travels and understood I could not tell him too much about my work. He was a good father to Brandy, and I relied on that. He suffered his first heart attack in 1987 and passed away four years later. Brandy and I both missed him.

Without John to help out, I put in for a more normal job at Langley, and then relocated to an office at Fort Meade, where Brandy now works. You should also know that after John died, I looked you up (The Internet made it easy). I saw that you had remarried, so I let it go. Our timing was always off.

Now back to Brandy. I wanted Brandy to know you, the real you. Of course, Brandy knew that John was not her biological father, and she often asked who her father really was. My mom would say it did not matter because her father had died in the Vietnam War. My mother's attitude was that any married man who would get her daughter pregnant was no good. Nor did my mom approve of my traveling as much as I did instead of being home to take care of Brandy. I fear that some of this attitude was projected onto Brandy when they talked.

When Brandy was about seven years old, we were at my mom's house, and I had an argument with my mom about whether Brandy should be forced to attend Sunday school. I wanted Brandy to have a say. Mom did not. The argument got loud. Mom reminded me that I had an affair with a married man and that I had left her in charge of Brandy for five years because I was never home. She did not want me and John to undo all the good she thought she had done for Brandy. Then she suggested that maybe the reason I had not been home was because I was still seeing you on the side. I did not know that Brandy had overheard the argument until years later, but it must have made an impression.

As she grew older, Brandy continued to ask about her 'real' father, about what I did in the war, and why I traveled so much. I could not tell her the truth. I repeated the lies about you having died and about what I did for a living, until when she was home after John had his heart attack. She was rummaging through my things, found your letters, and caught me in the lie. She was very upset with me. She blamed me for having an affair and for lying to her. I tried to explain, but then I think it upset her even more to think that I loved someone other than John. Then she said that her grandma was right and told me what she had heard. Brandy was pregnant, and she told me she was not going to do to her child what I did to her. (Yes, I was a grandma at 46.) All of this was happening in 1987 around the time when I received your letter. It was not a good time. I apologize for being so brief in my delayed response to your letter, but I hope you will understand after reading this.

My falling out with Brandy lasted until recently. She now knows I worked as a CIA operative, and why I was not home as much as we would have liked. I have apologized for not telling her the truth about you. I asked her to forgive me, but I think she deserves more. I want her to know what really happened, and that despite the circumstance she was conceived out of love, not lust. I want her to know that you did not take advantage of me as my mother believed. I know you never felt this way, but I always felt that if anything, I had taken advantage of you, not the other way around. I want Brandy to know the real you, the person I loved.

As you remember, before we left Saigon together, we had already understood that we were probably not meant to be together, and may not even see each other again, but we made a promise that we would always remember each other. You knew that Dona Rice was not my real name and you told me that you wanted to stay in touch and know that I was happy. You asked if you could send a Christmas card. When we parted at the airport in Hong Kong, I remember we both had tears in our eyes and we repeated our promises to remember each other, and I slipped my address and real name into your pocket, (A breach in protocol). Peter, I kept my promise. I always remembered you. Every day when I looked at Brandy, I remembered. She even has some of your features. You told me that you had no regrets about what we did, and you did not want me to have any either. You gave me Brandy. She's the best gift I ever received. I have no regrets.

Please help Brandy to understand and fill in the details of what happened in Saigon as you see fit. I always trusted your judgement.

Goodbye. I loved you both. —Donna

P.S. I know that you were trained to be skeptical, and Brandy often felt I had deceived her, so I am adding the following to what I wrote yesterday. Peter, I think you know that you were the only man I was with back then; but, if either of you have any doubts about your biological relationship, consider a DNA paternity test. Whether you let others know of your relationship, I must leave that entirely up to the two of you to work out.

P.S.S. I decided to make an extra copy of this letter so you could both have it.

After he finished reading the letter, Brandy could not help but notice that Peter was rattled and could no longer hide his emotions.

"Are you okay?" she asked sincerely.

"Brandy please excuse me for a few minutes, I need to use the restroom."

As he got up from the table, he pushed her copy over to her and said, "I think you should read the letter. We can talk when I return."

Peter washed his face with cold water, and took a few relaxing breaths before returning. When he returned, Brandy looked up at him and asked again, "Peter, are you all right?"

"Yes, please excuse me. This is sudden, and the memories are bringing forth many emotions. However, I want to tell you everything you need to know."

"I want to know if you loved each other, and why you stopped seeing each other. I think I know the answer to that." Her tone sounded almost like she was hoping for a different result. "I think she loved you, but I don't see how you could have loved her."

Before he could respond, she continued. "Peter, I read through the letter quickly. I don't understand what Mom meant when she said, '*I remembered how you comforted me after what I had done on that Friday. I have had to re-live that experience a few times, and I always felt something afterwards.*' Was Mom referring to having had sex with you and then other men later?"

"What? No . . . of course not!"

"What then?"

He could see the consternation in her face. He looked straight at her and calmly told her, "Brandy, your mom had just taken a life. It was the first time, and she was upset."

"Peter, I knew that Mom was a CIA operative. Is she telling us that she became a trained assassin and killed multiple times?"

Peter sensed some agitation.

"Brandy, it was self-defense. She had no choice. Your mother was concerned about having to kill someone again in the future. I told her that if she did and she did not feel anything, she may as well be dead herself. She would never have become a trained assassin."

"So, then what?" she said excitedly. "Are you telling me that you took advantage of her when she was upset and you comforted her by having sex with her?"

"No. I'm telling you that I didn't take advantage of her," he replied calmly. "It was not like that. Your mother and I already had strong feelings for each other."

"Peter, I know I should calm down, but I'm having a hard time with this."

"I guess that makes two of us Brandy. Look, we've been here for two hours and your kids and husband are probably wondering where you are. You probably need to get going, but I think that you and I should talk more. I would like us to meet again if you're willing."

"I don't need to be anywhere. I'm in no rush. I only have a teenage son and I'm divorced . . . .. I have something else I want you to see. I brought a large envelope with Mom's memorabilia. Do you have time to have a look?"

"Sure, what have you got?"

She reached into the envelope, pulled out a picture, and handed it to him. "Is this my mother with the motor bike? The print says April nineteen sixty-seven on the back."

Peter smiled and said, "Your mother loved that bike. She gave me many rides on the back. I took the picture. I mailed it to her in May after returning to New York, before I knew I would be going back to Saigon later in the year. Of course, she had to part with the bike when she left in August. What else is in here?"

She had a picture of Peter, the Christmas cards he sent in 1967 and 1968, and the note he sent in 1987 when he tried to reestablish contact. She even had the menu from *La Paix*, a French restaurant on the eastern side of Saigon. Peter smiled when he saw it. Donna also had kept a picture of herself when she was pregnant and one of Brandy when she was a baby. Peter smiled again and said, "Brandy you were a beautiful baby."

Brandy then asked, "Do you want to keep all of these memorabilia?"

Peter looked directly at her and replied, "I think you should keep it. I think your mother would have wanted you to have it."

It was Peter's view that continuity from generation to generation was very important, and seemed to be lacking in today's NOW culture. He felt like giving her a father to daughter lecture on the subject but restrained himself.

He continued, "Perhaps you came here to hear what I had to say and close the book on your mother and move on. However, your mother said she wanted you to know the real me and I think she wanted you to know her better too. She apologized to you and asked for your forgiveness. I think it's important that you forgive her and remember her in a good way. She tried to protect you, not just me. Her work was difficult both technically and emotionally. I want you to know that I am willing to spend as much time as you need to understand what happened in nineteen sixty-seven and why we were together. I would like us to meet again. I think your mother would want that."

"By the way," he continued. "I told my wife Carol about my affair with your mother. She says she's okay with it because it didn't happen on her watch. We've been married for almost fourteen years now and I have always been faithful. Of course, she doesn't know you're my daughter, but I feel like I'll need to tell her. I hope you're okay with that."

"That's fine."

"Before we part, I need to ask a favor of you. It's very important to me. Would you mind if I visit your mother's grave? I would like to say goodbye to her. Is she buried anywhere nearby?"

"Well, I suppose you are entitled to that," she responded. "The cemetery is nearby."

Then Brandy provided the details on where her mother was buried, and how to get there.

"I'll plan to be there tomorrow afternoon at one o'clock, unless that conflicts with others that may visit."

"Not a problem. That would be fine."

****

After meeting with Brandy, Peter brought Carol up to speed. He told her that Brandy was his biological daughter. He even had her read the letter from Donna. He told her about the mixed emotions he was feeling. A bit of sadness, some regrets that they were not together, a bit of happiness to know that he was remembered, a bit of comfort that a nice young lady had been brought into the world that gave meaning to Donna's life, and a bit of angst not knowing where any of this was heading in the future. He told Carol he needed to visit Donna's grave site. Carol said she understood and seemed to be supportive. She asked if Brandy was going to be there and he said he didn't know. He said he hoped that she would be, but that would be up to her. He just wanted to say goodbye and have some closure.

28

PAYING THEIR RESPECTS

The next day on Sunday, Brandy brought her son Brian to visit his grandma's grave. The cemetery was a forty-five-minute drive from their home in Ellicott City. It was off Route 355 just north of Bethesda. They arrived a few minutes after one o'clock that afternoon. The sun was out and the temperature was in the low 70s. In Maryland, spring brings out blossoms on many different trees including Cherry, Crab Apple, Bradford Pear, and Red Buds. Sometimes they are all in bloom at once. This seemed to be one of those times. It was a beautiful spring day.

Donna's grave was a distance from the roadway that wound its way within the park. As Brandy and Brian exited the car and began to walk toward the grave site, Brian noticed that someone was already there.

"Mom, who is that man kneeling in front of Grandma's grave?" he asked.

Brandy took a close look. Then she took Brian's arm and stopped their forward progress. She remembered how Peter reacted when they met at the coffee shop, and now he was at her Mom's grave. A warm smile came across her face. It was clear to her that he must have really cared about Mom. She was feeling very sympathetic and wondering if she could have been more sensitive when she had met with him.

"That's Peter Troutman," she said

"Who?"

"Brian, do you remember last Thanksgiving when Grandma started to talk about my biological father? Well, that's him. Grandma left letters for me and Peter and said she wanted us to know him. I met with Peter yesterday. I think he's alright. I want you to meet him."

Meanwhile, Peter had managed to find Donna's grave on his own. It was a family plot. Her mother and father were buried there, as was her brother. Peter looked around but could not find a marker for her husband, John Wolf. Donna's head stone said,

Donna Wolf nee Cinelli
1942 – 2004
She served her Country

As Peter paid his respects, a good feeling came over him. He became lost in his thoughts, remembering all the good things he could about Donna. He was thinking about the life she must have had, so different from his, when he heard voices behind him. He stood up and turned to face Brandy. She had someone with her.

They both were finely dressed. Perhaps they had been to church, he thought. He assumed this could be her son with her. He was tall, thin, and good-looking. He looked to be about 16 or 17 years old, consistent with when Donna's letter had said Brandy was pregnant.

"Peter, I would like you to meet my son, Brian. Brian, this is Mister Troutman. He knew your grandmother."

"Hello sir," Brian politely responded.

"Hello Brian, I'm pleased to meet you."

Then he asked, "How did you know Grandma?"

"I worked with your grandma many years ago in Saigon."

"Where?" he asked.

"Vietnam. Haven't you learned about the Vietnam war in school?"

"Oh, yes, a little. Were you and my grandma in the war?"

"Perhaps sometime I could tell you about it."

"Okay."

After quickly paying his respects by placing some flowers on his grandmother's grave, he told his mom he would come back in about a half hour.

As they watched him take off, Brandy said, "Brian recently got a driver's license and I let him drive me here. He volunteered to pick something up for me at a nearby store."

"Brian is a fine-looking young man. Your mother had a brother named Brian," Peter said as he gestured toward the grave marker.

"Yes, Mom was pleased that I named him after her brother."

"You must have been rather young when you had Brian. How were you able to manage?"

"After I graduated from high school I went to the University of Maryland for a year before I got pregnant with Brian. Mom and Grandma gave me enough support that I could work and eventually get an associate degree at the community college. I guess to be fair, my husband helped as well. Getting pregnant before I got my associate degree was not the wisest thing I ever did. However, I made a decision that I was going to be at home for Brian as much as possible. But before he was five, I needed to get out and Mom helped me to get the job at NSA. They paid for me to finish my education and get a bachelor's degree and a master's degree."

Then she changed the subject. "Peter, tell me something about you. According to Mom's letter, you and your wife had a child in nineteen sixty-seven. Do you have other children? What about grandchildren? According to Mom you're about her age, but you don't look that old."

"Well, thanks for the compliment about my age but I was born in nineteen forty-two, so what your mother told you is true. Yes, I have two daughters within a year of your age, and my current wife Carol has three children. We have seven grandchildren between us and there may be more to come. My oldest grandchild is twelve." Peter was pleased that she was beginning to show some interest in him but he saved a lot for future conversations.

Then he changed the subject. "You're dressed up. Did you come here from church?"

"Yes, we did."

"Your mother and I went to a Catholic Church in Saigon. We talked about religion. Are you Catholic?"

"No, we're Protestant. My grandmother was a devout Catholic and I remember my grandmother being very upset with Mom because she did not force me to go to a Catholic church. When we moved in with Dad, we began to go to a Methodist church. When I was about ten, Mom explained that it was important to have God in my life but she wanted me to learn about different religions so that when I got older, I could decide on what church I wanted to attend for myself."

Peter looked straight at Brandy and said, "I'm pleased to hear this. Your mom had issues with the feelings of guilt and unworthiness bestowed on her by the Catholic Church. I told her that I was going to expose my kids to multiple religions and give them a say. She told me she thought that was a good idea and wished that she had been given that opportunity when she was growing up."

Peter found himself looking at the gravestones again. "Your mom talked to me about your grandparents when I was with her. She said your grandpa had a construction business. According to the gravestone, he died in nineteen seventy-six. You must have been about eight. You lived with them, the first five years of your life. Were you close? Do you remember it?"

"Grandpa was nice to me but he wasn't home a lot. I was much closer to Grandma. Grandma allowed me to see the coffin at the service, but it was closed. I remember coming here to the cemetery with Mom and watching the coffin lowered into the ground. I asked Grandma how he died, but she wouldn't tell me. Later Mom said he was murdered, but they never found the person who did it."

"Wow, that must have been tough!" Then after a pause, "Did you know that I twice spoke to your grandma briefly on the telephone? The first time would have been the Christmas after you were born.

Your mom was not home; I don't think she ever got the message. The second time was back in eighty-seven when I was trying to locate your mom. All your grandma would give me was a post office box number where I could mail a letter to your mother, which I did. You have that letter in your memorabilia box. I was hoping to see your mother again, but it did not work out. I see that your grandma passed away in nineteen ninety-six. She was not that old, only seventy-six. May I ask how she died?"

"Grandma died of cancer, after a long battle, just like Mom. I guess it's what I have to look forward to."

"No! Brandy, you can't think that way."

Brandy sat with Peter for a few moments in silence, and then said, "I've given more thought to our meeting and to Mom's letter. I know I need to be able to forgive you and Mom. It's hard to reverse feelings that have built up over many years. I don't know if I can, but I need to try. I do want to understand you and Mom better." She looked at Peter and said, "You're different than what I originally expected. Would you help me to better understand?"

He looked at her and nodded yes. "Brandy, I don't want to intrude on your lives, but I would like to know you and Brian better too."

Meanwhile, Peter noticed that Brian had returned. "Brian is back, but I could come here again next Sunday," he said.

"Yes, I'd appreciate that."

It could never become a normal father-daughter relationship, but they both made an effort. Over the next month they became friends, and learned more about each other. Peter and Carol even had Brandy and Brian over for dinner one evening. Peter enjoyed giving him a short history lesson on Vietnam, followed by a friendly discussion of the morality of it all. He was a nice kid—said he wanted to go to college and become a lawyer.

29

HELP

Early one Friday evening, two months after Donna's death, Peter received a phone call at his townhouse. Peter and Carol were preparing dinner. Peter had his hands full, at that moment, so Carol answered. It was Brandy.

"Brandy, we're preparing dinner. Please don't keep him on the phone too long," she said to Brandy. Then, "Peter, your new daughter wants to talk with you," she said as she handed Peter the phone. The way she said it indicated some annoyance.

Peter talked to her for several minutes and then hung up. Having overheard part of the conversation, Carol was interested to know more.

"What did she want?"

"She wants to see me," he replied.

"Why?"

"I'm not sure. Although it has been two months since her mom died, she said that she was just now going through her Mom's things and she came upon some files that disturbed her. She thought that I could help her understand what she was looking at."

"What was she looking at?"

"She said that she came upon a scrapbook that had disturbing news articles and a picture of a dead person."

"How did she think you could help with *that*?"

"Not sure. I asked her that same question. She said that she saw my name mentioned in this book more than once. She thinks that although I had said otherwise, I may have been associating with her mom prior to her death."

"Were you?"

"No, of course not. I've been truthful to both of you. Other than knowing she was a covert operative for the CIA, I have no knowledge of what Donna was doing after 1967. I did try to contact her a few times prior to 1989 to have closure, but I was in love with you and I just wanted to be sure she was doing okay and let her know that I was doing okay. The last time I even had a glimpse of her was at Jon Wilson's memorial service way back in 1988. We both attended and I saw her on the other side of the chapel, but as I went toward her, she ducked out on me. Of course, I learned later the likely reason. She didn't want to lie to me about Brandy being my daughter. Anyway, after I married you and put thoughts of Donna aside until she passed away and I met with Brandy and learned the truth, and I've told you all that."

"Peter, I hope you can understand my uneasiness. This has all happened in a short period of time and Brandy works for the National Security Agency—not clear exactly what she does. I'm unsure of her motives . . . I'm still trying to adjust. I hope you aren't getting into something more than you can handle."

Peter had shared the entire story with Carol and Carol had accepted his affair with Donna. "It happened 36 years ago, not on my watch," she had said. However, in the letter that Donna had left for Peter, Donna had suggested a DNA paternity test if there were any doubts as to whether Brandy was his daughter. The two of them had only recently provided DNA samples to a medical laboratory, but the results had not yet come back. The delay was a cause of some tension between Peter and Carol. Meanwhile, over the past two months, Peter and Brandy had gotten to know each other and seemed to be forming a bond. Carol wondered if it all happened too fast. Carol was trusting, but she was also cautious.

"When did she want to see you?" Carol asked.

"Tomorrow morning. Is that okay?"

"I suppose you should meet with her, and see if you can help her, but don't forget, the lawn needs mowing." Her remark reminded Peter that his prime responsibilities were to Carol and their home.

"Yes. Why don't we plan to go out to dinner tomorrow night after I mow the lawn, and I'll tell you everything that I learn."

"Okay . . . fine. Tonight's dinner is ready now. Please help me serve." She had a tone of annoyance in her voice.

30

VISIT WITH BRANDY

On Saturday morning, Peter Troutman drove the seven miles from his house in Columbia to Brandy's house in Ellicott City. This was his first visit to her home. He arrived at nine. Summer weather had come early this year. It was going to be a warm and humid day and he hoped to be able to get back home and do the yard work later in the morning before it got too hot. He rang the doorbell. Brandy came to the door dressed in shorts and a T-shirt. At 36 years old she was still very attractive. She had a slim and shapely figure. Peter had to remind himself who she was. Nevertheless, he couldn't resist complimenting her.

"Brandy you are quite attractive. Good thing I'm your father," he quipped.

"You don't look old enough to be my father," she quipped back. At sixty-two Peter was also slim and had most of his hair with its original color.

"Peter come in. I have coffee for us in the kitchen."

"Okay, thanks."

"How do you like it?" she said as he followed her into the kitchen.

"Black . . . Nice house . . . How long have you been here?"

"I moved here shortly after I got married. After the divorce, I got the house."

"By the way, where is my new grandson today?" he asked.

"He's supposed to be with his father this weekend, but probably with friends right now."

"You said you were disturbed by some things you were finding in your mom's belongings. Did you want to discuss it?"

"I do, but before we talk about that I would like to talk about our relationship."

"What do you mean?"

"I'm getting a sense that Carol is uneasy about all this."

"You're right. She *is* uneasy about our situation."

"Tell me what she's uneasy about. I'm trying to be sensitive to this."

"Sure. We've been married for fourteen years and until you came along, I never told her anything about my experience in Vietnam, or about my affair with your mom. She probably wonders what else I haven't told her. She also knows that I was married when I was with your mom, and so now she probably wonders if I may have cheated on her. Her first husband cheated on her and he covered it up with lies. She was caught off guard. I think she also has some doubts that you're really my daughter."

"I see. I can't do anything about the trust issues she has with you. My husband cheated on me, so I understand her uneasiness."

"Hey c'mon. I hope you're not still uneasy about me and your mom."

"I'm sorry. I know you said it wasn't like that with Mom. I'm just saying I understand her uneasiness. I wish that paternity test I had us take will come back soon. That would resolve at least one doubt," she said in a matter of fact tone.

"Yes, I agree."

"I'll let you know right away when it does. How about more coffee?" she asked as she held the pot ready to pour. "We can take it into the den. That's where I have Mom's stuff that I want to ask you about."

"Okay, just half a cup."

Peter followed Brandy to the den being careful not to spill coffee on the carpet along the way. She had given him more than half a cup. He took a sip and set the cup on a small desk as Brandy began talking.

"Peter, I'll get right to the point. I'm finding things that make me wonder if Mom was legit."

"What do you mean? Like what?"

"Like documents that indicate that she had an overseas account with HSBC. Her friend Ed contacted me and asked me about it. I found a trust agreement, and an address in London where we need to send a death certificate—something I only recently received. If she was legit, why would she need an overseas account? And how is Ed involved?"

"Good question, but overseas accounts are legal. If she was a covert operative, it may be something that the CIA set up. I wouldn't read too much into it. You should probably ask Ed these questions."

"Okay, but there's more."

"Yes, on the phone you mentioned something about a picture of a dead person."

"This is what I wanted you to see," Brandy said, pointing to a loose-leaf binder in the center of the card table.

He took another sip of his coffee and then walked over to the table to have a look.

"Please look through it and tell me what it means."

He pulled a folding chair up to the table and proceeded to review the book page by page as Brandy peered over his shoulder.

The book displayed a sequence of events that began in the year 1987 and ended in April of 2003. Most of the events were described by newspaper articles and photographs with a few comments that Donna had scribbled onto the margin of the pages.

Peter turned to the first page. It was a newspaper article from April of 1987. Jim Hoffman, a resident of Colorado Springs, had died suddenly after having lunch with a real estate agent. The death was suspicious and being investigated as a possible suicide or even murder. The next page in the scrapbook had a news article about a body found in Boulder Creek. The body was identified as a student at the University of Colorado in Boulder who was also a suspect in an attempted break-in at a nearby missile defense system compound. Peter remembered reviewing these articles in 1988 when he was in Boulder, and he remembered how Carol—before he married her—had investigated the money flow to Hoffman's bank account. But why would this be of any significance to Donna and why would Brandy be concerned about it? Then he proceeded to the third page in the book.

When Peter saw the third page, he gasped. There was a newspaper article about an attempted car bombing in May of 1988 that took place in the parking lot of a Residence Inn in Boulder, Colorado. The article said that a bomb had been planted in a car rented to an unnamed IBM employee there on business. There was a photograph of the bomb-squad next to the car. Peter recognized it immediately. It was his rental car and he was the unnamed IBM employee. He and three auditors were about to go to the IBM site that morning. If he had not noticed the bomb before they got into the car, they would have all been dead. He wondered why this would be in Donna's book. What was her involvement? Then he noticed the hand-written note at the bottom of the page.

Peter, what had Jon gotten you into?

The past tense of the comment implied that she did not know about this at the time but learned about it later. Meanwhile Brandy could not help but notice Peter's reaction to what was on the page.

"Peter, you know something about this, don't you? Please explain," she said in a somewhat demanding voice.

Peter had to think for a moment. So far, nothing in Donna's book was classified, even the comments she wrote in the margins. Yet, at that time, Peter was working undercover on the Boulder Creek Project for Jon Wilson, a CIA officer. The project was highly classified. The bomb was an attempt to prevent him and his audit team from discovering that a virus was planted in software that IBM was scheduled to deliver to the Air Force that week. Peter was quite sure that Donna was not involved in that project.

"Okay, I'm quite certain that your mom was not involved in the bombing. I was working on a highly classified project for the CIA. The bombing was intended to kill me and the people on my team. I don't believe your mom had anything to do with the project."

"Why is all this in her book then?"

"Don't know yet. Let's keep going through the pages."

The next page was a news item about the death of an IBM computer room manager name Georgy Belinsky. According to the article, he died of an apparent suicide in his apartment over the Labor Day weekend in 1988. The article included a photo of Georgy.

"What can you tell me about this one?"

"I knew Georgy. He was a likable guy that got caught up with the wrong people. He did not commit suicide. It was murder."

"Did Mom have anything to do with this?"

"No."

"How do you know?"

"The person that murdered him tried to murder me later that same night."

"My God," she gasped. "Why is all this in her book?"

"I think your Mom found out about this after the fact. The person at the CIA that I answered to was Jon Wilson, and I think your Mom was in communication with him."

"I saw Jon Wilson's name later in the book. He died right? Who was he?"

"Your mom and I both worked for Jon in Saigon and I continued to do occasional contract work for him afterwards while at IBM. Jon and your mom may have continued a working relationship at the CIA, but I don't think she was part of any project I was involved with."

The next page had an obituary for Jon Wilson, followed by a memorial service program and a copy of the attendee list. Peter wondered how Donna obtained it. On the page with the program, Donna had circled the name Mary Lou McGuinness who was one of the speakers. Donna had handwritten in the margin:

I felt badly he had to die. She will pay.

"Why did he have to die?" Brandy asked. "Who killed him?"

"Mary Lou killed him."

"The attendee list shows that both you and Mom were present. You told me you had no contact with Mom after Saigon."

Peter knew he was being interrogated but he understood.

"Brandy, everything I told you was true. If you remember, I told you that I had tried to make a connection with your mom but she always managed to put it off. Yes, we were both at Jon's memorial service, but we never spoke. I noticed her on the other side of the chapel but before I could walk over to her, she ducked out the rear door. I did not understand why she was avoiding me until after she died and we read the letter that she left for us."

The next page had a picture of an attractive woman. Donna's note under the picture said:

Mary Lou aka Inga Sarnoff—Soviet Spy

The next two pages in Donna's book had newspaper articles about people who were murdered or died mysteriously over the next twelve years.

"Do you know anything about these people?" Brandy asked.

"Nothing."

"Do you think Mom killed any of these people?"

"No."

"Do you know who did?"

"Let's see what's next," he said as he turned the page.

The next three pages had articles about the elections in Costa Rica in 2002. One article included a photo taken at a political rally. The face of a female participant was circled. It resembled Mary Lou.

The final page had a news article dated March of 2003. It was about the murder of a woman named Maria Martin. The article suggested that she was a socialist with a Russian passport and that she was killed by the U.S. Central Intelligence Agency. There was a photo of the dead woman propped up in a semi-prone position with a bullet hole in her chest. On the bottom of the page, Donna had written:

Justice at last

The woman was the same one that was encircled on the previous page. She looked like Mary Lou.

"Peter, who is she?"

"It's Mary Lou. She was a Soviet spy."

"Did Mom kill her?"

"It's possible, but I don't want to believe it any more than you do. I also question if the CIA took her out. Do you know if your mother was in Costa Rica when this happened?"

"I checked the calendar and she was definitely not home then. She had asked me to feed Tabby while she was gone."

"What about her passport?"

"I had checked that. She probably traveled on her government passport. Her personal passport did not show anything."

"I agree. I think that if she went rogue, she would have used her personal passport. I don't know what else I can tell you except that Inga Sarnoff, or Mary Lou as I knew her, was a sociopathic Soviet spy who killed several people without any feeling of remorse. In my opinion she deserved to die. If your mother did it, I can't fault her."

"Peter, I have this need to know. I can't seem to shake it. Do you have any idea as to what my mother actually did for the CIA?"

"Not really. I suspect that much of what she did was covert. In addition to not wanting me to know about you, and not wanting to rekindle the flame, being covert may have been another reason why she avoided talking with me. Do you have anything else from your mother that may give us more answers?"

"I'll be right back."

She returned with a medium sized safe box with a built-in combination lock. It was obviously heavy. Peter took it from her and set in on top of the table.

"If you still have time, I would like you to go through the contents of this box with me."

Peter looked at his watch. It was only 11:00 a.m.

"Yes, Carol doesn't expect me home until around one, and later I need to mow the lawn and do some other chores around the house, so I have time."

"Where did you find this?" he continued.

"I found it hidden on the top shelf of the closet in Mom's office."

"Let's see what you have."

****

Brandy opened the lock box as she explained, "Mom left a letter for me with the letter she left for you in the safety deposit box at her bank. Her letter to me gave instructions for everything, including the combination for this box. It was in the letter that she said who you were and she said I should connect with you and that I should trust you to help me answer questions. She made all these preparations in 2002 after she got cancer and thought she might die. I'm glad she did—not the cancer . . . the preparations."

Peter smiled. "How would we have opened this lock box otherwise."

Peter looked inside the box. Among other items, he saw passports, a digital camera, memory cards, a burner phone, and a wad of cash.

"Wow, a regular spy kit," was about all he could say.

"I haven't removed anything. Everything is there the way I found it."

He thumbed through the cash, mostly fifty-dollar bills, perhaps a thousand dollars total. Then he looked at the passports, all personal ones but in different names. One of them was in the name of Donna Rice, a name he recognized, but it had recently expired. Then he removed a memory card from the box. It was labeled 'CR-01-02'. He inserted it into the camera, and began to scan through the large thumbnails. Almost all were photos. Most were pictures that included Mary Lou as Peter called her. They had dates imprinted on them, early 2002 for the most part. There was Mary Lou attending a political rally, Mary Lou having lunch at a café with another woman and some gentleman, Mary Lou walking into the Russian Embassy, Mary Lou walking into her house, and so on. These seemed to be surveillance photos. There was also a picture of the head of the PAC shaking hands with a local Socialist candidate in the 2002 elections. They were giving speeches surrounded by their entourage. Mary Lou was not in the background, but the gentleman she had lunch with was. As Peter scanned the thumbnails of the photos, Brandy stood behind him peering over his shoulder.

"Wait!" she said suddenly. "Go back."

"This one?"

"Yes, that's the one. Enlarge it please."

"Okay. What do you see?" he asked.

"It's Joe," she said looking at the picture of the three people at lunch. The gentleman appeared to be a handsome Latino. He had a cup of java in his left hand.

"Joe?"

"Yes, Joe Martinez. I know him."

"Really?" Peter said with surprise. "How would you know him. These pictures were taken in 2002 in Costa Rica."

"Oh my God. Peter, I dated him this past year—here in the United States."

Peter pushed the chair back away from the computer, turned toward Brandy, and gave her a hard look. "Brandy you need to tell me about him. How did you meet?"

"It seemed that we met by chance. It was at my fitness center. I was on a bike and he was on a treadmill just across the aisle. I caught him eyeing me and I returned the look. Obviously, we started talking. Things just seemed to mushroom from there. A year prior to that, I had been taking care of Mom. She was in the hospital, had surgery and was recovering. I helped with her meds, cleaned her house, took her to appointments. It kept me very busy, but by the spring of 2003 Mom was better. She was working and traveling again. I think it left a void in my life I needed to fill."

"You're sure this is Joe in the picture? It's not the most resolute picture."

"Yes, it's his tan skin, his hair, and his expression. It's definitely him."

"What did he say he did for a living?"

"He told me he was the co-owner of a company in Costa Rica that designed and marketed security systems. He said he was responsible for setting up new markets and that they had a contract with an international company in the United States. He said he traveled a lot."

"Are you still dating him?"

"No. I stopped seeing him in February after Mom got sick again. He told me that his project here was completed and he had a new assignment that required him to travel to Toronto. It didn't seem like our relationship could go anywhere. We had discussed this, and we parted amicably."

"Have you heard from him since then?"

"No. I hoped I would—I missed him terribly—but I never did after that."

"Brandy, did you sleep with him?"

"I don't like you asking me that. Mom asked that. Are you asking as my father? I don't think it's your business."

"Okay, I'm sorry. I'm just trying to get a feel for how close the two of you were. Did you introduce him to your mom? What did she think of him?"

"He celebrated Thanksgiving, Christmas and the New Year with us and he was also here for the Super Bowl party I held. Mom never said anything bad about him, but I think she had some reservations."

"Did Joe ever talk about his life in Costa Rica?"

"Yes, he told me he grew up there and went to school there."

Peter decided that this line of inquiry was leading nowhere, so he changed course.

"Let's see what else is in the lock box," Peter suggested as he reached in and pulled out the burner phone. "Interesting," he said. He turned it on and found two phone numbers in memory. The first was a U.S. phone number to be called from another country. The phone number was 00-1-703-555-9516 ext. 111. The second was a number with the foreign country code 506. The number was 506-2519-2099. Peter did not know the country but thought it might be Costa Rica.

"What are you doing?" she asked as he was about to dial a number.

"You're right. No dial-tone. No service."

"Here. Use my phone," she said and handed it to him.

First, Peter dialed the 506 number. This time it rang and rang. No answer.

Then, Peter put the phone on speaker and dialed the number in Virginia. A recorded message asked for the extension and he entered '111'.

They heard, "I'm not available. Please leave a message."

The message did not identify who they had reached, so he just hung up.

"Oh well. Let's continue looking through your mom's stuff."

"Peter, would it be okay if we continue this tomorrow? I need time to process some of this information. Besides, Carol is probably wondering what has happened to you."

Peter looked at his watch. It was already after one. He was late.

"Sure, what time tomorrow?"

"Around two okay?"

"Okay. See you then," he replied and hurried out the door.

****

Peter arrived back home around 1:30 p.m. Carol was not too happy.

They usually ate lunch at one, and he did not call to say he was going to be late.

"You're late. I just started eating my lunch, but I made a sandwich for you and put it into the fridge."

"Yeah, I'm sorry. Time got away from us."

"Did she show you the picture of a dead person?" Carol asked almost mockingly. "Who was the dead person?"

Peter looked hard at Carol. "It was Mary Lou!"

Carol's jaw dropped. "The Mary Lou we knew?"

"Yup. One and the same."

Peter could see the puzzlement on Carol's face so he continued. "Apparently Donna had put together a binder with news clippings about Mary Lou's activities starting in 1987."

"I still don't understand. What did Donna have to do with our project or with Mary Lou? Was she part of Boulder Creek? Was she spying on us?"

"I'm not sure. I can only speculate."

"What did you tell Brandy about it?"

"I had to tell her something. She had a picture and news clipping of the attempted bombing of my rental car in 1988 and she had knowledge of my association with Jon Wilson."

"I hope you didn't tell her too much. I don't want to lose my pension from the FBI," she quipped.

"Not to worry, nothing in Donna's binder was marked classified and I don't think anything I said was classified. There was nothing in the binder about you and I did not mention anything about your involvement."

"So, is everything okay with her now?"

"No. I agreed to go back tomorrow and help her make sense of what she found in her mom's safe . . .. Look, I know this is hard on you, but I figure the more we learn the better off we are. I'm also convinced that she's my daughter and I don't get the feeling we're being played."

"Hope you're right."

31

RETURN TO
BRANDY'S HOUSE

The next day, Brandy began the discussion. "Peter I've been thinking about what we discovered yesterday and I'm even more troubled than I was when we started yesterday. I didn't sleep very well last night thinking about it. Do you think that Joe could have had something to do with Mom's death?"

"I thought your mother died of cancer. Is there something you aren't telling me?"

"Mom had a checkup and blood test just before Thanksgiving. She was cancer-free. Then in January Mom suddenly became sick again. When Mom was in the hospital, I tried to get the doctors to tell me what they were finding. I got the feeling that I was getting a run around. They would say things like 'her organs are failing and we don't know what more we can do' but they would not provide me with specifics and they never said specifically that the cancer had returned. I also noticed that her boss had come to the hospital to visit her more than once with another CIA employee and they had several conversations that I was not privy to. A couple of days before mom died, I ask her what was going on. All she would say was that it was better for me the less I knew."

"I see," Peter responded. He was thinking that it would not be unusual for her boss to come visit and discuss things they needed to know about her job. Nor did Peter think that a sudden and unexpected return of cancer was so unusual, but he did not say anything.

Sensing Peter's skepticism, she said "Wait here. I'll be back in a moment."

When she returned, she had several sheets of paper which she handed to Peter.

"What are these?" he asked as he began to look at them.

"Those are the results of medical tests that Mom had. The first one was done just before Thanksgiving. They were perfect—no sign of cancer. The next two pages were tests that were done in late January when Mom started feeling sick. I'm not a doctor but the reports seem to indicate something other than cancer. In any case, I just found these when I was going through Mom's records."

"I see," Peter said somewhat unsure of where this was headed. "Could we take the report to a doctor now and find out what it means?"

"I already did," she responded.

"And?"

"He said that more tests were probably conducted after these, but based on this report, he said there was no sign of cancer cells and he expected poisoning. However, there were no traces of a specific poison."

"Was there a death certificate?"

"Yes, it took three weeks after she died before I was able to get a copy. It says that the *cause of death* was lymphatic cancer resulting in organ failure. It also mentions prior ovarian cancer. It says that the *manner of death* was indeterminate and pending investigation. The doctors asked if they could do an autopsy and I agreed. It's been a couple of months now since Mom was buried, but I still haven't received an autopsy result. I asked as recently as last week and they told me they were still waiting for lab and toxicology results."

"So, are they investigating the possibility of murder? Have the authorities talked to you?"

"No, and I wonder why not?"

"You said there were conversations between your Mom and the CIA just before she died. Perhaps they are involved. If it is murder, I could understand why they would want to cover it up, especially if it was murder by a foreign agent. But if it was murder, why do you think your boyfriend had anything to do with it?"

"I had trouble sleeping last night because I began to remember little things that did not seem important at the time, but may be important now that I have seen her scrap book and these pictures. I'm trying to connect the dots."

"I see. What are some of those dots?"

"Well . . . the morning after Mom went into the hospital, I went to her townhouse to check on her cat. I made sure that Tabby was fed and did a few other things while I was there. Mom liked iced tea and she made batches of it each week and stored it in the refrigerator in a large pitcher. I recall that at some point I opened her refrigerator and everything seemed to be in order. Well, four days later, that pitcher was not there. At the time I thought it odd, but maybe I just hadn't noticed it missing four days earlier. I gave Tabby a splash of milk and brought him back here with me along with the milk. The milk was fine, as is Tabby. But I wondered about the iced tea."

"Any other dots that you recall?"

"Yes, I'm angry that I never heard from Joe after he left. He left three days after Mom went into the hospital. I would have thought he cared enough to ask about her after that. Two weeks after he left, I tried to call him. I called his cell and it was no longer in service. I called the Maryland office of International Security Systems, the company he said he had a contract with. They had no record of a Joseph Martinez. Then I called the number on his business card in Costa Rica. They would not give me any information except that he was out of the country on a special assignment. I realized he played me."

Brandy's voice began to show some agitation as she continued. "Then I remembered the day he left. I had spent the night with him—yes, and I apologize for my reaction yesterday when you asked.

Anyway, he was in the shower and I was in his living room where he had his laptop and his shoulder bag. He had printed out a few pages on a printer that he had connected to his laptop and the papers were sitting on top of his laptop. The top page was an airline itinerary with the name Joseph Garcia and a flight to Toronto. Joe had told me his name was Joseph Martinez, so that was confusing. However, I also noticed that a sheet of paper had slid off onto the floor underneath the table, so I retrieved it and was about to put it with the other papers when I noticed that it was also an airline itinerary for that evening. The only thing is the name was not Joseph Martinez and the destination was not Toronto. It was for Alexander Sarnoff and the destination was Moscow via JFK."

"Did you ask Joe about this?"

"I did. He told me that his full name was Joseph Ricardo Garcia Martinez and that it was customary not to refer to a person's last name in Costa Rica. He also told me that the itinerary was for Alex, a colleague that he needed to meet with before they both left, and that Alex had sent him a copy of his itinerary so that they could fit it in. Joe also said he had agreed to drive him to the airport."

"What was Joe's demeanor when he said all this? Did he seem upset with you for noticing this or anything like that?"

"No. He smiled and thanked me for retrieving the page and he spoke calmly. What he said seemed very plausible to me at the time and I didn't think any more about it until about a week later. I thought I would have heard from Joe. I thought he might want to know how Mom was doing, but I never heard from him again. That made me so curious that I used my position at NSA to follow up. Peter, neither he nor Alex ever boarded a flight to Toronto or to Moscow!"

"Anything else?"

"Yes. Joe had said I could have anything he left in his townhouse. Specifically, he told me I could have his printer, but he also said he had some clothes in the closet that I could give to Goodwill. I took them home, but before I gave them away, I checked the pockets and found a slip of paper with a phone number. It had the initials *BM*' followed by a phone number. I can't remember the number precisely, but I do remember the area code was 703 and I think the extension number was 111, but I'm not sure. The number we found on Mom's burner phone yesterday was similar. Now I'm trying to put two and two together—may not mean anything."

"Do you still have the scrap of paper?"

"I may. I think I put it back into the pocket, and I have the jacket. It's hanging up in the closet. Let me go look."

When she came back, she had the slip of paper. "Here it is," she said excitedly. "The number is *identical* to the 703 number on the burner phone. I guess all we need to do now is determine who the number belongs to."

"The 703 number is in Northern Virginia. My suggestion is to call it tomorrow, a work day. My guess is that it's someone at Langley, perhaps her boss. But that begs the question, why would Joe and your mom need to call the same number in Langley?"

"Okay. What about the other number on the burner phone?"

"You could try and call it tomorrow as well. Perhaps someone will answer. I checked out the 506 country-code last night on the Internet. Just as we thought, it is Costa Rica. Could the number be Joe's number in Costa Rica?"

"I have Joe's business card and when I called it, two months ago I'm pretty sure I dialed a 506 country-code, but I don't think it's the same number. Let me go get it just to be sure."

She returned waving Joe's card in her hand.

"Does the business card agree?"

"Nope, same country code, different number," she said and showed him the card. "I thought it might be the number for Mom's friend Ed? He lived and worked in Costa Rica. But, it's not the number he gave me when I spoke to him at the funeral."

"Again, call the numbers tomorrow and see where it leads you. Do you remember anything else that would help us connect the dots?"

"I don't know. I just have so many unanswered questions. Peter, do you think we should go to the police and start an investigation?"

"Hmmm . . . I don't think it would be wise."

"Why not?"

'Well think about it. If they found evidence of foul play—and we have none now—I think you would be their prime suspect. You had the means, and they could also argue motive."

"**Motive**? **How so?**" she said loudly."

"They could argue that you wanted the life insurance money. They could also investigate your many years of estranged relationship with your mom."

"Ugh!" she moaned as she got up and began to pace.

"Hang on. I believe you said your mom had conversations with her boss before she died. It's possible that the CIA is already investigating this. Did you talk to them at all?"

"Only after she passed. Her boss expressed his condolences. He seemed sincere and he left me with a business card—said I could contact him if I needed to talk, but the number on his card was not the one on mom's burner phone."

"Well, I think you should take him up on his offer. Don't know if you will learn too much more, but I think it would be a safe avenue to pursue. What's his name?"

"Brian Matheson . . .. *BM*' were the initials on the slip of paper in the jacket pocket. You don't know him, do you?" she asked inquisitively.

"Actually, I do know who he is. I met with him once in 1988 and again in 2000," Peter said and then paused. "Matheson was Jon Wilson's second in command and took over for him when Jon was killed. We crossed paths again when I was doing telecommunication consulting work for a large corporation. The CIA was interested in phone calls between someone who worked for my client and a certain party in Central America. He said he did not have enough for a warrant or to bring NSA into it, so he came to me. I thought it had to do with exchanging drugs for classified technology information. I gave him what he needed . . .. I would be happy to go with you to see him."

She didn't respond. Her mind seemed to be elsewhere.

"Peter . . . I'm thinking about Mom's friend Ed. He came to visit her both times when she was sick and he came to the funeral. I talked to him briefly. He gave me his contact information, but no phone number with a Costa Rican country code. He said he was a long-time friend—told me how Mom had good things to say about me, and so on. I think he may be more that a close friend, and I'd like to know how he fits into all of this."

She paused and then continued.

"Last night, I searched through her personal email accounts. She had two personal accounts, a regular one, and another that was reserved for 'junk'—you know, one she used for vendors and people that might put her on a mailing list. She and Ed must have had some way of staying in touch, but I didn't see any emails from him in either account and if he sent letters, I didn't find them which is strange unless he was CIA and Mom tossed them to protect his identity. Anyway, I did come across an email in the 'junk' account. It was addressed to Sally Mae from the proprietor of a coffee plantation in Costa Rica. Mom once told me she would use phony names like that to hide her real name. Anyway, the proprietor was responding to a survey she answered indicating how much she enjoyed the tour of his coffee plantation. The survey was dated the Saturday before the newspaper said they found Maria Martin's body. So, now I'm certain that she was there at that time. I'm also guessing that she was with Ed. I really hope Mom was not the assassin. Perhaps I should talk with Ed about that."

"Did you say he gave you his mailing address?"

"I'll find the contact information he gave me at the funeral. Maybe I could send him a letter in the mail."

Peter looked at his watch. "Brandy, I'm sorry but I need to get home. Just give me a call and let me know how I can help. I'm willing to go with you to see Matheson."

"Okay. I'll call you as soon as I set something up with him."

****

Two days later, Peter received a call from Brandy. She had set up a meeting with Matheson at CIA headquarters. Unfortunately, it was not right away as he was going to be traveling, but the meeting was scheduled for Friday afternoon in the first week of June. She told Peter that Matheson remembered him, and he was invited. She would pick him up at his house and they would drive to Langley together. Brandy also mentioned that she found the home address for Ed Perez in Costa Rica and had written him a personal letter expressing her concerns and asking him a whole bunch of questions.

32

DRIVE TO LANGLEY

B randy had arranged the meeting with CIA Officer Brian Matheson for a Friday afternoon early in the month of June. She took off work and drove from her office at Fort Meade. She picked up Peter at his home in Columbia and together they drove to CIA headquarters in Langley. The day was sunny with temperatures in the mid-seventies and the traffic was not bad. The drive was relatively pleasant, and took less than an hour.

"Peter, I received a response from Ed Perez," she said gleefully. "It came in today's mail. I've already read it, but I thought you may want to read it while we're driving. It's in the glove compartment."

The envelope contained a two-page letter and a thumb drive. Peter pulled out the letter and began to read.

> *Dear Brandy:*
>
> *It was such a pleasure to hear from you. I hope I can help with some of your concerns, but please understand that I can only speak to personal matters relating to you and your mom. I have known your mom for about 15 years as a friend. Due to the nature of our work I think we had a special and unique relationship, one which became intimate more recently. We were*

both close to retirement and we discussed retiring together. Your mom was a wonderful person, and I miss her terribly.

You should know that your mom loved you and that you were the world to her. She told me how over the years she struggled with balancing her job and her role as a mother. She also told me how proud she was of your accomplishments and how much she loved you for standing by her when she was sick both in 2002 and recently. I believe she died with a clear conscience about the decisions she made during her life and was at peace with herself and her maker.

I am very pleased to know that your mom told you who your birth father is and that you have connected with him. I urged your mom to tell you because my own mother disappeared when I was three, and I understand the need to know about birth parents. In my case, she was my mother, and although we never really hit it off, I had a sense of closure after I met her. Although I never met Peter, your mom and Matheson had many good things to say about him and the work he and Carol did for us. I would very much like to meet him. I don't get back to the States that often but I will contact you when I do.

You asked why your mom was here in early April last year. You wondered if the news reports of the murder of Maria Martin, believed to be a Russian spy, may have been more than coincidental to her presence here. Let me say three things. First, the CIA has denied any role in her death. Secondly, I can't imagine your mom killing someone except in self-defense. Finally, Maria's body was discovered on a Sunday morning. I had dinner with your mom Friday night, and I was with your mom 100 percent of the time from Saturday morning to early Sunday evening. As you discovered, we went touring on Saturday. In addition to the coffee fincá, we also toured Poás and a hummingbird park, and we had dinner and went dancing later. We had a very enjoyable and romantic weekend. (As I write this, I find myself becoming emotional. Please understand.) Yes, the news did suggest that Maria may have been murdered earlier on Friday. However, your mom gave me a very plausible and verifiable account of where she was. Unfortunately, the Costa Rican OIJ has not yet arrested anyone for the crime, and the news media and the Russians believe that your mom was the assassin.

Regarding your boyfriend, Joe. In December, your mom had expressed a suspicion to me about his intentions. She expressed a concern for your welfare as well as her own. Unfortunately, I was not able to tell her much at that time. Then in early January, she sent me a photo and asked me to investigate. I recognized Joe as the operator of a security firm in Costa Rica and I contacted him. He told me he was involved with a highly classified operation. Details could not be revealed. I asked about his involvement with you. He told me he cared about you and you were not in danger. I could not reveal Joe's involvement at that time. However, your mom's concern increased after there had been attempts on her life and she became ill. She thought he may be a Russian agent who was poisoning her. I did not want her to pass away without knowing what was going on. Matheson agreed to read me in and I told your mom everything I knew, and reassured her that you would not be in danger.

I know it must be disconcerting to have Joe vanish on you the way he did, but Joe is in custody. The OIJ arrested him when he returned to Costa Rica. He faces serious charges. I met with him on several occasions and he admits to no wrong doing. While in Costa Rica there were attempts on his life. To protect him, he is now in U.S. Federal protective custody and held at an unknown location in the States. During my visits, he reiterated his frustration that he can't see you again to apologize and explain. I told him I would see what I could do.

You told me that you had a meeting scheduled with Matheson. I hope that will be productive. I talked with him and requested that he read you in on certain matters that will resolve some of your remaining concerns. Whether or not he can

be trusted to do that remains to be seen. Don't expect him to
admit to anything that is illegal or that would expose an asset.
    The enclosed thumb drive will explain a lot. You will need
a password: CIOP410BM.
Fondly, Ed Perez

After reading the letter, Peter folded it back up, put it back into the envelope with the thumb drive, and set the envelope in the tray between the seats.

"Very nice letter. I'm curious though. He didn't say anything about the overseas account. Had you asked him about it?"

"I did. Perhaps he chose to ignore it."

"Have you seen the contents of the thumb drive?"

"No. Let's do that as soon as we get back home," she responded.

****

As soon as they crossed the American Legion Memorial Bridge into Virginia, they took the George Washington Parkway. They passed an exit to the CIA that was labeled employees only and Peter asked if she could use it. "After all," he said, "You are an employee of NSA." Brandy mused that she wished they allowed employees of NSA to use it as it would save a few miles if they did. However, they continued, exited onto Route 123, and drove to the main entrance.

Matheson had put their names onto an authorized visitor list and given them an access code that they could present to the guards protecting the entrance roadway. A guard came out of the booth and asked for ID. Brandy gave him her NSA ID and then he turned to Peter.

"And you sir?"

"I'm with her," Peter replied

"Could I have your ID please?"

Peter passed him his driver's license.

"Were you given a code?"

"Yes." Peter fumbled through his pockets for the code that Brandy had just given him no more than 40 minutes ago, as Brandy rolled her eyes. "Here it is."

The guard took the license and the code to his booth, checked something on his computer, and returned with their IDs.

"You guys are free to go. Have a nice day," he said with a deadpan expression.

As they passed through the gate, Peter noticed the black uniformed guard off at the side of the road. He had an automatic rifle pointed toward the gate.

33

MEETING IN LANGLEY

They parked the car and walked into the main lobby. After they were screened and signed in at the lobby, an administrative assistant named Jeannette escorted them to Matheson's office. On the way, they passed by the Memorial Wall with stars that represented the agents and operatives that died in the line of duty. Brandy wondered if her mom would qualify for a star and to have her name in the Book of Honor that sat on a pedestal in front of the wall. When they arrived upstairs, they found Matheson standing at his office door.

Matheson had been with the agency for at least twenty years. Titles and positions were not generally made known, but Peter knew that Matheson had replaced Jon Wilson in 1988 and now he was probably a Deputy Director of something related to counter intelligence. He was probably around fifty years of age. He looked very average and ordinary, but when he spoke, he captured your attention. His tone was sincere and compassionate, but direct and commanding at the same time. He was well liked. Donna had reported to him.

"Hello Brandy. And Peter, haven't seen you in a while," he said as he looked at Peter. "How is Carol?" he asked referring to Peter's wife.

"She's fine . . . said to tell you hello."

"Brandy told me on the phone that she's your daughter. I must admit I was very surprised to hear that. Although, it does explain why you and Donna often asked about each other . . . I didn't see you at Donna's funeral—"

Brandy interrupted. "Mom kept our relationship a secret from both of us until after she passed. It's a long story, but she had her reasons."

"Well anyway, please, let's sit down. What is it that I can do for the two of you today?"

"Mr. Matheson, you said I could call—"

"Brandy, please just call me Brian," he interrupted.

"Yes Brian. I have concerns about what my mother was involved with. I need to know how to remember her, and we have lots of questions."

"I see. What sort of questions?"

"Like who killed Mary Lou," Peter replied and handed Matheson the news clippings he had of Maria Martin from the Costa Rican newspapers.

Matheson took a quick look at the news clipping and then looked at Peter. "I'll tell you what. We have a sensitive compartmented information facility, a SCIF. Let's go there."

They followed Matheson into a small conference room. "Our conversation will be totally secure and private in here. Please sit."

Peter spoke. "The news implies that the CIA took her out, and we know that Donna was there at the time. Did she do this?"

Matheson looked directly at Brandy. "Brandy, your mom was a good woman and a patriot. That's how you should remember her. To answer your question—No! The CIA does not assassinate people," he said, quoting the official line.

"Did she have an alibi?" Brandy wanted to know.

"I don't know how you feel about this sort of thing, but your mother spent the weekend in question with a gentleman friend."

"Was his name Ed?"

"Yes. How did you know?"

"He sent flowers when she was in the hospital. I traced the order back to an Ed Perez in San José. He also came to the funeral," Brandy responded.

"He must have cared a great deal about your mother for him to risk revealing his identity." Then after a pause, "Did you have any other questions?"

"We do," Peter responded. "We need to know the truth about Donna's death."

"What do you mean?"

Brandy began to explain. "In January, Mom said she wasn't feeling well. I asked her if the cancer could be coming back. She told me she hoped not, but if it was, she didn't want to fight it again. We agreed to go to the doctor and find out, which we did. She got worse and we spent several days doing appointments and getting tested. She told me that the doctors thought she had been poisoned. She thought so as well."

Brandy continued her explanation. "I went back to her townhouse with the intent of finding the source of poisoning. She always kept a pitcher of iced tea in the fridge and Mom thought that could be the source. Well, there was no iced tea in the fridge. Was I losing my mind? I could swear it was there before she got sick. Then I noticed that the pitcher had been emptied and washed. It was sitting in the clean dish drainer. My thought was someone else had been there. Maybe the person who tried to kill her had come back and destroyed the evidence. Meanwhile, just prior to this time, her townhouse was broken into. They disarmed her security system, but it was not clear if anything was taken. Perhaps they added poison to her food. I'm sure she reported it to you."

"Who did you think poisoned her?" Brian asked.

"My boyfriend!" Brandy replied emphatically.

"Your boyfriend? How—"

Peter interrupted and tried to lure Matheson into saying more. "We have evidence that her boyfriend, Joe Martinez, was a spy and that he poisoned Donna. We have enough evidence that we're considering going to the FBI and requesting an investigation. However, we wanted to alert you beforehand in case the CIA had an objection."

Matheson stared at Peter as he gathered his thoughts about how to respond.

"I can tell you with one-hundred percent certainty that Donna died of cancer, not poison. The death certificate and the medical reports are now released and that's what they say. We delayed these being made public until we finished our own investigation."

"Investigation or cover-up?" Brandy snapped back.

"Brandy, surely you must realize that national security may be at stake here and there are certain things I can't reveal. Peter you understand that, don't you?"

"We have information that we're willing to share with you," Peter responded. "If you also share with us. It would be better than sharing it with the FBI, don't you think?"

"I don't want you going to the FBI."

"Then read us in." Peter suggested.

"Give me something first."

"Okay, we have a picture that Brandy's son took of Joe and Brandy on Thanksgiving. Then, Donna's friend took another picture of Joe on New Year's Eve," Peter said, and handed the pictures to Brian.

Realizing where Peter was going with this, Brandy interjected. "At Thanksgiving, Joe didn't seem to appreciate having his picture taken, but we didn't think much of it at the time. Then on New Year's Eve, he told Mom he didn't want her to take a picture and pulled away, but I think by then Mom was starting to get suspicious of Joe, and Mom had a friend take the picture of him with everyone else later in the evening when he was off guard. But after that, I wondered why he wouldn't want his picture taken."

"Okay, not so unusual is it?" Matheson said.

"After Mom died, we found this newspaper picture taken in 2002 at a socialist political rally in Costa Rica. Apparently, Mom was suspicious and she circled the head you see in the crowd. Who do you suppose that is?" Brandy asked sarcastically.

Matheson kind of nodded his head but didn't comment on the picture. It was obviously Joe in the picture. "Anything else?"

"Here's another picture," Peter said. "It's a picture of Joe and Mary Lou together with a third person in Costa Rica. We know Mary Lou was a Russian spy. Who is the third person? The implication is that Joe worked with them."

Matheson seemed alarmed. "Where did you get this?" he demanded.

"Donna left it for us. It's not marked classified . . . just three people having lunch. I was hoping you could verify the identity of the third person."

"So, you think Joe came here to poison your mom?"

"Yes, I do! I had invited Mom, a few friends and Joe to watch the Super Bowl at my house. On the day of the Superbowl, Mom was at my house helping to get ready. I think Joe went to Mom's townhouse earlier in the day and poisoned the pitcher of iced tea that she kept in her fridge, and maybe also the orange juice. The next day, Mom was very sick!"

"Do you have any evidence that he was actually in your mother's house?"

"He was in Mom's townhouse several times in December and January with me, but on that particular day, when he arrived at the party, I noticed cat hair on his pant legs where Mom's cat Tabby would have rubbed."

"Did he have a key? And what about your mom's security system?"

"He knew Mom had a key hidden in the downspout. He could have gone back after his first visit with me and copied it. At some point Mom removed the key from the downspout, but I still had a key in my purse, and Joe may have taken it, copied it, and returned it without my knowledge. Even without the key he probably could have picked the lock. Peter showed me how easy it is to do that. As far as the security system, he could have watched me enter the code when we went there together. But just before the break-in, Mom changed the code. If Joe went there after that and didn't know the code, it may have been the reason why Mom knew there was a break-in. An alert was never sent to her or the alarm company, but she said that when she arrived home that day, she found that the alarm system was totally disconnected. After that, Joe either learned the new code or learned how to disconnect it and reconnect it without the code. He was a security expert, wasn't he?"

"Anything else?"

"Brian," Peter interjected. "We have been forthcoming with you. Now it's your turn. Please tell us who is Alexander Sarnoff."

"I need to know how you heard of that name?" he responded.

Brandy replied. "On the morning that I said goodbye to Joe, I found a travel itinerary for Alexander Sarnoff. Joe said he was a colleague. Was that Joe's real name?"

"Okay, but before we go any further with this, I need to know that neither of you will reveal to anyone what I'm about to tell you."

"Of course, you have our word."

"Please understand, not only is this a matter of national security, but your lives could be endangered if you leak anything."

"Okay." Both Peter and Brandy responded simultaneously.

"Sarnoff, also known as Aleksei Chaban reports to Ivan Markov, an intelligence officer in the Russia's SVR-RF, the Russian equivalent to our CIA. Markov is a member of an elite group called *Dignity with Honor*. He's the third person in your picture. He oversaw the operation Maria Martin—Mary Lou to you Peter—was working on in Costa Rica to influence the 2002 elections and increase the socialist influence in the country. They were somewhat successful. He also oversaw an operation intended to take out your mom."

Matheson continued. "Early in 2003 your mom went down to Costa Rica to arrest and interrogate Inga Sarnoff, aka Mary Lou, who used the name Maria Martin at this point. Finally, after all these years," he said as he looked at Peter, "she surfaced and was revealed. Donna met with high-ranking officials at the OIJ to discuss the plan. We believe that either one of those officials leaked information to the Russians, or that the meeting room was bugged. We think that it was from what Donna said about herself at that meeting that the Russians learned of her responsibilities at the CIA. Your mom was a tracker," he said as he looked at Brandy. "She tracked down Russian spies, been doing it for fifteen years. Unfortunately, Inga Sarnoff was murdered before we could arrest her."

Matheson continued to look at Brandy. "Your mom became a target. Our intelligence sources told us that the Russians wanted to find out who your mom's contacts were, who her intelligence sources were, and what Russian agents she was still tracking. The Russians believed your mom killed Maria Martin. Once they got the information they wanted, they planned to kill your mom in retaliation. Markov was responsible for the operation. We believe that Maria Martin reported to him, so it may have been personal for him as well."

"Did they succeed?"

"No. They did hack into your mom's CIA accounts and they did steal your Mom's Blackberry. However, we were able to plant fake information and fake files on the CIA server, so what they got was not what they thought they were getting."

"What about the poison?" Peter asked.

"We thought we intercepted the poison before Donna imbibed it. However, when she had symptoms of cancer, we went to her townhouse and searched for it. We took samples of the iced tea, the juice, and the milk, and then we dumped what was left. We washed out the pitcher and left it in the drainer. Brandy, your mind was not playing tricks on you when you discovered that. It was us. However, the doctors could not find evidence that she had poison in her system."

"If that's the case," Brandy interjected, "then why did it take so long do produce a valid death certificate?"

"Well, your mom definitely died of cancer. However, our intelligence said that Markov's plan was to poison your mom with cancer cells. I know that sounds preposterous, but the Russians may have developed a way to trick the immune system into fostering the growth and spread of cancer cells through the lymphatic system. Supposedly the chemical would be difficult to trace unless the medical examiner knew what to look for. We needed time to analyze the chemical and we also wanted the Russians to believe that their plan succeeded. It would give us more leverage when we interrogated Markov and threatened a charge of murder."

Brandy looked puzzled. "Were you able to arrest him?"

"Of course. We set up a sting operation and arrested him. He may have had diplomatic immunity in Costa Rica, but he did not have it here in the United States. He was here illegally. We charged him with several counts of espionage and one count of conspiracy to commit murder."

"Doesn't sound as if you can prove attempted murder," Peter suggested.

"Actually, we have a recorded conversation in which Markov orders the kill and provides the lethal chemical to do it."

"What about Chaban? I saw his itinerary. Didn't he escape?" Brandy wanted to know.

"We arrested him at the airport. We charged him as an accomplice."

"And what about Joe? Where did Joe Martinez fit into this," Peter wanted to know.

"We arrested him too. He was Markov's inside man. He used Brandy to gain access to her mom."

"He used me alright," she muttered.

"It seems as if you had someone on the inside yourself. You had a great deal of intelligence that you were able to act on, and I think I know who your inside man was," Peter surmised.

Matheson and Brandy both looked at Peter. "It was Joe. Wasn't it?"

"Sorry, I can't comment on that," Matheson responded.

"Yes. It's all starting to make sense now," Brandy said excitedly. I was with Joe, at his townhouse on the morning that he left, I stayed at his place for another hour before I left to go home. He asked me to take some clothes he had left to the Goodwill. In one of the pockets, I found a scrap of paper with a phone number on it. I didn't think anything of it at the time and put it back into the pocket where I found it. But this past week Peter called the number and heard 'Hello, I'm not available, please leave a message.' The number was 703-555-9516 ext. 111. Sound familiar?" she said excitedly. You could tell by her tone that she was also angry.

"Okay look," Matheson responded. "I have no idea about that and I never received a phone call from Joe Martinez."

"Did my Mom know that my boyfriend was working with the Russians in a plot to kill her?"

"We couldn't let her know. If we did, it would have jeopardized our ability to catch the Russians in the act of espionage and attempted murder . . . but we——"

No sooner had he said this than he realized the impact his revelations must be having on Brandy.

Brandy was livid. "How could you do this to me and to Mom? You allowed an agent to take advantage of me and you allowed my mother to be used as bait?"

"I'm sorry. I can only imagine how you must feel," he said, but it was too late.

"I feel like I was raped! Can you imagine that?" She immediately got up and stormed out of the room.

"Brian, I'm with Brandy on this," Peter said and followed Brandy out of the room.

When he caught up with her, she was crying. He put his arm around her and tried to comfort her. She resisted at first but then they hugged. "I told him I was with you on this. I think what the CIA did was deplorable. Are you going to be okay?"

"I'm sorry. I guess I let my emotions get the better of me," she said as she looked up at Peter and forced a grin. "Peter, I want to go home."

"Yes, of course. I understand."

As they turned to go, Matheson stood in front of them blocking their way. "Brandy, I had no intention of hurting you. I did not know that you and Joe were intimate. If he forced himself on you, I need you to tell me so that I can take appropriate action."

"He did not force himself, but if I had known who he was, it would not have happened. I was taken advantage of. I need to leave now."

Matheson didn't know what else to say. "Please wait here and I'll have Jeannette usher you out."

34

RESTING PLACE

Brandy and Peter didn't say much as Brandy drove north on the Beltway toward the Maryland state line. But when she approached Route 355 in Maryland she slowed down and turned onto the exit ramp—several miles before they would normally turn off to head back home.

"Where are we going?" Peter asked.

"I want us to visit Mom's grave. I hope you're okay with that." He thought he detected a bit of residual anger in her voice but took note that she had said, *us*.

"Yes, of course."

They entered the cemetery grounds, parked on the roadway as close to the site as they could, and walked up a slight hill to Donna's marker. Brandy was about to set herself on the ground a few feet in front of the grave stone, but the ground was damp. And newly grown grass was beginning to take hold, so she remained standing. Peter remained a few feet behind her.

They remained silent for what seemed like ages, staring at Donna's tombstone. Then Brandy looked back at Peter and motioned for him to come next to her. She had tears in her eyes.

"Peter, I need to apologize for letting my emotions get the better of me."

"It's understandable."

"I'm still trying to figure things out . . . Do you think that Matheson was telling us the truth?"

"Well—"

"I mean, isn't it possible that Joe really did poison Mom. How do we know that Matheson himself wasn't working for the Russians?"

"Well, I think—"

"Or, on the other hand, maybe Joe was really working for the United States . . . like a double agent or something?"

Then she took a breath and turned her head toward Peter.

"Brandy, nothing is absolute, but in my opinion, it's most likely that everything Matheson told us is true, but I don't think he told us the whole story, and he was very vague about what Joe's involvement was. Ed's letter seemed to imply that Joe was not out to kill your mom, but if that was true—"

"Either way, I was used and I'm having a hard time getting over it." She turned her head back toward the grave stone. "Mom, how were you able to tolerate this duplicity all those years?" she said in an agitated tone as she stared at the tombstone.

Peter put his hand on her shoulder to calm her down.

"Peter, you've worked with the CIA in the past. Did you have to deal with this sort of thing?"

"Yes, I did. After Mary Lou, aka Maria Martin, killed Jon Wilson, I swore I would never do another assignment with the CIA. But, unlike your Mom, I had a choice, or so I thought. Ten years later, Carol and I won a telecommunications consulting contract with a large company. It was a big win for us. Then two weeks into it, our client's Vice President called me into his office to give him a status update. As I entered his office he motioned to his left, and lo and behold, who is standing before me? None other than Matheson. Turns out that our contract was a guise by Matheson to get us to secretly do some intelligence work for him."

"Is that the same assignment you mentioned when you were at my house?"

"Yes, it is."

"Did you do it?"

"Didn't have much of a choice at that point. I had a contract. It wasn't illegal, and the additional twenty-grand for the intelligence work didn't hurt. Yes, we did it. I didn't like how they had manipulated me, but after I began to see the bigger picture the way Matheson did, I got over it."

"What was the bigger picture?"

Matheson explained that his job was to accomplish certain objectives for God and Country, while minimizing collateral damage, and while keeping his actions legal. I didn't necessarily like it, but I understood it, and I accepted it. I think your mother got it as well."

"Are you saying that I was collateral damage?" she mumbled.

Peter didn't answer. He put his arm around her and pulled her close.

"I think," she continued, "what I'm most upset about is falling for Joe only to find out he was lying to me. I had real feelings for him. I wonder if he had any for me."

"It's quite possible he did, Brandy. Things are not always cut and dry. Either way, you're not doing yourself any good by dwelling on it."

"You're probably right," she said as she went directly up to her mom's tombstone. Peter watched as she crouched in front of the gravestone and put the palm of her hand over the engraving on its face. "I love you Mom," she said softly. Then she turned back to Peter. "I'm ready to go now."

35

MORE TRUTH

They left the cemetery, and arrived at Peter's house around three thirty in the afternoon. Before getting out of the car, Brandy motioned to the envelope. "I thought you would want to see it too."

"I do. Why don't you come inside with me? We can view it on my desktop."

"What about Carol?"

"Not to worry."

Carol came down the stairs from her office and greeted them at the door. Peter detected that look of *where have you been.*

"I'm home. A little later than I thought . . . I know. We stopped at her Mom's gravesite on the way home."

"Oh, hi Brandy. How did the meeting go?" Carol asked the two of them.

"Okay, I guess," Peter replied halfheartedly. "Oh, Matheson said to say hello for him," Peter added in a cheerful tone and then said, "I hope you don't mind, but Brandy and I need to review something on my computer before she goes home. We won't be long."

And before Carol could respond, Peter headed down the stairs to his office with Brandy in pursuit.

Peter removed the thumb drive from the envelope and plugged it into the USB port, while Brandy pulled up a nearby chair. They sat there in front of the computer screen, eager with anticipation, like two kids about to go on a carnival ride.

"Here goes," Peter said as he entered the password required to open the thumb drive. The thumb drive contained two folders: Folder A and Folder B. Peter clicked on folder A.

Folder A

Brandy:

Here is my understanding of Joe's involvement.

Your mother was aware that the Russians had targeted her and she had agreed to Matheson's plan to entrap them. However, Brian Matheson is a strict believer in the "need to know" philosophy. Up until she passed, your mother was unaware of your boyfriend's role in the operation. Prior to January, I was totally out of the loop and unaware of the operation that your mother was involved with. Interestingly, Joe was not aware that neither I nor your mother knew of his role.

Joe's role was to work with the Russians to gather intel and set them up. It was also his job to protect your mom, but when your mom got sick, it was not clear if he had succeeded. This all came out after I had met with Matheson and Joe in late January. Bottom line, Joe is one of us. I informed your Mom of Joe's role just before she passed. However, she was sworn to secrecy.

Folder B contains transcripts of correspondence between Joe and Matheson. I trust that you understand the sensitivity of the contents. Matheson used the initials BM and Joe used the initials JGM. You may want to destroy the thumb drive after you read it.

"So! Joe was a double agent under deep cover? Matheson never indicated ***that*** when we talked to him," Brandy exclaimed. Peter could see the agitation in Brandy's face.

"Take a breath," he advised. "We'll get through this. Are you ready to see the contents of folder B?"

"I'm ready. Let's do it."

<u>Folder B</u>

████████████

Text message 8 a.m. April 5, 2003

BM:

Enclosed is a transcript of what I observed on Friday evening April 4. As you approved last night, I did report to Petrov the death of Maria Martin and that the possible assailant was Officer Wolf. As you can see, my observations do not fully support what I reported to Petrov. He has requested a full report within the week. As of now, the authorities have not been notified. Please advise as to what else I should report to Petrov. (See Enclosure.) JGM

████████████

TRANSCRIPT OF OBSERVATIONS
ON FRIDAY APRIL 4 2003

I am tracking Donna Wolf, aka Donna Rice, a known employee of the American CIA. I follow her from the InterContinental Hotel in Escazu to La Copa Máxima, a coffee shop and eatery in the city of Heredia. She is driving a rented late model white Toyota Camry, plate number 8537161. Wolf is wearing casual business attire consisting of a white blouse, a silky neck scarf, black slacks with a black belt, and black slip-on shoes. She has dangling earrings, shoulder length brown hair and is not wearing glasses.

We arrive at La Copa Máxima at 5:15 p.m. Wolf enters the establishment. I follow her in. I go to the counter and order a coffee. While standing there I see Wolf walk over to a table in the back corner. Two men are there. I don't know the one. Let's call him Mystery Man. She says hello to the other man and there is an exchange of words. I recognize him as a Deputy Director of the DIS, Jafeth Balladares. He reports directly to DIS Director Geraldo Alverez. Wolf seats herself at a table on the other side of the room. I return to my car.

At 5:30 p.m. Mystery Man leaves the coffee shop. I think I have seen him before but I can't quite place him. He looks to be in his mid-thirties. He is about 5 feet 9 inches tall, slender, but with an athletic build. He is dressed more casually than the Deputy Director. He is wearing a white short-sleeved shirt, a tie but no jacket, black slacks, and black shoes. I notice he has a tattoo on his left forearm. I believe it to be symbolic of a faction of the Nicaraguan Resistance movement. He turns to his right and goes to the parking area around the side of the building out of my line of sight.

A half-hour later, Wolf exits the rear door of the café and comes around the building to her car. She has a small cardboard carton in her right hand. She sits in her car a few minutes before leaving. I'm too far away to see what she is doing. Perhaps she is primping, I think. While I'm waiting, I see Balladares leave the café and go to the back of the building and out of sight. At 6:10 p.m. I follow Wolf out of the parking lot onto Route 3.

I follow Wolf to the Rohrmoser area of San José. Wolf makes a left turn from Via 104 and enters the neighborhood, but a black Ford sedan with tinted windows cuts in front of me and prevents me from following closely. I miss the light and must wait a few more minutes before I can continue. As I finally enter the neighborhood, Wolf is no longer in sight. However, I know the neighborhood and I know where Maria Martin lives, having once been to her house when I worked with her. I assume that may be where Wolf is headed. I drive to Maria's address at 23 Thirteenth Avenue. At 6:45 p.m. I pass by the residence and don't notice any activity at the house. The sun has already set and the only light is an outdoor driveway lamp. Then I notice a parked car, a white late model Toyota Camry. After a quick glance at the license plate, I determine it to be Wolf's car. The car is empty. After I pass by, I circle back and park where I have a view of both the residence and Wolf's car.

I sit in my car and wait 25 minutes before Wolf comes back to the Camry. Wolf returns to her car carrying a large shoulder bag. In the dim light I can't see her face, but I notice she is now wearing a black top and glasses. I follow Wolf out of the neighborhood, back to Via 104, and I follow her to the Grano de Oro Hotel.

We arrive around 7:25 p.m. Wolf parks on the street near the entrance to the lobby and I do the same. She has her shoulder bag with her as she exits the car. I exit my car and follow her into the lobby. She stops at the front desk, removes a small carton from her bag, and hands it to the desk clerk. They exchange a few words and then she proceeds down a hallway, toward the bar and dining area, presumably to use the ladies' room. Judi had mentioned that Wolf was planning to meet a friend there. I reason that Wolf could have altered her appearance and was now heading to the ladies' room to change back before meeting her friend.

If she's meeting a friend or staying for dinner, I expect her to return to the lobby. But, the light in the lobby area is revealing, and after no more than 15 seconds, I sense that the woman that went down the hallway does not look like the Donna Wolf that I remember seeing at the cafe in Heredia. Of course, the black top and glasses are different, but other details like her hair and her gait seem different as well. I also wonder why she would park on the street if she were planning to stay for dinner. I become suspicious.

I slowly make my way down the hallway. When, I come to the end of the hallway, a new hallway goes off to the left. I see no ladies' room, and I don't see Wolf, but I do notice a side door far down the hallway that leads back outside the building. She must have gone out the side door and walked around to the *front of the hotel where she left her car. I immediately run back through the lobby and out the front door of the hotel. I arrive just in time to see the woman drive off in the same white Camry that I had followed here. Damn, I've been played. The time is now 7:30 p.m.*

I jump back in my car, a bit angry, and not knowing what else to do, I give chase. She had a good jump on me and with the traffic and the darkness I temporarily lose her. However, two blocks later, there's a break in the traffic and I spot her white Camry up the road ahead. I follow the car to a nearby fast-food restaurant on Via 104. The car sits for a few minutes in the rear parking lot before the woman exits the car. I watch her make her way to a nearby dumpster at the rear of the restaurant carrying her shoulder bag. She is in the shadows and has her back to me, but she is now wearing a white top like she wore when she left La Copa Máxima. I watch her drop the shoulder bag into the dumpster. Then she turns as if to come back to the car, but heads for a side door of the restaurant instead. My view is partially obstructed by other cars and people. I wait in my car until she exits the restaurant two minutes later. She is facing me as she passes through a lit area near the door and heads back to the car. My view is unobstructed. I see clearly that she is no longer a woman! She is now Mystery Man!

I now have a choice. Do I follow the Camry, or do I find out what was put into the dumpster? After the Camry drives off, I go to the dumpster where I discover the contents of the shoulder bag and the gun case. The bag contains items of disguise, latex gloves and black ladies' shoes. I look for blood spatter, but it's too dark. I open the gun case and find a small hand gun, an ammo clip, and a silencer. The time is now 7:45 p.m.

Judi said that Donna was planning to have dinner at the Gran de Oro with a friend who worked at the Embassy, so perhaps I would find her there. I'm also curious to know who will pick up the carton left at the lobby desk. As soon as I find a place to turn around, I head back to the Grano de Oro. I drive to the rear of the hotel and park in the guest parking area. As I start to walk to the nearest entrance, I notice a Toyota Camry that looks exactly like the one that Wolf drove—same color, same model. I place my hand on the hood and in front of the grill and determine that the engine is still hot. I peek into the car window and see nothing on the seats. Of course, I don't know what might be in the trunk. Then, I check the license plate and it's identical to the one I had followed.

How can this be? I ask myself. *How could the car that Mystery Man is driving have the same plate number as the one that Wolf is driving? Did I misread the plate on Mystery Man's car?* Perhaps I mistook a 6 for a 9 or reversed the order of the numbers in my head, but I didn't think my eyes or my dyslexia were that bad. I thought it more likely that the plates on Mystery Man's car were altered or forged. Wolf's plate number became public when she rented the car Wednesday night. The number 3581767 could easily have been altered to be 8537161. Black ink and white-out would probably do the job. If the DIS were behind this, I think they could even have manufactured new plates for Mystery Man in the two days they had before tonight.

I go inside the hotel and I see Wolf. She's wearing the same outfit she wore when she left La Copa Máxima. She is seated at the bar next to a man who I identify as a U.S. embassy courier. Another man, who I identify as Ed Perez, a U.S. government employee, appears and walks away with the courier. Perez heads up the main staircase while I follow the courier to the front desk. I watch him take possession of the carton, and I follow him up the staircase to room 299. I keep my distance so as not to be seen. Perez is waiting at the door and they both enter the room. Then at about 8:15, Perez rejoins Wolf at the bar and the hostess seats the two of them in the dining area. Later, I verify that Donna Wolf is back at her hotel, the InterContinental, before 11:00 p.m.

****

███████████

Text Message April 6, 2003

JGM:

Langley wants you to report to your Socialist client the portions of your report that are not *redacted (see attached).*

We want you to convince your client that CIA officer Donna Wolf was Inga's assassin, and that they will need your help to retaliate. Our objective is to identify Inga's puppet masters and expose their plans to retaliate—whether it be espionage or attempted murder—against Wolf and the CIA on U.S. soil. If on U.S. soil they will be subject to arrest and/or death. Please consider the following to be your official report.
BM

███████████

REPORTED OBSERVATIONS ON
FRIDAY APRIL 4 2003

I am tracking Donna Wolf, aka Donna Rice, a known employee of the American CIA. I follow her from the InterContinental Hotel in Escazu to La Copa Máxima, a coffee shop and eatery in the city of Heredia. She is driving a rented late model white Toyota Camry, plate number 8537161. Wolf is wearing casual business attire consisting of a white blouse, a silky neck scarf, black slacks with a black belt, and black slip-on shoes. She has dangling earrings, shoulder length brown hair and is not wearing glasses.

We arrive at La Copa Máxima at 5:15 p.m. Wolf enters the establishment. I follow her in. I go to the counter and order a coffee. While standing there I see Wolf walk over to a table in the back corner. ███████████
███████████ *She says hello to the* ███ *man and there is an exchange of words. I recognize him as a Deputy*

Director of the DIS, Jafeth Balladares. He reports directly to DIS Director Geraldo Alverez. Wolf seats herself at a table on the other side of the room. I return to my car.

A half-hour later, Wolf exits the rear door of the café and comes around the building to her car. She has a small cardboard carton in her right hand. She sits in her car a few minutes before leaving. I'm too far away to see what she is doing. Perhaps she is primping, I think. While I'm waiting, I see Balladares leave the café and go to the back of the building and out of sight. At 6:10 p.m. I follow Wolf out of the parking lot onto Route 3.

I follow Wolf to the Rohrmoser area of San José. Wolf makes a left turn from Via 104 and enters the neighborhood, but a black Ford sedan with tinted windows cuts in front of me and prevents me from following closely. I miss the light and must wait a few more minutes before I can continue. As I finally enter the neighborhood, Wolf is no longer in sight. However, I know the neighborhood and I know where Maria Martin lives, having once been to her house when I worked with her. I assume that may be where Wolf is headed. I drive to Maria's address at 23 Thirteenth Avenue. At 6:45 p.m. I pass by the residence and don't notice any activity at the house. The sun has already set and the only light is an outdoor driveway lamp. Then I notice a parked car, a white late model Toyota Camry. After a quick glance at the license plate, I determine it to be Wolf's car. The car is empty. After I pass by, I circle back and park where I have a view of both the residence and Wolf's car.

I sit in my car and wait 25 minutes before Wolf comes back to the Camry. Wolf returns to her car carrying a large shoulder bag. In the dim light I can't see her face, but I notice she is now wearing a black top and glasses. I follow Wolf out of the neighborhood, back to Via 104, and I follow her to the Grano de Oro Hotel.

We arrive around 7:25 p.m. Wolf parks on the street near the entrance to the lobby and I do the same. She has her shoulder bag with her as she exits the car. I exit my car and follow her into the lobby. She stops at the front desk, removes a small carton from her bag, and hands it to the desk clerk. They exchange a few words, and then she proceeds down a hallway, presumably to use the ladies' room. Judi had mentioned that Wolf was planning to have dinner there with a friend. I reason that Wolf could have altered her appearance and was now heading to the ladies' room to change back before meeting her friend.

I slowly make my way down the hallway. When, I come to the end of the hallway, a new hallway goes off to the left. I see no ladies' room, and I don't see Wolf, but I do notice a side door far down the hallway that leads back outside the building. She must have gone out the side door and walked around to the front of the hotel where she left her car. I immediately run back through the lobby and out the front door of the hotel. I arrive

just in time to see the woman drive off in the same white Camry that I had followed here. Damn, I've been played. The time is now 7:30 p.m.

I jump back in my car, a bit angry, and not knowing what else to do, I give chase. She had a good jump on me and with the traffic and the darkness I temporarily lose her. However, two blocks later, there's a break in the traffic and I spot her white Camry up the road ahead. I follow the car to a nearby fast-food restaurant on Via 104. The car sits for a few minutes in the rear parking lot before the woman exits the car. I watch her make her way to a nearby dumpster at the rear of the restaurant carrying her shoulder bag. She is in the shadows and has her back to me, but she is now wearing a white top like she wore when she left La Copa Máxima. I watch her drop the shoulder bag into the dumpster. ▇▇

I now have a choice. Do I follow the Camry, or do I find out what was put into the dumpster? After the Camry drives off, I go to the dumpster where I discover the contents of the shoulder bag and the case. The bag contains items of disguise, latex gloves and black ladies' shoes. I look for blood spatter, but it's too dark. I open the case and find a small hand gun, an ammo clip, and a silencer. The time is now 7:45 p.m.

Judi said that Donna was planning to have dinner at the Gran de Oro with a friend who worked at the Embassy, so perhaps I would find her there. I am also curious to know who will pick up the carton left at the lobby desk. As soon as I find a place to turn around, I head back to the Grano de Oro. I drive to the rear of the hotel and park in the guest parking area. As I start to walk to the nearest entrance, I notice a Toyota Camry that looks exactly like the one that Wolf drove — same color, same model. I place my hand on the hood and in front of the grill and determine that the engine is still hot. I peek into the car window and see nothing on the seats. Of course, I don't know what might be in the trunk. Then, I check the license plate and it's identical to the one I had followed.

I go inside the hotel and I see Wolf. She's wearing the same outfit she wore when she left La Copa Máxima. She is seated at the bar next to a man that I identify as a U.S. embassy courier. Another man, whom I identify as Ed Perez, a U.S. government employee, appears and walks away with the courier. Perez heads up the main staircase while I follow the courier to the front desk. I watch him take possession of the carton, and I follow him up the staircase to room 299. I keep my distance so as not to be seen Perez is waiting at the door, and they both enter the room. Then at about 8:15, Perez rejoins Wolf at the bar and the hostess seats the two of them in the dining area. Later, I verify that Donna Wolf is back at her hotel, the InterContinental, before 11:00 p.m.

"Wow!" Peter exclaimed. "It's amazing how the meaning of something can be totally different after it's redacted. This whole thing was a counterintelligence operation devised by Matheson. I wonder if he even had approval from higher up. It makes clear that Joe was not here to kill you or your mom. And if you believe Joe's unredacted report, it also exonerates your Mom. Looks like she was set up—she's no killer."

"I wish I could be sure. The DIS and the CIA could have been in it together. One of them pulled the trigger and the other disposed of the evidence."

Could she have a point? he asked himself. *What if these reports were fabricated to cover up what really happened? Not likely.*

"Don't be so cynical," he quickly responded. "She's your mother!"

"Peter, I've had it with all this secrecy and subterfuge," she said angrily. "I'd like to leak this report to the media, or maybe to the OIJ in Costa Rica?"

"I think you know what would happen if we did. As you suggested, this report implicates the DIS and the CIA in illegal activity, including murder. The source of this information would be known. Both you and Joe would be targeted and would likely end up dead . . . and look at the security classifications on this document. They were redacted, but my guess is that the classifications on these memos are far above what we should be looking at. You never saw this . . .. Ed could be in trouble for sending it to us—could lose his job and go to jail."

"I think he and Mom were very close." She started to cry again. "I'm sorry. They took advantage of Mom and me. Mom was anxious about being targeted and about my welfare, and I was dumb enough to fall in love with a hardened covert operative. I just can't seem to get over it."

"Did you really fall in love? In his letter, Ed said he met with Joe and that Joe wished he could see you one last time to make amends. Would you be willing to do that?"

She paused . . . "I'm not sure. I'm so angry at him right now. Yet another side of me says maybe It would bring closure."

"Brandy, it's all going to be okay," he said. As he put his arm around her to comfort her, they became aware of Carol having come down the stairs to go to the food storage area in the other room. She probably overheard much of what was being said.

"Listen, we had best wrap it up." He unplugged the thumb drive, put it back in the envelope with letter, and handed it to her. "Keep this in a secure place."

They walked up the stairs to the front door. "You're going to be okay," he said as he pecked her on the cheek and held the door for her.

Carol had followed them up the stairs and watched them say goodbye.

"Did Brandy get all of her questions answered?" She asked.

"Some, but not all. She's upset."

"About what? Not with you, I hope."

"Not with me. I can't tell you much. Our meeting took place in a SCIF and the discussion was highly classified. However, I will tell you this. She's upset that she hasn't heard from her boyfriend since her mom got sick, and she's upset with Matheson for not telling her everything about the circumstances of her mom's death."

"I see, and I assume you're the one who consoled her," Carol said somewhat sarcastically. If I didn't know you better, I would think the two of you were having an affair," she mocked.

"Sounds like you're jealous. We had our appointment for a paternity test and we're hoping that the results will be back soon, but there's no question in my mind that she's my daughter. In any case, you know I love you," he said and gave her a hug.

"Carol, I just thought of something I need to do," he added and headed back downstairs to his office."

It was only four forty-five. Although it was Friday, Matheson would not normally leave his office before five. As soon as Peter got to his desk, he dialed Matheson's number.

36

GENETIC PROOF

O n Tuesday the following week, Brandy received the results of the DNA paternity test. She was excited. She immediately called Peter. Carol answered the phone.

"Carol this is Brandy. Good news. The paternity test results are back. It's definite! I'm Peter's daughter! Is he there?"

"No, he's not, but that *is* good news."

"Well, I would like to bring you the paperwork. I know you have been a little uneasy about our relationship. I hope this will help."

"Well yes. Peter and I were a bit wary at first, thinking that you may be conning him in some way. As Peter probably told you, I had a bad experience in my first marriage. My husband lied to me and covered up an affair, and I was totally unaware until the end. And I know I should not have felt suspicious of the two of you, but I did."

"Carol, I fully understand your feelings because the same thing happened to me in my marriage, and recently I was upset because my boyfriend turned out to be someone other than who I thought."

"You're welcome to come over whenever it's convenient."

"Thursday evening okay?"

"Would you like to join us for supper?"

"Yes. I'd love that. What time?"

"Six thirty okay?"

"Yes, I'll come directly from work."

****

Brandy's jubilation changed dramatically Thursday morning when she received the following message from Matheson:

> *Joe wishes to see you. He has suggested the boutique hotel near*
> *Dupont Circle. I can arrange it. Please respond yes or no by 2*
> *p.m. Friday. Details will follow.*

Brandy became emotional as she read this. She remembered that weekend. It was just before Christmas. The air was crisp and cold that day. She and Joe had toured the city and many of its sights like the monuments, museums, embassies, etc. They had used the Metro system whenever possible but had also done a lot of walking. By the end of the day they were cold, and they were hungry. They came across a small hotel with a restaurant not far from the Dupont Circle Metro stop. They were seated at a small table, ordered food, and continued to enjoy each other's company. While waiting for the meal to be served, Joe excused himself—men's room? When he returned, he said the hotel had a cancelation and persuaded her to stay in the city overnight. It hadn't taken much persuasion. At this point she was head over heels for him, and the opportunities to spend the night together were limited as they were not ready to publicize to Mom or Brian that they were sleeping with each other every chance they had. Later, Joe admitted to planning this overnight ahead of time. She didn't mind. It turned out to be a very romantic evening.

Now she had a decision to make. Was the message for real or could it be a trap set by the Russians trying to find out where Joe was? Could she trust Matheson? She wondered if she should let Peter know about this development. *In any case*, she told herself, *it won't be a conjugal visit. I need closure, not sex.*

****

Thursday evening, she arrived at Peter's house with a bottle of wine. Peter greeted her at the door and took possession of the wine.

"Come in. Dinner is almost ready. How are you feeling?"

"I'm feeling great," she said and gave him what he interpreted as a forced smile.

"Carol said you seemed very happy about the results of the DNA test when you called on Tuesday. I sense that something else is going on. Did something happen between Tuesday and now?"

Once again, she smiled. "Yes, but I'm dealing with it."

Peter gave her a curious look. "You heard from Joe, didn't you?"

She wondered how he knew, but nodded in the affirmative and put her finger across her lips.

"I received this message this morning," she said and handed him a copy. "I'm not sure what to do. It could be a trap."

Peter took a quick look at it and handed it back.

"I'm *glad* you heard from him. It's not a trap. I think you should go. You both need closure."

"You seem very sure of this," she said almost taken aback by the quickness of his response and the certainty in his voice.

"I am, but you don't need to decide tonight. Tonight, we celebrate."

Peter put his hand on her shoulder and escorted her into the kitchen where Carol welcomed her.

"Brandy brought us a bottle of wine," Peter said and showed her the bottle.

"Oh, thank you . . . very nice of you."

"Can we open it?" Peter asked, looking at Brandy.

"Absolutely," Brandy said, "If it's okay with Carol. Will this go with supper?"

"Pinot noir goes fine with pork tenderloin," Carol replied. "Peter can get the wine glasses. Dinner's just about ready."

After they were seated and the food served, Peter poured the wine and offered a toast. "To new beginnings," he said and raised his glass.

Dinner conversation was cheerful and friendly between the three of them, but at some point, the conversation turned to Brandy's mother Donna. Carol asked Brandy how she was doing after dealing with so much.

"Well, looking back on it, I wonder how I got through it," she replied. "First Mom got sick, then my boyfriend disappeared, then Mom died unexpectedly, and then I find out I have a new father—all within a two-month period. However, I'm coming to grips with it now. I want to thank Peter for helping me—perhaps even more than he's let on. Everything Mom wrote about him is true." She raised her glass. "Here's to Peter and to Mom."

"And here's to you Carol for your patience and understanding," Peter added.

"Yes, to Carol," Brandy repeated.

They clinked glasses and then they each took a swallow of the Pinot Noir.

"You know, Mom had a very interesting life. Doing what she did for the CIA while raising me must have been very challenging for her. I only began to fully understand her in recent years when she got sick the first time. I began to understand her and we became close. I was thinking that her story would make for a very interesting biography, a way to celebrate her life from the eyes of others."

"How much wine have you had?" Peter asked.

She giggled. "No really, what better way to honor someone than to write their life story?"

"Okay, have you ever written a book?" Peter asked.

"Nope. That's why I want you to help me write it," she said looking at Peter.

Peter played along. "You mean like co-authors?"

"Yeah. It could be her story seen through the eyes of those who were close to her. Besides us, we could talk with my stepbrother, my son Brian, and maybe even Matheson could add something not classified . . ."

"And what would the title of this book be?"

"I don't know. How about '*Mom's Final Project*' . . . what do you think?"

Carol who had remained silently amused by all this, now decided to say something. "I think you've both had too much wine."

37

FORGIVENESS

After much deliberation, Brandy replied "yes" to Matheson's offer to arrange a meeting with Joe, and received further instructions.

Come to the hotel on Sunday. Take the Metro. Arrive at 2:00 p.m. Ask the front desk for a message in your name.

On Sunday, she drove to the Greenbelt Metro station and took the Metro to Dupont Circle. She walked from the station and arrived at the boutique hotel at 1:50 p.m., ten minutes early. As instructed, she went to the lobby desk and asked if there was a message for Brandy Evans. The lady behind the desk looked down and pulled out an envelope and handed it to her. Brandy opened it. The message was short.

Come to Room 354 and knock four times.

Strange, she thought, but she took the elevator up to the third floor, found room 354 and knocked four times as instructed.

The door opened a crack and a husky woman's voice said, "Come in. Joe is expecting you."

Brandy could feel her heart beat faster as she cautiously stepped into the room. A man that had been sitting on the other side of the room got up and approached her. Was that Joe? The man had a full beard and long dark hair tied in a ponytail. He wore jeans, tennis shoes, and a short-sleeved golf shirt. A pair of dark glasses dangled on a strap from his neck.

"Hello Brandy. Thank you for coming," he said as he stood in front of her.

Her jaw dropped as she stared at him. Even his eyes were a different color.

"Joe, is that you?"

Meanwhile, Brandy was startled by the sound of the door slamming behind her. She turned quickly to see a stocky woman next to her. To Brandy, the woman looked like a German female prison guard in an old war movie.

"Who are *you*?" Brandy asked excitedly.

"Brandy, meet Greta. Greta, meet Brandy," Joe said as Greta was in the process of displaying her ID. "Greta is with the U.S. Marshals Service."

"Turn around and put your hands up against the door," Greta ordered.

"What? No!" Brandy protested

"Greta, stop!" Joe shouted. "There's no need for that."

"Whatever you say sir. It's your life. You two behave yourselves. When you're done, bang on the door. I'll be right outside in the hallway." Greta left.

"Sorry for that. She was just assigned to me for the day. She can be over the top. Please sit."

Now almost speechless, she took a seat on the chair, while Joe sat on the edge of the bed.

"Brandy," he began. "Please forgive me. I know I have hurt you, but I really care about you and needed to see you. Please allow me to explain the situation." He sounded sincere.

"I've been in hiding. It's the CIA's version of witness protection. By now you probably know that I was working as an agent of the CIA. I want you to know I haven't been charged with a crime. I'm being held as a material witness to crimes committed by Russian agents. Until now, I've not been allowed any communications to the outside world. On Friday evening, Matheson told me you had met with him and he gave me a stern lecture about becoming involved with you. He said you told him that you felt like I raped you. That was not—"

"No," Brandy replied. "I was angry and I said I felt like you took advantage of me. You lied to me about who you were."

"Okay, you were right to feel that way, but it was not my intent to take advantage of you. I never wanted to hurt you. I was under deep cover. If I told you who I really was, it would have put you and others at risk. My feelings for you are real. I'm in my late thirties and my work doesn't allow me to live a normal life. This was the first time in my life that I felt like a normal person who could have a normal relationship with a woman. You made me feel that way, but I was wrong to think that was possible. I care deeply for you, but I realize now that I misled you and hurt you. For several weeks, I have been telling Matheson that I wanted to talk with you and ask for your forgiveness. He advised me against it, but said that after he met with you, and after he talked with Ed Perez and with Peter Troutman, your father, he decided he would not stop me. He said that both Ed Perez and your father had been very persuasive. By the way, when did your mom tell you that Peter Troutman was your father?"

"After she died, in a letter she had left for me."

"But you're glad to know, right?"

"Yes, he's been a big help to me."

"I also told Matheson that when this trial is over, I want out. Don't know if that's possible though. I don't know where I'll be, what my job will be, or what my name will be three months from now. I don't know if the Russians will figure out that I betrayed them and track me down—in fact they probably already have. There was an attempt on my life a month ago but it may have been the Costa Rican DIS. Anyway, after the courts are done with me, I may go into WITSEC for the rest of my life."

"That's the Federal witness protection program isn't it?"

"Yes, it is, and that means you can't know where I am. I needed to see you now while it was still possible."

Brandy was stone silent.

"I'm sorry. Please forgive me."

Brandy stared at him and remained silent.

"Maybe this was not a good idea. You should go now," he said as he rose from the edge of the bed and motioned toward the door.

"Wait!" she said. "I need to know something."

"What?"

"Did my mother know who you really were?"

Joe sat back down.

"No, not until after she was in the hospital. Apparently, Matheson never told her what my role was. I didn't know this when I started my assignment, but it became obvious to me after a while. Do you remember we visited her in the hospital just before I fled? And do you remember she asked to speak to me alone for a few minutes? She accused me of killing her. I told her who I was and what my role was. I was not authorized to do that, but I thought she should know. I don't know if she believed me at that moment, but Ed Perez also told her about me when he saw her a few days later."

He paused, but Brandy remained silent.

"Matheson had kept Perez in the dark also. Perez did not know the whole truth either until sometime in January. Your mother became suspicious of me—thought I was a Russian spy and suspected I was trying to compromise you in some way. Apparently, your mother expressed her concerns to Perez about me, so he met with me to find out more. You recall I had gone back to Costa Rica for a few days in January. I didn't realize until he spoke to me that neither he nor your mother knew what was going on. Officially, I couldn't tell him, but he appealed to my conscience and convinced me that he cared about you and your mom. He had the ability to expose my cover, but I didn't think he would have done it, I already knew who he was and I felt I could trust him. So, I gave him a document that spelled out the total plan that Langley had contrived."

Again, Brandy said nothing so he continued.

"According to Perez, your mother also went to Matheson and expressed her concerns about me. When she started to feel ill, she thought perhaps I was there to poison her. She told Matheson what she thought she knew. She threatened to act if he didn't. Matheson never told her the whole truth though. Perhaps he was trying to maintain my cover in case the Russians showed up at the hospital—don't know. Matheson promised her I would be arrested and you would be safe. Apparently, he later lied to her and told her they had arrested me at the airport before I could flee. In fact, I was arrested in Costa Rica three weeks later. I felt badly that I couldn't be there for you at your mom's funeral, but I was in custody. So, no, I don't think she knew the whole truth until after Ed talked to her in the hospital."

Brandy finally responded. She rose and went over to him.

"Joe, thank you for helping me to understand. I fell in love with you and you hurt me. I don't know if I'll be able to forgive you. If in the future your situation changes, perhaps we could start over—I don't know."

"Brandy, I'm so sorry."

They both had tears in their eyes as she walked out the door.

38

SAFE HOUSE

After the meeting with Brandy, Greta took Joe back to his safe house. He had been kept there since they brought him back from Costa Rica near the end of May. The safe house was a large brick two-story home with an attached garage and it was in an upscale neighborhood. It stood on a half-acre of land. From the outside no one would know that a prisoner was kept there—and yes, although he had not been charged with a crime, he was a prisoner. Each morning that he needed to be taken somewhere, he would enter the garage and get into the car. The garage door would remain shut until he was inside the car. A push of a button on a key-fob would open the garage door and they would be off to court, the FBI, the lawyers, CIA, or wherever that day's agenda dictated. No one would see who he was as he came and went.

Joe was also impressed with the state-of-the-art security system. Cameras monitored activity on the grounds outside, while sensors monitored all the doors and windows on the inside. If anything occurred, notifications were sent off-site to the U.S. Marshals and alarms went off inside.

On the inside, it was heaven—especially if you compared it to the alternative, a prison cell. Joe had everything a prisoner could want and a lot more. He slept in one of the three bedrooms upstairs, while his guard slept in the bedroom on the main level. In case there was a house invasion, there were two safe rooms, one on the second level and one on the basement level. These rooms were bombproof and impenetrable. Each room could also serve as a SCIF. They were soundproof and impervious to electromagnetic waves.

Right now, Joe was on the main level watching the news on TV with his guard, Bill. Bill had been his guard since they moved in a month ago. Joe was beginning to view Bill as a friend. They often engaged in friendly chit chat. Who else could he talk to? However, Bill was a professional. Joe knew he could rely upon him in case of an emergency. Bill had told him how once he saved a whole family from a planned hit by the Mafia. Bill was ex-special forces, was in perfect physical condition, had an IQ above 140, packed a 9 mm semi-automatic, and kept a fully automatic military assault rifle in the hall closet just in case. He was the best!

Not much on the news—same old, same old. Then, Bill asked how his day went.

"Did you close things out with your girlfriend? You still seem down."

"It went as well as I could expect, but I still can't get over her."

"Want to talk about it?" I'm a good listener," Bill offered.

As much as he emotionally wanted to, Joe had been advised not to talk about his assignment or about those involved.

"No. Thanks, but I'll be okay," he replied.

Shortly after that, Joe decided to retire and went upstairs to his room. He couldn't sleep and began to think about the conversation he had with Brandy that afternoon. He wished he could have told her everything he had endured over the past two months. Perhaps she could better understand and she could forgive him. As he lay there on his bed, he also began to recollect his experience after he left the BWI airport in February.

Joe had planned to go to Toronto, cool off, and decide what to do next, but he made a last-minute change and flew to Quebec instead.

Then, after three days he decided to fly to Costa Rica. Perhaps he could resume his normal life. Not being able to sleep, Joe thought about the two and one-half months he had endured in Costa Rica before ending up at the safe house.

39

TESTIMONY IN COSTA RICA

Joe closed his eyes and recalled his escape from BWI. The original plan was to return to Costa Rica after he completed his work in the USA. Never, was the plan to fall in love with Brandy, or to be responsible for the death of her mother. This weighed heavily on his mind. However, after he arrived in Costa Rica, things got even worse. The OIJ was investigating the Socialist and Russian influence on government officials, and his name had surfaced as a supporter of those activities. He was only there three weeks before the OIJ wanted to bring him in for questioning.

He recalled how he was afraid of what would happen to him if he allowed the OIJ to question him, and what would happen if they arrested him. The Russians would know he betrayed them, and certain elements in Costa Rica would not want his knowledge of corruption in the government to be made known. Joe remembered how he feared that testifying in Costa Rica could easily result in his death. The United States had procedures in place to protect witnesses like Joe—Costa Rica not so much.

He had gone to Ed Perez at the U.S. Embassy for advice. After all, he was really working for the CIA and he was not sure what he could say or could not say regarding his undercover assignment. It was from Ed that he learned that yet another shoe was about to drop.

The FBI had hoped to turn Chaban and have him testify against Markov. However, this was not about to happen. Joe learned that the case against Chaban and Markov for conspiracy to commit murder would be weak without his testimony. The CIA and the FBI wanted him back in the States. He was a material witness and possibly a co-conspirator. At the advice of Perez, he surrendered to the FBI within the next week. While he waited to be transferred back to the United States, he was kept in a room in the basement of the U.S. Embassy. This was for his own protection they told him. Ed advised him to seek witness protection and apply for admittance into WITSEC. Ed provided him with legal counsel and helped him through the process.

Joe's legal counsel explained everything about WITSEC and gave him the following summary about the program:

The federal Witness Security Program WITSEC was originally created as the Federal Witness Protection Program in the mid-1960s by Gerald Shur, when he was Attorney in Charge of the Intelligence and Special Services Unit of the Organized Crime and Racketeering Section of the United States Department of Justice, (DOJ). The program was formally established under Title V of the Organized Crime Control Act of 1970, which in turn sets out the manner in which the United States Attorney General may provide for the relocation and protection of a witness or potential witness of the federal or state government in an official proceeding concerning organized crime or other serious offenses.

The program was improved in 1984. The Witness Security Reform Act of 1984 extended the authority of the Attorney General to provide protection and security by means of relocation for persons who are witnesses in official proceedings brought against persons involved in organized criminal activity or other serious offenses where it is determined that an offense involving a crime of violence directed at a witness is likely to occur.

Originally the program was intended to encourage testimony in the prosecution of organized crime, like the Mafia. After the attacks on the World Trade Center and the Pentagon on 9-11-2001, the program was increasingly applied to witnesses involved in any serious federal felony for which a witness may be subject to retaliation by violence or threats of violence.

WITSEC is administered and operated by the United States Marshals Service, (USMS). The USMS is an organization within the DOJ that has been around since the days of George Washington. The USMS is responsible for protecting witnesses that are in the program and not incarcerated in a federal prison.

Applications to the WITSEC program go to the Office of Enforcement Operations (OEO), a department within the DOJ, that is responsible for authorizing or denying admittance into WITSEC.

Joe found that the WITSEC application process was quite rigorous. There were interviews, forms, and paperwork, as well as psychological tests. The application process even considered what he might say to a grand jury. He had to prove that he was in danger and needed protection. Finally, after two weeks, Joe was admitted to the program.

Meanwhile, the OIJ pressured the DOJ to release Joe to them. A negotiation ensued and finally, after another two weeks, and with the help of Ed, an agreement was reached. Joe would testify to everything for both the Costa Rican OIJ and the U.S. DOJ. In exchange he would receive full immunity from prosecution by both, but he would be given protection by the USMS. It was also understood that he would not answer any questions from the OIJ that would implicate the CIA or Donna Wolf. The deal had been made by early April.

Joe remembered the room he stayed in at the embassy—nothing like the quarters he had now in the safe house. It was his home for about two months. The room was down a set of stairs and at the end of a hallway lined with concrete walls. The room was sparse with a bed, a small closet to hang clothes, a chest of drawers, a table and chair, and a private bathroom with shower. There was adequate lighting but no windows.

The procedure had been the same each day. he would be up at 6:00 a.m., shower, dress in business attire, have breakfast delivered to him in his room, and then be escorted to a black van waiting in the drive way. The van belonged to the OIJ, but one body guard from the USMS would also be in the van. The van would make its way to the OIJ complex on the other side of San José. He would be escorted to a secure conference room in a building adjourning the courthouse where he would wait until the first of a stream of Counselors came to question him. All the interrogations were recorded, often with video. His testimony would later be used in court. He cooperated. It was in his best interest to do so.

Lunch had been brought to him around noon each day. Lunch typically consisted of a burrito and a fruit drink in a carton with a straw. It wasn't much, but he didn't complain. However, on the sixth or seventh day, he had just opened his burrito and was about to take his first bite, when the guard burst into the room.

"Stop! Don't eat that," the guard had said excitedly.

"Why? What's going on?"

"We just found the regular food delivery boy. He's dead! Your food could be poisoned."

"Well thanks," he had responded. "Don't think I'm hungry now. Take it away."

Sure enough, the next day his lawyer told him that his burrito had been laced with cyanide. "You're lucky," his lawyer had said.

I'll be lucky if I ever get out of here, Joe had thought.

That night, like most nights, Ed Perez had come to visit him in his room at the embassy. The two of them had worked together as business colleagues—as spies, but now they were getting to know each other on a personal basis. They were almost friends. Ed had just sat down when a guard brought Joe his dinner. The embassy had no cook and any meals were prepackaged like those you would have on an airplane. Ed had watched him remove the tinfoil cover from the tray and the utensils from the napkin, and he had watched him pick up his fork with his left hand, scoop up several peas, and lift them to his mouth. After he set his fork back down, he turned his head and looked hard at Ed.

"Ed, I need to know something."

"What's that?"

"I need to know if I'm responsible for Donna's death."

"No. She died of cancer but your poison did not cause it. If it had, you would not be sitting here and I would not be helping you."

"Why are you helping me? Did the CIA instruct you to be sure I didn't say anything that would damage their reputation?"

"No that's not it."

"What then?"

"I was very close to Brandy's mom, Donna. Neither she nor I had been read in to your role. In December Donna had become suspicious of you and she sent me a picture of you. She wanted me to determine who you really were. I went to Matheson. It took a while, but he finally agreed to read me in. Donna wanted Brandy to be safe and happy, and before she died, I told her what I knew and assured her that I would help. But Matheson didn't tell me everything and Brandy needs to know more. She thinks her mother could have assassinated Inga Sarnoff, and that you may have assassinated her mother. She has enlisted the help of her biological father to help. She needs to know the truth, but I'm not sure she will get it from Matheson."

Joe listened attentively as he continued. "And . . . I also understand your situation. You and I have some things in common. I see myself in you when I was about your age."

"Yea, how so?"

"Both of us are well educated and highly intelligent; We both lost our birth mothers at a young age; We're in similar lines of work; We're both caught up in the quagmire of government bureaucracy; We're both Catholic; and, we both have ethical and moral conflicts between our work requirements and our personal relationships. I had a wife once, but couldn't handle it. You sacrificed a lot and deserve another chance."

"And how did you resolve those conflicts Ed?"

"I changed my expectations. Between moral and immoral, black and white, there are infinite positions you can be in. You will need to decide for yourself where in the gray area you are most comfortable."

"We're not normal people, are we?"

"No, we're not. Look, I understand your frustration with Brandy. We have kept in touch. Anyway, she's trying to understand what happened and why her mom died and what you had to do with it. She has asked me for help. She also told me she has a meeting set up with Matheson. Perhaps there is some way that the two of you can meet to clear the air. You both need closure. Can't promise anything, but I'll see what I can do. You do want to see her again, don't you?"

"Yes, I do and I appreciate your help." He then wrote something down on a sheet of paper and handed it to Ed.

"What's this?"

"It's the decryption code for a document that will help you and Brandy with the truth about her mother. I will ask my lawyer to retrieve it from my office and send it electronically to your office here at the embassy."

Then, Ed changed the subject. He asked Joe what he thought would happen to him when he returned to the States.

"As much as I wish I could live in my home country, Costa Rica, I have too many enemies here, and Costa Rica has no witness protection program like the U.S. does. So, I'll be glad to return to the States. I'll testify and put the Russian spies in jail where they belong. After all, that was the whole point of the operation, wasn't it? Beyond that, I don't know."

"Joe, I detect anger in your tone."

"Yes, I'm angry! I gave up my career, I gave up my heritage, and I gave up the only woman I ever loved more than my mother, and then if I'm lucky to still be alive after I testify, I'll get a whole new identification and be relocated to a strange place so that I can start my life all over again, and today someone tried to kill me for my efforts," he said excitedly and slammed his left fist on the table. Then he stood up and began to walk slowly around the room. After he calmed down, he said, "I'm sorry. I'm letting my emotions get the best of me."

"Joe, if you are relocated, where do you think you will be?"

"Don't know. I've heard that if they ask and you tell them where you would like to be, that's the last place they will send you." He was being cynical but it was probably true. "But if I had a choice, I would like to live in Albuquerque, New Mexico."

"Really. Why?"

"I've never been there, but I've read about it—medium sized city surrounded by beautiful country—good job opportunities—large Spanish speaking population—and the weather there is suitable for me as well. I can't stand the cold damp winters in the D.C. area."

"Maybe you'll get your wish. Look, as far as your career is concerned, you can still do what you know. They will create documents and references for you and help you get employment. You're smart. You will do alright. I know you will."

"Thanks for the encouragement, Ed. You're turning out to be a good friend. Maybe after this is over, I can start over and have a normal life."

After four more weeks had elapsed, Joe had told the OIJ everything they wanted to know. He told them how he provided surveillance—often illegally—to catch important government officials in compromising situations. He described situations that included everything from sex to drugs to bribery. He told them how the Russian spy Inga Sarnoff, aka Maria Martin, would then use the information to extract political donations. These donations would then sponsor socialist causes, and help elect socialist candidates into office. The information that Joe provided was very useful to the OIJ, and helped them to clean up the political corruption.

After his testimony in Costa Rica was complete, Joe was flown back to the States. It was in the middle of the night when two armed guards from the USMS escorted him from his room out the delivery entrance and into a black van. He was taken to the *Tobías Bolaños* airport in Pavas, only about one and a half miles away from the embassy. The Pavas airport was not very well known, but in 2004 it was the second busiest airport in Costa Rica. The airport was served by only one public airline that connected several cities in Costa Rica. However, the airport was primarily used to transport executives, freight, government employees, and foreign officials on privately owned aircraft. Four hours after boarding, they landed at Andrews Air Force Base near the District of Columbia and were quickly whisked away in another black van.

Now he was in the safe house and in the process of providing testimony to the DOJ that would be used in court to prosecute Markov and Chaban. Tomorrow would begin his third week here. He finally gave in and fell asleep.

40

TESTIMONY IN THE
UNITED STATES

Joe had been back in the States for two weeks now. Each day he had been brought from the safe house to an interrogation room at the FBI headquarters. Joe willingly cooperated. The CIA had provided a lawyer, the USMS had provided him with temporary witness protection, and he had been given full immunity.

Joe was pleased that he was given full immunity. In the U.S. he could have been charged with a range of criminal offenses, including breaking and entering, theft of classified information, and conspiracy to commit murder. These were also the offenses that Aleksei Chaban and Ivan Markov were charged with. The medical examiner's reports had not been made public and The DOJ also intended to charge Markov and Chaban with murder. It would provide leverage to get them to plead guilty to a lesser crime. If it went to court, they needed Joe to testify against them.

Starting today however, the preparation for Joe's testimony would take place in his safe house. He had asked Bill about the change in venue, and was told that the Marshals had uncovered a plot to intercept his transport, and they were concerned about his security.

Counselors would come to the safe house and record the details about how he worked undercover to reveal the Russian plan for the theft of classified information and the murder of Donna Wolf. Each day, an FBI agent and two counselors were brought to the safe house and went to the SCIF in the basement. Joe was brought in while Bill guarded the door. The FBI agent and their counselor sat on one side of a conference table; Joe and his assigned lawyer faced them on the other side. A transcript of some of Joe's testimony follows:

> *Counselor: "We want to know how you became involved in a Russian plot to steal classified information and assassinate CIA Officer Donna Wolf. Please tell us everything you know from the beginning."*

> *Joe: "My allegiance has always been with both the United States and Costa Rica. I did a great deal of covert intelligence work for the Costa Rican DIS and in 2002 supported a joint effort between the DIS and the CIA to ferret out corruption and illegal communist influence in Costa Rica. This led to the discovery of who Maria Martin was. Her Russian name was Inga Sarnoff, and she was wanted by the CIA for past crimes. She was also wanted by the OIJ for helping to rig the 2002 Costa Rican elections. Unfortunately, the OIJ was not able to make a strong enough case with the courts to get a warrant for her arrest. Officials who would support the OIJ in this endeavor would often turn up dead and evidence would disappear. Meanwhile the CIA wanted her to be extradited for trial in the United States. That approach was also blocked by corrupt Costa Rican officials. The only choice left was to have her assassinated."*

> *Counselor: "When was Sarnoff assassinated?"*

> *Joe: "April the fourth, 2003."*

> *Counselor: "Were you the assassin?"*

Joe: "No."

Counselor: "Do you know who the assassin was?"

Joe: "Yes."

Counselor: "Who was it?"

Joe: "It was an agent of the Costa Rican DIS."

Counselor: "Was the CIA involved?"

Joe: "I don't know if the CIA was party to her assassination."

Counselor: "Please tell us what role you and the CIA played after her death."

Joe: "I was instructed by the CIA to make the Russians think that she was killed by the CIA, specifically by CIA Officer Donna Wolf."

Counselor: "Who instructed you?"

Joe: "Brian Matheson,"

Counselor: "How did you get the Russians to think that the CIA was responsible for killing Sarnoff?"

Joe: "I met with the head of Russian intelligence in Costa Rica, Vladimir Petrov, and with Ivan Markov, a Russian intelligence officer from the Sluzhba vneshney razvedki or SVR. I gave them credible evidence based on my surveillance. This plus the news reports were enough to convince them."

Counselor: "Why do you think the CIA wanted you to do that?"

Joe: "I think they were trying to set a trap to catch the big fish they knew as Ivan Markov."

Counselor: "Please explain how you would help with that."

Joe: "The CIA wanted me to help the SVR obtain classified information that Wolf was authorized to receive, and they wanted me to help the SVR assassinate her. It was my understanding that they would be arrested before anything could actually happen."

Counselor: "I see. So, if I understand this, the CIA wanted you to act as a Russian agent."

Joe: "That's correct."

Counselor: "Please take me through the process. Tell me everything you did."

Joe: "Sure. In early September, I met with Ivan Markov and Aleksei Chaban We agreed upon a course of action which I would then execute. The first part of the plan was to clone Wolf's laptop and give them access to classified information on the CIA network. The second part of the plan was to assassinate Wolf using a poison they had that they said would mimic cancer."

Counselor: "Was anyone else at that meeting?"

Joe: "Yes. Markov had a body guard."

Counselor: "Where did this meeting take place?"

Joe: "It took place in Markov's room at the Washington Court Hotel in D.C."

Counselor: *"Was there a recording of what was said at this meeting?"*

Joe: *"Yes. I had a hidden microphone and transmitter."*

Counselor: *"Didn't they pat you down?"*

Joe: *"Yes. They did, but the device was inside my undershorts. They never thought to check there."*

Counselor: *"What happened to the recording?"*

Joe: *"The recorder was in my room at the hotel. The next day after we met it was turned over to the FBI."*

Counselor: *"Then did you execute the plan you were given by the Russians?"*

Joe: *"I did."*

Counselor: *"Please explain what you did."*

Joe: *"The first thing I did was determine where Donna's daughter Brandy lived. My colleague had already gotten Brandy's phone number from Wolf's contact list when she was in Costa Rica. I did a reverse look up and got the address of Wolf's daughter, Brandy. She lived in a four-bedroom house in Ellicott City just off Route 29 and just north of Columbia Maryland. Then, I made a point of accidently meeting Brandy at her fitness club. I established a rapport and we began dating. This afforded me access to Donna Wolf's residence which was a townhouse located about five miles from Fort Meade near I-95 and just north of Route 32. It was about ten miles from Brandy's house. I was also able to make copies of Donna's door key without Brandy's knowledge, and by making visits with Brandy to Donna's townhouse, I was able to learn the key code* to Donna's security system. Meanwhile I rented a townhouse for myself about two-thirds of the way between Brandy's house and Donna's house."

Counselor: "So tell me how you managed to steal classified information."

Joe: "Please understand . . . I didn't steal any classified information. What I did was to provide the means by which Markov and his agents could access classified information using Wolf's access authorizations. She used a laptop computer from home and when on the road. This laptop was authorized by the CIA to access the CIA's Virtual Private Network (VPN) on which resided her email and certain classified documents. All communication links were encrypted and access required multiple passwords. Wolf used a password manager that resided on the laptop. Backup was on a USB thumb drive that she gave Brandy to keep. All I needed to do was to crack the master password and I had all the others. The master password turned out to not be very strong. It was 'TabbyCat1.' I decoded it in less than eight hours with the help of special computer apps. Once I had all the passwords, I basically cloned her laptop, and everything on it, onto another laptop. The cloned laptop I delivered to Markov. The CIA network then viewed him as Wolf every time he accessed the network. Markov was able to access everything that Wolf was authorized to access, or so I thought—"

Counselor: "Or so you thought?"

Joe: "I later learned that the CIA had modified what could be accessed by the Russians, as a security measure. A cookie I buried in the log-in code allowed the CIA network to distinguish which laptop was requesting access. I also modified the network log-on authorization so that it would communicate and store

*the IP address that the laptop was coming from. That allowed
the CIA to know where the user of the laptop was located after
the fact."*

*Counselor: "Please give me the time frame. When did Markov
begin to have access to classified information?"*

Joe: "It was mid-November."

*Counselor: "Okay, but I don't understand. Why did you want
to allow the Russians to have access to classified information?
Isn't that not only risky but also illegal?"*

*Joe: "Well . . . I was just following orders, but my understanding
was that Markov would be misguided by being shown false
information that would cause him to take actions for which he
could be arrested. I had no role in what that information was
or how it was used."*

Counselor: "Do you know who did?"

*Joe: "I would guess that Wolf and her boss may have
orchestrated that."*

*Counselor: "Okay, let's take a fifteen-minute break and then
come back."*

Joe welcomed the break. They took turns in the small restroom,
and then returned to the SCIF where Bill greeted them with fresh
bottles of cold water. Joe took several swallows of water and the
interrogation, as he referred to it, resumed.

*Counselor: "Okay, so I want to talk about your role in the
attempted murder of Donna Wolf. Tell me what the Russians
asked you to do."*

Joe: "*The Russians decided that after they got all the classified information they could, they would assassinate Wolf. This would be revenge for taking the life of Maria Martin . . . uh . . . Inga Sarnoff. However, they wanted it to be low key, to look like a natural death, with no publicity—*"

Counselor: "*Sorry to interrupt, but why low key? Why not send a loud message to the U.S.?*"

Joe: "*Good question. I raised the same question. They told me they wanted to avoid public animosity toward their country. They also said that they would still make the message very clear to the CIA. In addition, they had this new chemical that supposedly caused cancer, so maybe they wanted to try it out.*"

Counselor: "*Okay, please continue.*"

Joe: "*The idea was that this poison, or whatever it was, could be added to a beverage like iced tea. Wolf was a tea drinker and she usually kept a pitcher of tea in her refrigerator. Since I already had a way to get into her townhouse, I was selected to be the one to add the poison to the tea.*"

Counselor: "*When did they select you to do this?*"

Joe: "*Markov ordered Aleksei Chaban to meet with me. This meeting occurred the first week in December at the Italian bar and grill in Glenmont near the Metro station. Chaban gave me a small bottle of this poison with an eye dropper top. He told me to administer five doses over a two-month period. I also recorded the conversation at this meeting. Again, I had a transmitter in my sock and a recorder outside in my car in the parking lot.*"

Counselor: "*Okay, so please tell us what you did to execute your orders from Markov and Chaban.*"

Joe: "I went to Wolf's house when she was at work, and I pretended to add poison to her tea. However, what I actually did instead was to send that first dose to the FBI Lab for analysis."

Counselor: "Excuse me again but when was this?"

Joe: "The first time was early December 2003 on a weekday. Then I did the same thing two weeks later and sent the second dose to the FBI lab as well."

Counselor: "How did you send these to the FBI lab?"

Joe: "It had all been prearranged. I had been provided with sterile capsules that I could deposit the poison into. I kept these in my house. When one was ready to be sent to the lab a special courier came to my door and he transported it to the lab."

Counselor: "Okay, then what was Markov's response when there was no change in Ms. Wolf's condition?"

Joe: "Chaban called me and told me that Markov was getting impatient. I tried to get ahead of it by asking him if there was something wrong with the poison. I told him I used 40 percent of the bottle already. 'Should I have used more? Is this something that takes time to have an effect?' I asked. 'Cancer doesn't happen instantly does it,' he said. He told me that Markov wants to verify that she was drinking the tea and put the next dosage into something else that she would drink. The liquid was clear and he said it would not have taste. I'm not sure he totally trusted me, because he instructed Aleksei to accompany me on the next visit and assure that everything was done correctly."

Counselor: "So how did you handle that?"

Joe: "*The next visit was on New Year's Eve. Aleksei took the Metro up from D.C. I picked him up and we drove to Wolf's house. I told Aleksei the alarm code while I went to the refrigerator. Either the alarm code had been changed or Aleksei punched it in wrong. The alarm went off. I scrambled to disconnect the system before the alarm company was alerted. I think I was successful. Meanwhile, Aleksei found that the tea level was low, which means it was being drunk, so he put a dropper full of the poison into the orange juice.*"

Counselor: "*So how did you deal with the fact that her juice had poison in it. Did she drink it?*"

Joe: "*After I drove Chaban back to the Metro stop, I sent a text message to Wolf using a special burner phone that Matheson had given me. Caller ID was disabled so she would not know who sent it. The message said that the orange juice may be poisoned and that she should not drink it. I also notified Matheson of the situation.*"

Counselor: "*Why didn't you go back to the house and dump the juice?*"

Joe: "*I thought that the alarm company would possibly detect that the system was down, and alert Wolf of this, and possibly send the police. When she got back to her house, she would know there had been a break-in anyway. I had not been able to reset the alarm, and had left the alarm power and phone line disconnected.*"

Counselor: "*Is it possible that Wolf drank some of the poisoned tea . . . I mean juice?*"

Joe: "*I don't think so. But as it turned out, she stayed overnight at Brandy's house and was not back until morning, so it's possible.*"

Counselor: "Please explain something. Who had the remaining poison at this point? You or Chaban.?"

Joe: "I did, except when Chaban put some in the juice. I had the bottle when we left."

Counselor: "If Chaban used it to put some in the juice, would Chaban's finger prints be on the bottle?"

Joe: "I don't think any finger prints were found on the bottle. Both Chaban and myself were very careful to wear gloves."

Counselor: "What happened the next time you went to Wolf's house?"

Joe: "It was on Martin Luther King Day in mid-January, Monday the 19th. Chaban and I went there in the morning while Wolf was out shopping with her daughter. This time I had done my research on the alarm system and I disabled the system and restored it again before we left by using factory override codes. The orange juice was low. I watched Aleksei add poison to the tea. There was no way for me to know if the old orange juice from two weeks prior had been drunk, or tossed and replaced. Obviously, I didn't want Wolf to end up drinking her tea when she came home from shopping that afternoon. My thought at the time was that I could double back later in the day and dump the tea. However, after I dropped Chaban off at the Metro and drove back, Wolf had already returned home. So, I sent another text message from my burner phone telling her not to drink the tea."

Counselor: "So how do you know that she saw your messages and didn't drink the tea?"

Joe: "Once again, I also contacted Brian Matheson, I assume he contacted Donna and told her not to drink her tea."

Counselor: "But you don't know for sure what he actually did?"

Joe: "No."

Counselor: "Did you see Wolf after that?"

Joe: "Not right away, but I saw Brandy, and Brandy mentioned that she was concerned because her mom had complained recently about sore glands and abdominal pain, and had scheduled a doctor's appointment for early February. I didn't think she had actually consumed any poison so I wasn't sure what to make of it."

Counselor: "Did you inform Markov of Wolf's condition?"

Joe: "Yes I did, but he decided to use the rest of the poison to be sure things continued to progress."

Counselor: "When was that?"

Joe: "Brandy was hosting a Super Bowl party on Sunday February the first, and we decided to do it earlier that day when she would be at Brandy's house helping her mom get ready."

Counselor: "Did you?"

Joe: "Yes, Chaban put the remainder of the poison into both her tea and her juice."

Counselor: "Were you able to warn her?"

Joe: "Yes, I immediately left a text message on her phone and another for Matheson."

Counselor: "But it was Sunday. How do you know if either of them received the message in time?"

Joe: "I was concerned about that. I knew that Wolf would be back home in the afternoon and I didn't want her to drink the tea."

Counselor: "When did you next see Ms. Wolf?"

Joe: "At a Super Bowl party at Brandy's house that evening."

Counselor: "How did Ms. Wolf seem?"

Joe: "Not all that well. She complained of stomach cramps after the game, and Brandy had her stay at her house for the night. I politely said good night and headed home."

Counselor: "Did you go directly home?"

Joe: "No. The possibility that she may have had tea earlier bothered me, so I went to Wolf's townhouse and checked the tea. It did not appear to me that any of it had been drunk and I tossed the tea and the juice. She would know that someone did that for her, and by now I thought, she may have been told who I really was."

Counselor: "Do you think that anyone saw you go there?"

Joe: "No, it was early in the morning, around two."

Counselor: "Did you see Ms. Wolf again after that?"

Joe: "I saw her once more about two weeks later when I went with Brandy to the hospital to visit her. Her condition had deteriorated rapidly. This bothered me and I wondered if in fact she had been drinking the poison."

Counselor: "What did you tell Markov?"

Joe: "I told him that his mission was accomplished—Ms. Wolf was dying of cancer."

Counselor: "Did he believe it?"

Joe: "Yes he did."

Counselor: "When did you last contact Markov?"

Joe: "February sixteenth. It was President's Day."

Counselor: "When did you last contact Aleksei Chaban?"

Joe: "February twenty-third, Monday afternoon at the airport just prior to his arrest."

Counselor: "Thank you That's all for now. The guards will escort you back to your quarters."

Joe's testimony lasted another week. Joe's entire testimony was recorded. In the recordings, and in the transcripts, he was always referred to as J. Doe, never his real name. Only portions of his recorded testimony were presented to the Federal Grand Jury. The prosecution only needed to present those parts of testimony that made their case. The prosecution wanted a murder indictment, so they did not present the portion of Joe's testimony about him warning Donna not to drink the juice and tea. In a grand jury there is no defense or cross examination, like in a trial, and all proceedings are secret. In addition to Joe, others testified, including a medical examiner, an FBI agent, the young newspaper reporter, and a CIA employee who was working with Donna. By the end of the year 2004, Ivan Markov and Aleksei Chaban were indicted. The indictments included murder, theft of classified information, and several other lesser charges.

However, the prosecution took the death penalty off the table in exchange for a guilty plea to various counts of espionage and attempted murder. The prosecution knew they could not prove murder. The CIA and the FBI knew it, but the grand jury and Markov did not. Everyone new that Donna had died of cancer but the manner of death was never known with certainty. During the grand jury proceedings, a medical examiner testified that the FBI lab had identified the poison used by Markov and that it could cause the type of cancer that killed Donna. This was true. What the medical examiner didn't say was that they had not detected it in Donna's body. An indictment of murder allowed the prosecutor to bargain with Markov. Markov and Chaban were eager to avoid death and the bad publicity that a public trial would bring to their country. They pleaded guilty to attempted murder and to the other charges. A trial was avoided.

Joe was also pleased that a trial was not needed. For him, it meant less public exposure and less chance of an attempt on his life. It also meant no cross-examination, something that he was not comfortable with.

****

Now that the Joe had completed his testimony and the Russians were in a federal prison, Joe contemplated the decision he would need to make. He could drop out of WITSEC and go back to being the old Joe Martinez, or he could accept a totally new identity and be relocated to a place where he could start over. Joe was faced with the reality that he would be a marked man unless he was given a new identification. Surely the Russians would know he betrayed them, and he had already been subjected to attempts on his life. He would need the protection. Even if he continued to be an agent of the CIA, he would need to have a new identification.

He had been told that as a condition for being in the program, he would have to say goodbye to all his friends and family and never have contact with them again. He considered the ramifications of this. He had no family left, so that was not a problem. Did he have any friends? Was Bill a friend? Was his business partner a friend? They certainly got along. Although he was working counter-intelligence, he had thought of Maria Martin as a friend—until he discovered she was also a serial assassin wanted by the U.S. DOJ. Perhaps Ed was the closest one he still had to being a friend. He would miss him. Ed had shown compassion, had helped him get through the ordeal in Costa Rica, and had convinced Matheson to allow him to say good bye to Brandy. Then there was Brandy. She had been a friend—it still hurt to think about her. Perhaps not having anyone close would be a blessing in disguise, he thought. It would mean fewer complications.

Joe was friendly and people seemed to like him and enjoy his company. But the job he had seemed to run counter to long term close relationships. Now that he was no longer working covertly as a triple agent, he felt confident that he would make friends wherever he ended up. He welcomed the thought of starting over. Perhaps he could look forward to having a normal life after all.

So, he decided to stay in WITSEC permanently. By the time Chaban and Markov were sentenced, Joseph Ricardo Garcia Martinez became someone else. It was a popular name and would not stand out or arouse unusual interest. Joe was given a new birth certificate, new college records, new work history, and a new bank account. Joe was instructed to memorize who he was and be ready to act the part.

A prerequisite to joining the WITSEC program had been that he would attend two orientation meetings. These meetings were intended to help the transition. The first occurred when he entered the program. The second of these meetings occurred after he had his new identification, but before he knew where he would be relocated. The meeting took place at a secret location in D.C. and was attended by several others that also had new identifications.

One exercise was for each initiate in the program to introduce themselves to another person—using their new identification of course. This might be someone you meet at a cocktail party, or at a meeting, or while interviewing for a new job. It was important that the initiate feel comfortable doing this. A U.S. Marshals employee would supervise and give suggestions afterwards. Typical questions that one may be asked would include:

"I'm so and so, and you are?"

"Tell me about yourself. What do you do?"

"Where did you live before you moved here?"

"Why did you leave?"

Etc.

Joe had studied his new history the night before. He felt very comfortable with this. Afterall, he had been living semi covertly for several years. This was just another cover, he reasoned. He passed the test without any help.

A Marshal ended the meeting by emphasizing the importance of staying with the program. "No one in the program has been exposed and killed," he said, and then added, "so long as they followed the rules and stayed in the program."

The USMS provided Joe with $75,000 in a checking account in his new name. This was a customary amount to allow him to have money to live on while he looked for new employment consistent with his prior income. Lawyers with powers of attorney closed out the accounts he had in the name of Joseph Garcia Martinez. That money was legally transferred through a third party and deposited in his new account. This accounted for another $100,000. The CIA also gave him another $75,000 as compensation for the work he had done for them. So, he had about $250,000. It was more than enough to tide him over while he found employment at his new location.

Within the week, the USMS relocated Joe to an unknown location. They would monitor him periodically and provide a local USMS contact in case he had an issue. Other than that, he was free to begin his new life.

41

LIFE GOES ON

B randy continued to stay in touch with Ed Perez. Two years after Donna's death, Ed retired from the CIA. Although not the life he envisioned having with Donna, he opted to become a permanent resident in Costa Rica. After he retired, he moved to a house in a gated community on the outskirts of San José, and began to attend the local Catholic church more frequently. The idea of a country setting within reach of the city and the airport appealed to him. He already knew more people in Costa Rica than back in the States. Although none were close or intimate friends, he did have a few buddies that he could go to the gun range with, go golfing with, or go fishing with off the coast and have intellectual conversations with. These included prior colleagues from the DIS and the OIJ. His connections afforded him opportunities for consulting work with agencies of the Costa Rican government. He registered as a foreign agent with the U.S. government. He kept busy, but not too busy to pursue his photographic hobby.

Ed was happy in retirement. He took pictures of nearby scenes using an expensive high-resolution digital camera. He improved his skills at mounting and framing his photos and managed to get a part time job in an art and photo gallery and store. He learned about the best backing materials, the best matting material and the best wooden frames to use. Working in the store afforded him discounts on the materials and equipment he needed to make the job easier and faster. After only two years of retirement he already had the first showing of his work. The theme was Costa Rican volcanos. It was a success and a touring company offered to buy some of his pictures. But there was one photo he would never sell, one that had the view of Poás that he shared with Donna two years earlier.

When Brandy mentioned that she was thinking of a vacation in late June of 2005, Ed convinced her to bring her son Brian, her father Peter, and Carol to Costa Rica. Brandy's son Brian would graduate from high school and would enter Stanford in the fall. Ed had suggested this trip as a graduation gift. He said he would pay for the trip. Brandy asked how he would have the money to do this. He told her not to worry about it. He would explain later. Peter and Carol agreed to join them but said they would pay their own way. Ed would arrange for a one week stay at a resort in Sarapiqui. The resort was in the mountains north of San José, where temperatures would remain desirable.

Ed met everyone at the San José international airport with a small van. The first night was spent at Ed's new house in Escazu, not very far from the airport. The house had four bedrooms. Ed used the master bedroom for himself. Two others he planned to rent out for tourists. Peter and Carol would have one of those bedrooms, and Brandy would have the other. He used the fourth bedroom as a studio and workshop for his photography. For this night, he would set up a cot in the studio for Brian. The first thing that Brandy and the others noticed when they entered were the framed photographs that lined the walls. Ed was eager to show them off. Brandy found one of her Mom, and another of the Poás volcano that she especially liked. "We will visit Poás tomorrow," Ed commented.

Early the next morning, they set out for the resort with Ed acting as their tour guide. On the way, they stopped at the Poás Volcano. Ed told them it was one of his favorite places and that he had been here with Brandy's mom three years earlier. Brian was impressed with the view. "Awesome," he said.

The resort consisted of multiple circular units; each unit had eight private rooms. Peter and Carol shared a room and the other three each had a room of their own. There was no TV or other amenities, but the shower was nice, and each room had access to a balcony with lounge chairs that circled the unit. The resort also had a pool and a bar. It was there that he pulled Brandy aside and kept his promise to explain the overseas account that provided the funds for their vacation.

****

Ed and Brandy found a quiet table near the poolside bar where they could talk. A roof over the bar area protected them from the sun. There were no walls. The pool was visible on one side, rain forest on the other. It was a sunny afternoon and some people were in the pool, very few in the bar area. Ed went to the bar and returned with two bottles of cold water—too early for liquor.

"Brandy, I want to talk to you about how I am paying for this trip. You deserve to know the full story. The money is from the overseas HSBC account that you asked me about. Your mom and I set the account up twelve years ago." Ed watched Brandy's eyes widen as he talked.

Brandy had discovered the existence of the overseas account two years ago. She had asked Ed about it but never got a complete answer. She looked at Ed with anticipation as he continued.

"We were on a temporary two-year assignment in Europe. We barely knew each other before that, but the assignment drew us together. Each of us was given extra pay to cover our living expenses. Your mother was the one that came up with the idea that we could save a lot of money if we pooled our resources and shared our living quarters. The idea fit well with our cover stories and we decided to do it. We rented a two bedroom flat on the outskirts of London and that became the base of our operation. Please understand, we maintained our privacy, and there were many days that only one of us was there. We also got by with only one rental car while in the

London area. The bottom line is that after two years we had each saved more than 50,000 pounds. The money was gained legally, and we had paid income taxes on it."

Not knowing what to say or ask, Brandy remained silent.

"However, during that two years we had also become good friends, and even more the week before we parted. We had learned to trust each other. I was the one that suggested that we pool our money and set up an offshore account. We did. We were already doing business with HSBC under our cover names Donna Rice and Edward Gardner, so that is where we went. We invested all of our extra money into a deferred annuity index fund and named each other as beneficiaries."

Ed could see the question mark on her face. "The account is legally under our real names, but our pseudo names appear on correspondence. HSBC is good at maintaining privacy."

He continued. "When your mom passed, I became the sole owner of the account. However, the law required me to begin taking minimum payouts each year. I've taken about 6,000 dollars so far, and some of that I used for this vacation. But now we have a decision to make."

"What do you mean?"

"Half of the account was your mom's and is rightful yours. I've also added your name as sole beneficiary for when I die, but in the meantime, if you or Brian needs money, like for college, I could help with that now. No need to wait until I die."

"Ed, how much money are we talking about?"

"There's about 400,000 US dollars in the account right now. Tell me what Brian needs for college."

"Ed, I really appreciate your generosity, but Brian and I are really doing okay. I have a good salary at NSA. I received money from Mom's life insurance and Brian's father is supposed to pay half his college expense—at least that was the agreement we had. And, Brian had scholarship money too. But what about you Ed? You're retired now. Don't you need income?"

"I really don't. If I stay here in Costa Rica, I have more than I need and I have no family or heirs. You and Brian are the closest thing I have for family. Your mom wanted you to benefit from this account and I want the same thing."

"I see . . .. Why don't you continue taking as much as you're required to take each year—more if you need it? Then when you die, whatever is left can come to me. That would be good with me if acceptable to you."

"Okay, that's what I'll do. What do you say we go for a swim before the others get back from the Pineapple plantation?"

"Sounds good."

****

It seemed like one week was not enough and went by too fast. During their stay at the resort, they enjoyed hikes in the rainforest, spotting howler monkeys, a lecture on bats, swimming in the pool, sipping *pura vidas* at the bar, feasting on the native cuisine, and more. In addition to the tour of a pineapple plantation, Ed had arranged for them to all go white-water rafting in the nearby Sarapiqui River. The rafting trip was one of the highlights. When Brian was asked what he enjoyed the most, he didn't hesitate to say "The whitewater rafting and the Poás volcano. They were awesome!"

42

A NEW LIFE

Brandy continued working for the NSA and attained the title of Associate Director of Information Technology. But despite her success, she was tiring of her work. To make it more interesting she began writing technical papers and gave presentations at a few conferences. Her lively personality made her an entertaining speaker.

In the fall of 2010 Brandy spoke at a major information technology conference in Las Vegas, sponsored by the SIA. Attendees and speakers were from both industry and government. It took much preparation, review, and security screening, but she was cleared and now she was in a large meeting room facing an audience of more than 100 people. She breathed deeply, let out a long breath, and delivered one of the best talks of the conference. People applauded loudly and afterwards a group of 'fans' surrounded her to compliment her on a great talk, tap her for more information, ask more questions, impress her with their own knowledge, exchange contact information, and to just plain schmooze.

As the size of the group surrounding her dwindled, a well-dressed middle-aged gentleman introduced himself.

"Hello. Ms. Evans? Allow me to introduce myself. I'm Joseph Ramirez," he said while using his left hand to point to the name-tag he wore below his right shoulder. "I found your idea about multi-dimensional surveillance to be of great interest. I'm the marketing manager for a security business and can relate to those concepts." He reached into the left pocket of his jacket and handed her one of his business cards. She looked at his card and then at him.

Joseph Francisco Ramirez had short receding curly black hair, and a neatly trimmed beard and mustache. He wore glasses that gave him an air of dignity. Brandy stood looking at him, her mouth agape. She was almost speechless . . .. "Joe?" She finally uttered weakly.

"Call me Joey. If I were to ask you to join me for coffee, would that be too forward of me?" he asked.

"Uh . . . of course, I'd love to," she said

They went to the break area and took their coffees to a table for two.

"Joe, I mean Joey, may I ask where you're from?" she asked playing along.

"Albuquerque, New Mexico."

"You said you managed a security business?"

"Yup, the marketing manager for five years now. While I've been there it's grown from a three-person operation to eight employees and six contractors. I'm doing quite well and I really enjoy the work . . .. And you? I saw on the conference brochure that you're an employee of the US government at Fort Meade, where you manage information technology.

"I'm an Associate Director of Information Technology at NSA."

"Impressive!"

"The title is more impressive than the job . . .. Joey, could I ask you a personal question?"

"Sure."

"Are you alone? I mean are you married or with someone?"

"No, I live by myself in a nice garden apartment with a pool. No girlfriend . . . and what about you?"

"No, just me, a cat, and my work. Joey, you're a very handsome man, eye candy to many women, I'm sure. I 'm surprised you aren't spoken for."

"I appreciate the compliment, but six years ago I was in love with a wonderful lady and it just wasn't going to work out at that time, but I remembered that when we parted, she said that maybe someday we could start over. I don't expect things to be the same, but I was hoping to take the first step . . . but only if she's willing."

"How could this work?"

"Could we talk about the possibilities over dinner tonight?"

Although hesitant, she agreed.

That night they had dinner at a local restaurant and they talked. He told her who the new Joey was. He told her that before moving to Albuquerque, he had worked with the General Services Administration headquartered in Washington D.C. He told her his job was to work with building contractors on security and he also helped to develop security related standards. He often traveled to the various regional offices of the GSA as part of his work.

"What kind of education did you need for that kind of work?" she asked. "Do you have a PhD?"

"No, I have an engineering degree and a masters in computer science. I considered a PhD but I ran out of money and decided to work."

"Where did you get your degrees?" She was obviously testing him and of course he knew that.

"Cal Tech," he proudly stated.

"I'm detecting a slight accent. Is it Spanish?"

"You're very perceptive. I was born in Texas and grew up there, but both my parents were from Central America. For many years I lived in the El Paso area. There were many people in my neighborhood and the school system who spoke Spanish, and I still speak it when I need to. I find that being able to speak more than one language can be very useful for work."

"Are your parents still alive?"

"No, sorry to say. They passed away many years ago now."

After a pause she smiled. "Joey, I'm impressed."

Then, after dinner, they retired to her hotel room where they could talk more privately. The chemistry was still there but they both resisted the temptation. They needed to come to an understanding and an agreement on how they could move forward. He told her that he still loved her and how much he wanted to be with her. Their conversation extended into the next evening. He told her he was taking a big risk revealing that he was in WITSEC, the Federal witness protection program, but that he trusted her. He told her that to remain in the program and remain protected, he was not supposed to associate with anyone from his past or even be where someone from his past might recognize him. She said she understood and agreed to keep their conversation a secret. No one else would know they had met.

"What happened to the old Joe," she wanted to know. "Did he die?"

"No, he's still out there somewhere, but no-one knows where. He disappeared," Joey stated facetiously. "Apparently it's not like in the movies where the person fakes their death before going into WITSEC."

Joey told her how much he wanted them to have a long-term relationship together. He invited her to come see him in Albuquerque in a month. He said, he would understand if she decided not to pursue it, but really hoped she would. "In any case," he said, "regardless of your decision, please don't reveal our prior relationship to anyone." Once again, she promised.

By the close of the second evening together, they could no longer hold back. The fire between them was reunited. He spent the night in her hotel room and they made passionate love.

Over the next ten months, Brandy visited Joey three times in Albuquerque. Joey introduced her to his work colleagues and his friends. She was the girlfriend that he had met at a recent security conference in Las Vegas. It took time, but they got to know each other—again. More importantly, Joey was real, his business was real, and his participation in the community was real. People that knew him liked him, and Joey liked his new life. It was not long before Brandy fell in love with him all over again.

He asked if she would be willing to relocate to Albuquerque. They both wanted to be together and make it work, but there were some serious questions that needed to be resolved before she could agree. Mentioning a new boyfriend who she occasionally saw was one thing, but moving to be with someone in a close relationship was something else. She didn't want to lie to her son. Brian had already met Joe on several occasions in the year 2003 and early 2004. Eventually he would need to know the whole truth. Same thing with her father, Peter, and what about Ed Perez? And then there was her ex-husband. He had met Joe once. What if he found out? Could he be trusted? And what about the life she would leave behind in Maryland?

Brandy decided that before she made such a monumental decision, she needed advice. She would talk to Peter. She could certainly trust him, and besides, Peter had been very instrumental in helping her learn the truth about her mother and about Joe. She called him and asked if he would come over to her house so they could talk. Of course, he agreed.

****

Over the years, Brandy's relationship with Peter remained about the same—occasional visits, emails, and phone calls.

It was now the summer of 2011. Although they had talked on the phone a few times, it had been more than a couple of months since she had seen Peter. They were both busy with their own lives—not unusual. He was glad to hear from her and be invited over, but he wondered why. It sounded important. She greeted him at the door with a hug and she ushered him into the living room where they were seated.

"Peter, I'm so glad to see you. We don't see each other often enough and it seems like when I do see you, it's because I need something."

"So, what's up? It sounded important."

"I need to make a very important life decision, and I want your advice."

"Okay."

"As you know, I met someone when I gave my presentation at the security conference in Vegas last year. We have kept in touch, and I have flown out to Albuquerque where he lives to visit him three times now in the past year. He wants me to move out there and be with him. I would need to sell my house, retire from NSA, get a new job, and move. I need your advice about that."

"Okay . . ."

"Do you think I should do that?"

"Could I ask you a few questions?"

"Sure."

"You must feel very strongly about each other to want to do this."

"We're in love and want to be with each other."

"It sounds like you have only been with him three or four times. How can you be sure that you will have a future with him?"

She seemed to be unsure as to how to answer. "We're sure," she finally said.

"Brandy, are you pregnant?"

"No! No! Nothing like that."

He looked at her and detected some deception. "What then? I sense that there is something you haven't told me."

"Peter, his name is Joey Ramirez . . . .. He's the same Joe that I was in love with in 2004. He just happened to be at the conference, and we talked and we really care about each other."

"So . . . is he still a covert operative? Does he still work for the CIA?"

"No. He stayed in WITSEC and they gave him a new life."

"If Joe is in WITSEC, and the Marshals Service gave him a new identity, the two of you are taking a big risk. You know that, don't you?"

"You don't approve, do you," she said despairingly.

"I'm not saying that. It's your decision, and I'll support you no matter what. It's just that I care about you and don't want to see you get hurt."

"What about Carol?"

"What about her?"

"Will she know? Will she approve? She was FBI. Will she keep it under wraps?"

"I never told her the details of our investigation into the circumstances surrounding your mom's project or who Joe was, and she never tried to find out. But, if she did know, I'm sure we can trust her to keep the secret."

"I'm not sure what to do."

"If you do this, I suggest you take it one step at a time. Move out there and get your own apartment. Make it look to the outside like a slowly developing relationship. Don't reveal his prior identity to anyone. If it doesn't work out, no one will be the wiser, and you can continue with your life independently. If it does work out, and you end up living together, you will need to decide how you deal with people that are close to you, like your son."

Peter stood up, walked over to her, put his hands on her shoulders and kissed her on the forehead. "Bottom line . . . I think you should follow your heart."

She jumped up and hugged him. "Thank you, thank you!"

****

After talking with Peter, Brandy decided to retire from the NSA. She would have more than 20 years of service and would receive a decent pension. She would move to Albuquerque. Aside from Peter, a couple of girlfriends from work, and her mom's grave, there was nothing keeping her in Maryland. They would understand, she reasoned. Her son had just started a career as a lawyer in the Los Angeles, California area, and her stepbrother now lived in Kentucky and owned an auto body shop, and her cat—really her mom's cat— had passed away. She already knew she had support from Peter. So, she decided to sell her house and move to Albuquerque. She took Peter's advice to avoid suspicion, and rather than move in with Joey, she would rent an apartment for herself. She was only 43 years old and an experienced manager with IT systems knowledge. It would be easy for her to find a job in her field, she reasoned. But even if it took a while, the money from the sale of the house would bridge the gap.

So, in August of 2011, Brandy retired from NSA and moved into her new apartment in a fashionable suburb of Albuquerque. For convenience, her apartment was not far from where Joey lived. Within another month, she had a management job in her field of information technology.

Brandy looked forward to her new life.

43

ED'S VISIT

Ed received an email from Brandy telling him that she left had
left her job and had moved to Albuquerque. She enclosed the
new address and telephone number and wished him well, but didn't
say much else. After reading the email, Ed wondered what would
motivate her to move, and why Albuquerque. In his reply email, he
asked her that. She wrote back telling him how great a place it was
to retire, and listed some of the things that were great about the state.
She also told him she got herself a job, so apparently, she really wasn't
retiring, and then she mentioned she had met a guy and was dating.

A couple of months later, Ed decided he needed to disrupt his
routine. Throughout his career, he was not only busy but he dealt
with the unexpected almost daily. He thrived on the uncertainty. Yet
during those years with the military and the CIA, he often longed
to have a normal life. Now in retirement, life was slower and not so
exciting. Of course, there was the photography, the golf game once
a week, the gun club once a week, the church group, etc. But life
had become routine. If this was normal, he needed to spiff it up. He
needed to get away.

Ed recalled that in her email, Brandy had praised New Mexico,
so he got on the Internet and researched what it had to offer as a place
to visit. Turned out, it had quite a bit. There was the famous annual

International Balloon Fiesta in the fall. There were balloon rides over the Rio Grande Valley. There was Roswell, where aliens supposedly landed in 1947 and an associated museum with artifacts to make you wonder if it was true. There was the White Sands Monument where the first Atomic bomb test took place and a nearby museum displaying missiles and other legacy weapons of mass destruction. There was the Silver City mining town, the Sandia Peak Ariel Tramway, and the reminders of the Spanish cultural heritage in the old towns of Albuquerque, Santa Fe, and Taos. To top it off the scenery matched that of Costa Rica. How could he resist.

He found a small group tour company and booked a trip for October of 2011. There had been a cancelation and he would get a great price if he could be ready to go in three weeks. His plan was to fly into Albuquerque, participate in the tour, and then rent a car and visit Brandy at the end of his trip before flying back home. He sent an email to Brandy to let her know his plan and assure that it would work for her. It was short notice, only three weeks away, but he could still modify his booking if necessary.

> *"If I come there on Sunday October 9, would that interfere with any plans you or your boyfriend might have?" he asked. "By the way, I would like to meet him. Will he be around? I could take the two of you out to dinner."*

> *"That would be fine. See you then," she responded.*

****

Three weeks later, on Sunday morning, Ed drove into the parking lot of Brandy's apartment complex. Although she was expecting him on Sunday, they had never agreed upon an exact time. He didn't exit the car, but called her on the phone to let her know he was in the area.

"When can you be here," she asked.

"Any time now," he answered. "What would be convenient?"

"Can you give me an hour?"

"Not a problem. See you then."

Ed put his phone aside and set the satellite radio to a station playing country-western music. After a few minutes, he decided to take a short drive while he waited out the hour. He was about to start up the car when he noticed a man leaving Brandy's apartment. He was probably about 250 feet away, so it was difficult to see his face, but Ed thought there was something about him that seemed familiar. He watched as the man got into a Honda sedan and drove away. He considered the idea of following him, but decided against it. It was probably Brandy's boyfriend who spent the night. Perhaps she wasn't ready to make it known that they were sleeping together. He could respect that. So, to kill time he drove around the area. Very nice upscale developments, he thought. After a while, he stopped at a local Mr. Donut and bought six jelly filled to go. Then, he returned to Brandy's parking lot and parked closer to her apartment this time.

Well, here goes, he thought as he walked up to her unit and pressed the doorbell.

"Hello Ed. Come in."

They hugged politely with no kiss.

"What do you have in the bag," she asked.

"Oh, I brought a couple of doughnuts from Mr. Donut."

"Yummy. Let's go into the kitchen. I have fresh coffee in the pot. We can have coffee and donuts while we talk."

Ed took a seat at the kitchen table.

"Jelly donuts?" she said peering into the bag. "Looks like you have six."

Brandy went back to the counter and was about to pour the coffee, when Ed spoke up.

"Brandy, before we dig into those donuts and coffee, would it be okay if I used your bathroom and washed up?"

"Oh sure, down that way and to the right."

While washing up, Ed could not help but notice the extra toothbrush and the small travel bag on the counter. He took a closer look and noticed the handwritten identification tag attached to the handle. It belonged to Brandy's boyfriend, he thought.

However, it was not the name, address, and phone number that was of interest. It was the fact that the writing all slanted to the left like someone who was left-handed would do.

Back in the kitchen, Brandy had already positioned a full cup of coffee, a plate with a jelly doughnut, and a napkin and fork at his place.

"One reason I brought extra donuts is because I thought you were living with someone now. Will he be here?" Ed asked, sounding curious.

"Oh, no. We have separate apartments."

"Perhaps he could come over later. I'd like to meet him and take you both out to dinner."

"I'll call him and see if he can do that."

"How serious are you about this guy—what did you say his name was?

"Joey . . . Joseph Ramirez. We're serious, but we're taking things slowly, one step at a time."

"I see. What does Joey do?"

"Do?"

"You know, for work."

"Oh . . . He's in charge of marketing for a small security systems company."

"How did you meet?"

"Ah . . . well—"

He was aware of her hesitation.

"Brandy, I hope I'm not asking too many questions? You seem nervous?"

"No, it's okay. We met at a security conference in Las Vegas about a year ago. I was giving a presentation and after my talk he approached me and we began talking."

"Interesting—"

"Ed why are you looking at me like that?"

"I remember you had a boyfriend named Joe just before your mom passed away. He also had a Spanish last name. I find it interesting that you went with him to a security conference, and that he also was a marketing rep for a security company. And, I think that the guy who shared your bathroom this morning is left-handed just like that Joe. As I had told you, I knew that Joe, spent time with him when he was brought back to Costa Rica to testify. He knew he would be relocated and get a new identification. I asked him where he would like to live and he told me Albuquerque. He also told me how much he cared for you and how he needed to meet with you to clear the air before he disappeared into WITSEC. Peter and I influenced the powers to be to allow that to happen. I want you to trust me. The coincidence is too much. Sounds to me like Joey and Joe may be the same person."

"Ed . . . Joey and I discussed this. We were still trying to decide if we would need to let you know, and how and when we would do it. Then, when you said you were coming to visit, our time-table moved up. We were not totally prepared. Joey has taken a big risk. You understand that, right?"

"More than you think. But it's a risk for both of you. You must love each other a lot to take this risk."

"Please promise you'll keep our secret."

He didn't respond to that right away but kept talking.

"I can't help but wonder what your mom would have said about this. Your mom knew how unhappy you were in your marriage. She never liked your husband—thought he was a jerk—said he cheated on you. She always wanted you to meet someone who you could be happy with. Then when Joe came along, she hoped he would be the one, that is until she learned that Joe was a double agent and that you were being used. It upset her, and when she knew she was dying, I told her I would look out for you. If you or Joe had asked my advice, I probably would have advised against it. On the other hand, Joe's a good man, and I know he must love you to take such a risk. Look . . . bottom line . . . what's done is done. I'll support you and you can trust me to keep your secret."

"Ed, Mom always spoke highly of you. I can see why. Thank you."

They spent several more hours talking, talking about Ed's life in Costa Rica, talking about Brandy's job, talking about Albuquerque, etc. They went for a walk in the neighborhood and enjoyed the warmth of the sun. The neighborhood seemed nice. At some point Brandy called Joey, and he said he would come over in the late afternoon.

Joey rang the doorbell shortly after four. Ed stood on the other side of the room as Brandy let him through.

"Ed, please meet my friend Joey. Joey, this is Ed."

Joey and Ed looked at each other and Joey was the first to speak.

"Hello Ed. You don't seem surprised to see me. Perhaps Brandy has already revealed our secret."

"I really didn't have to," Brandy piped in. "Ed pretty much figured it out himself."

"Welcome to our new inner family circle, Ed," Joey said and held out his arms.

The two of them walked towards each other and hugged each other in a manly manner. Then the three of them had a drink—a ginger ale for Joey—and they talked. Ed learned that at present, the "new inner family circle" consisted of himself, the two of them, plus Peter. They knew that they would need to expand that to include Brandy's son Brian, and possibly Peter's wife Carol. That evening, the three of them went out to one of Brandy's and Joey's favorite restaurants. Ed was happy to treat.

44

WEDDING PLANS

By 2012, Peter and Carol had retired their consulting business. Peter began doing volunteer work and writing novels. With the help of Brandy, he was writing a novel titled *Her Final Project*, a biography of Donna's life. Carol had become a master gardener and began teaching an adult education course at the local community college in Howard County, Maryland.

One day in February of 2012, Peter sorted through the daily mail. There was an envelope addressed to both him and Carol. It was from Brandy. "Carol, come look at this," he called as he carefully opened the envelope and removed the contents.

Brandy Evans
and
Joseph Ramirez
request the honor of your presence
at their marriage
on Saturday the sixth of June
two thousand and twelve
at six o'clock in the evening
Sandia Resort and Golf Club
30 Rainbow Road, NE
Albuquerque, New Mexico

In addition to the wedding invitation, Brandy had also enclosed a short note.

> *Peter:*
>
> *To Mom's disappointment, I was married by a justice of the peace in a dingy back room when I married Dan. I think Mom would be pleased that this time Joey and I will be married by a member of the clergy in a beautiful setting.*
>
> *Joey says he gave up on Catholicism long ago and is okay not to be married in a Catholic Church. He has made arrangements with a local resort that is one of his clients. The Sandia Resort provides the venue for the wedding, the reception, and the overnight all at one convenient location. And there is free shuttle service to and from the airport. No need for a car.*
>
> *We hope you and Carol will join us, and I would be honored if as my father you would walk me down the aisle.*
> *Love,*
> *Brandy*

****

Brandy and Joey planned for their wedding to be small, perhaps twenty people in total—very close family members, Joey's employees, and a few of Joey's local friends. There would be no big newspaper announcements or any other media publicity. For it to be otherwise would be too risky for Joey. Aside from herself, Ed and Peter, only one other person was invited to the wedding who knew what the old Joe looked like. That was her son Brian.

Brian had graduated from law school in 2011 and was in his first year working for a law firm in Los Angeles, California. The money from Donna's life insurance had helped to pay for his six years in college. Brandy and her ex-husband Dan had attended the graduation, but that was the last time Brandy and Brian had seen each other. Peter and Carol thought about going, but although they had friends in Los Angeles, it was a long way and Peter was involved with clients. They sent a card and a gift.

Brandy could not be married without her son being there. Three months before the wedding she called him and convinced him to come visit her in Albuquerque. She said she needed to discuss some very important matters regarding her upcoming marriage and she wanted him to meet Joey. Brian wondered why they couldn't discuss it over the phone, but she insisted and he agreed.

Brandy met her son at the airport and they drove back to her apartment.

"Mom, where's Joey?"

"You'll meet him later. Right now, he's still at work."

Brian looked around the apartment and commented, "I don't see any indication that Joey lives here."

"We both have leases that we can't break yet, but we have plans to buy a house together as soon as we marry."

"What was it that you needed me to come all this way to hear in person?"

"I'm going to reveal something to you that you must promise never to repeat."

"What's that?"

"I'm dead serious," she said with a raised voice. "You must promise that you won't repeat any of this to anyone, no one at the wedding, none of your friends, not your father, not your girlfriend— No one!"

"Okay Mom, relax. I promise."

"Do you remember my boyfriend Joe from years ago?"

"Yeah . . ."

"Joey is the Joe you met eight and a half years ago. Aside from you and Grandpa Peter, no one else at the wedding will know this."

Brian appeared stunned and it seemed like ages before he could respond.

"Mom, I don't understand. Grandma thought Joe was trying to poison her. She had me take a picture of him. She told me her fears and said she was sending the picture to a friend who could find out who Joe really was."

"Yes, and she did that. She sent the picture to Uncle Ed. You probably know that Grandma and Uncle Ed were more than just friends, and I'm sure you remember that vacation he arranged for us in Costa Rica. Well anyway, Uncle Ed found out what was going on, and informed your grandma."

"Didn't Joe poison her?"

"No, he didn't."

"How did she die then?"

"She really did die of cancer. I think you know that your grandma worked for the CIA. It seems that Uncle Ed did also and he knew who Joe was. Turned out Joe was part of a covert CIA operation. Joe was put into witness protection and that's why he disappeared, but I didn't learn any of this until a couple of months after your grandma died."

"How did you find out?"

"Grandpa Peter helped me coordinate an investigation, and Uncle Ed was very helpful as well."

"So, did you say that Grandpa Peter and I will be the only ones at the wedding that can identify who Joe really is? What about Uncle Ed?"

"I heard from Ed. He doesn't think he should attend. He and Joe were both stationed in Costa Rica prior to 2004. Ed said his prior association could result in too much risk for Joe . . . and of course Peter knows, and speaking of him, there's something else you should know. I've asked Peter to walk me down the aisle . . . if that's okay with you."

"It's fine Mom. You deserve to be happy and I promise that you can trust me to keep the secret," he said, and gave his mom a big hug.

****

Brandy and Joey had received a wedding card and a note from Ed Perez indicating that he would not attend. He said that they should be on the lookout for a wedding gift that would be shipped to them shortly. Ed's gift arrived on Friday two weeks before the wedding. It came in a rigid carton about three feet by two feet and four inches thick. Joe and Brandy open it together. They opened one end of the carton and carefully slid out two foam protection sheets. A note had been taped to one of the sheets:

> *Dear Brandy and Joey:*
>
> *I hope you enjoy your wedding gift. The picture is my favorite. Your mom was with me when I took it. All of us have shared this image of Poás, and I hope it brings you the same warm feelings that it brings me . . . Ed*

Then they slid out the framed picture that was inside and propped it up against the coffee table.

"Wow. It's beautiful! Just like I remember it," Brandy exclaimed.

"Brandy, the note says that we have all shared the image. When were you there?"

"Oh, I never told you. Yes, Ed invited me and Brian to come down for a vacation. Peter and Carol also came. One of the places we went was to Poás."

"When?"

"June of 2006. When we were at his house, he had a picture of Poás on his wall. Photography is his hobby. He does all the framing himself and he's displayed his photos in several exhibitions. When we went to the volcano site, Ed told me that he had brought my mom there in 2003, and that he asked her to retire with him. I think he really cared about Mom."

"Yes, when I was incarcerated in the U.S. Embassy, he told me how much he missed her . . .." Joey's voice trailed off and he began to gaze at the picture, almost in a trance.

"Joey? Are you alright?"

She got his attention. "Sorry I was just remembering the times *I* was there. I grew up near there and I often visited the Poás National Park with my father and stepmom. Those were enjoyable times. The volcano site is also where I first met Ed in 2001. That's when he recruited me as a CIA asset. I have good memories, but it's part of the life I'm supposed to bury."

"Joey, you don't have to bury all of it. If someone were to ask about the picture, you could truthfully tell them that you went there with your parents when you were young . . . like on vacation as a tourist."

Joey turned toward her and smiled. "Yes, you're right," he said emphatically and gave her a kiss. "I think the picture will look fine in our bedroom on the wall at the head of our bed in the new house."

"I agree," she said.

45

WEDDING JITTERS

The following Monday, a week and a half before the wedding. Joey received a phone call from a woman who said her boss was interested in hiring him for a security project.

"This must remain confidential," the woman said. "Please meet us in the Roosevelt Park off 544 Coal at eight o'clock in the morning this coming Wednesday. I'll be seated at a bench near hole fifteen of the Frisbee course. We can talk there. Please come alone. I'll bring a ten-thousand-dollar deposit check for you if you decide you want the project."

The woman spoke with a slight Spanish accent, but did not give a name. "I'll be wearing a droopy wide-brimmed hat," she added. Security and secrecy went hand in hand and this approach was not all that unusual. Joey had other projects that started the same way.

Joey had been feeling on edge lately and had been having trouble sleeping. Was it the stress of the upcoming wedding or the search for a house that he and Brandy would both be happy with? Or, was it that he was having second thoughts about the risks he was taking with everyone's security? On Tuesday evening he went to the lock box he kept in his bedroom closet. He had a concealed carry handgun permit and he would take his 9 mm with him in the morning. As he retrieved the gun and the ammo clip, he noticed the sheet entitled The Ten Rules. He pulled it out and quickly perused the words, reminding himself of the rules for keeping his prior identity a secret.

The Ten Rules
To Avoid Revealing Your Prior Identity.

Recall the "Seven Deadly Sins." (Lust, Gluttony, Greed, Sloth, Wrath, Envy, and Pride.) The last one on the list is "Pride" which closely resembles vanity and arrogance. Don't think you can take risks and never fail. The seven deadly sins are called deadly for a reason. Committing them can lead to your downfall. To avoid committing them, follow the ten rules below:

1. *DON'T correspond to the wrong person. Never mention anything in your correspondence about your prior life. Phone numbers, email addresses and U.S. mail items can be traced. To avoid having your phone number traced back to you, consider an unlisted number and/or a burner phone. Be careful who you copy on emails and who you give your address to. Packages and letters sent via the U.S. mail have return addresses, postmarks, finger prints and DNA. Fingerprints and DNA can be compared to samples from known contributors, including records from your prior identity.*

2. *DON'T be visually spotted by someone who is looking for you, or by someone who can be persuaded to tell the person that is looking for you. Avoid promotions and publicity that include your picture. This means no pictures on Face Book or similar social media. Consider Altering your appearance.*

3. *DON'T purposely reveal your prior identity to someone you think you can trust. For example, you may be tempted out of love to avoid lying to a new partner. Then that person either purposely or inadvertently reveals your identity to a person who is looking for you.*

4. *DON'T purposely reestablish or maintain contact with people you associated with prior to changing your identity. If someone is looking for you, they could coerce people you have contact with to reveal whatever knowledge they have about you. Coercion could be by force or by bribe.*

5. *DON'T commit a felony. Fingerprints and DNA will be compared to law-enforcement and other government data-bases. If you had a record prior to changing your identity, that record is likely still there and will expose your prior identity.*

6. *DON'T assume that because you are in protective custody, either in WITSEC or in a state-run program, your information cannot be hacked or leaked.*

7. *DON'T do a poor job of creating your new identity. Anything short of the Federal WITSEC program is probably not good enough. People who don't want to be found have new identifications with new documents like birth certificates, driver's licenses, work background, etc. If these new personal histories and documents are not perfectly created, a background check could turn up inconsistencies and cause suspicion.*

8. *DON'T apply for a job that requires an extensive background or security check, unless prearranged with WITSEC.*

9. *DON'T travel to a place, or belong to an organization, where people from your past may recognize you.*

10. *DON'T keep memorabilia from your prior life, on your person or in your new residence, where housekeepers, guests, partners, or thieves can find it.*

WARNING: The consequences of mismanaging your identity can be anything from you appearing to lack credibility, to blackmail, or death.

Clearly, he had violated Rules 3 and 4 multiple times now, once for each person that he reestablished contact with. And could his wedding take place without violating Rule 2? Surely people would want to take pictures. He was beginning to question his own judgment. Were his emotions, his pride, his over confidence in himself causing him to assume too much risk?

Tuesday night, Joey retired early. He had recently told his doctor that he was having trouble sleeping, possibly due to the stress of his upcoming wedding, and the search for a new home. According to his doctor, this was perfectly understandable and he was prescribed Ambien. So, he took the recommended dosage and set his clock radio for 6:00 a.m. As he lay in bed, he began thinking about the possible discussion he might have with the woman who spoke with the slight Spanish accent. He fell asleep wondering how his meeting the next morning would turn out.

****

Joey arrived for his meeting at the agreed upon time, and as he approached hole #15 noticed that his prospective client was already sitting on the bench. Joey expected she would come with her boss, but she seemed to be alone. Joey approached her from the side and said good morning, but the woman did not respond and remained silent. Her droopy hat disguised much of her face. As Joey got closer, something did not seem right. The woman's head was slightly cocked. Had she fallen asleep? Joey moved around in front of her and looked straight at her face to face.

"Oh my God!" Joey said aloud.

"She's dead!" he heard someone say behind him.

Joey turned around quickly. His jaw dropped. It was Ed Perez.

"What's going on? What are you doing here?"

"Do you recognize who she is? Take another look."

Joey looked again and thought for a moment. "No, I don't think so . . .. Wait. Is that Judi? Did you just kill her?"

"I had to. She knew who you were, and was planning to kill you."

"What? . . . after all this time, why?"

"She said that she had a thing for you, and that you betrayed her. She said she is convinced that you lied about what happened that Friday night when Maria was assassinated—thinks you're the one that killed her—been hunting for you ever since you left Costa Rica."

"How did she find me?"

"You broke the rules."

"Did she come alone?"

"Don't know—We should move away from here before the body is discovered. None of this ever happened—not a word," Ed said sternly.

They walked toward Joey's car.

"Thank you for saving me," Joey said sincerely.

"Nada," Ed responded, "I'll always protect you and Brandy." Then before he disappeared down a side path, Ed had one more thing to say. "You and I will never be like normal people. Our past lives will always be with us. Watch your back amigo. *Hasta luego.*"

Joey got back into his car and started up the engine. The sooner he got out of there, the better. Hopefully, no one saw him.

****

Joey felt a sudden shot of adrenalin course through his body. He was wide-eyed and staring at his window air-conditioner in the wall across from the foot of his bed, and he was listening to a male voice giving a news report about a dead body that was found in the park. It was 6:00 a.m. He had been dreaming!

He took a deep breath and headed for the shower. He was still thinking about his dream. Could it have been real? Could something like that really happen? Would agents of the Russians take revenge for testifying against them? Or, would someone from the U.S. CIA or the Costa Rican DIS come after him? There had been a conspiracy between the DIS and the CIA. Both the CIA and the DIS violated their own rules and what they did was not legal in either country. Officially, the CIA and the DIS never acknowledged that he worked for them, and the DIS never admitted their involvement in the death of Maria Martin. Was he a loose end that knew the truth?

More chilling was the possibility that there could be a leak and that he could be found. He thought about the rules and the guidelines he was given and the ten possible means by which he could be exposed.

He wondered if Brandy would be safe. If something like this ever happened, should he even tell her? A good marriage is based on honesty and trust. However, he wanted her to feel safe and secure. This should be *his* problem, not hers, he reasoned. Perhaps after the wedding, they could have another discussion about the risks.

After Joey had breakfast and coffee, he drove to Roosevelt Park and met with his prospective client as planned. Everything seemed to be on the up and up. Joey signed a non-disclosure agreement and they came to a tentative contract agreement for which Joey received a check in the amount of $10,000 as a sign of good faith. They agreed to meet again, in the client's office, not the park. That afternoon Joey celebrated the initial success with his boss, and later that evening with Brandy.

46

THE WEDDING

Brandy and Joey had chosen to have the wedding at a local golf club and resort where Joey was a member. Playing golf was one way to make deals, especially when he could demonstrate his work at the same time. Joey's company had installed their entire security system, video cameras, member ID cards, entry scanners, alarm systems, etc. The location was also ideal for a wedding, even a small one. The outdoors was picturesque with mountains in the background, and afterwards the hotel offered overnights with plenty of amenities.

The day was beautiful—sunny, warm, and dry. Twenty guests would sit in two sets of white folding chairs on an outdoor lawn with an aisle in between. A small gazebo in front of the chairs would serve as an altar. Guests included work colleagues, local friends, Peter Troutman and his wife Carol, Brian and his girlfriend, Eva, and Jennifer, a local friend of Brandy from work. Brandy had asked Jennifer to be her Maid of Honor and Joey had asked Brian to be his Best Man.

When Peter joined Brandy at the head of the aisle, he told her how gorgeous she looked. She was wearing a baby blue blouse, dressy black slacks, and black high heels. A pair of blue sapphire earrings dangled from her ears. The stone was cut in the form of an elephant.

Peter noticed this right away, but did not say anything. The wedding-party outfits were coordinated. Joey was wearing a black suit, a baby blue shirt matching Brandy's blouse, and a black and blue striped tie. Peter and Brian wore charcoal gray suits, light gray shirts, and silver and gray striped ties. Jennifer wore charcoal slacks, a silver blouse, and heels.

Peter escorted Brandy down the aisle. Joey, Brian, and Jennifer were waiting for them at the altar. Recorded music played as they walked. When they arrived, Peter gave Brandy a kiss on the cheek and took a seat next to Carol. A non-denominational minister conducted the ceremony. Joseph Ramirez and Brandy Evans recited their vows and became husband and wife.

Joey and Brandy had discussed the possible risks of taking pictures, but people expected to be able to take photos at weddings. No way they could forbid it. It would look very suspicious if they did. However, they did request that the attendees not post pictures on social media. But who knows, people will probably do that anyway. They also decided to further minimize the risks by having Peter be the official photographer. Only family members would receive those photos. They also figured that over the past eight years, Joe had aged and changed his looks. Unless someone knew what they were looking for, the risks were small. So, pictures were allowed.

Before moving inside for the reception, the guests had time to mingle on the grounds while Peter took pictures of the wedding party. Brandy and Joey had reserved a private room and had sprung for a full course dinner with wine for their wedding guests. Peter and Brian gave toasts to the bride and groom. That was followed by Joey's boss Jeff, who told everyone that Joey was a hard worker that rarely took time off, but joked that if he didn't take the next week off, he would fire him.

"Where are you going on your honeymoon?" people asked.

"We have reservations for a lodge in the Taos area," Joey responded, and then added, "After we get back, we plan to close on a new house and finally move in together. I want to thank all of you for participating in our wedding and making it a joyous occasion for both of us."

Peter and Carol met Joey for the first time. Having had common experiences in the fields of security, communications, and detective work, they had much to talk about. Although Peter had seen an old picture of Joe, and knew what had transpired, he kept his knowledge to himself. The only person attending who had met Joe in his prior life was Brandy's son Brian. Brandy had been nervous about that, but Brandy had coached him ahead of time and Brian kept his promise not to reveal anything. His girlfriend Eva seemed nice and Brandy secretly hoped she might be the one for him.

After the dinner, the wedding guests were able to join the public in a lounge where they had live music and dancing. When Joey and Brandy entered the room, the band began to play "Here Comes the Bride," prearranged by the club owner. Peter danced with his daughter for the first time. As they danced, he commented on the earrings.

"The earrings look very attractive on you," he said.

"Thank you. They were Mom's. She showed them to me when I was only five. The stones are in the shape of elephants. I was impressed by that because I had just been to the zoo and had seen real elephants for the first time. I remember her telling me that in Asia the elephant is a symbol of good luck, happiness, and longevity. I remember asking her where she got them. She told me a special friend gave them to her before I was born and that they were very special to her. She told me that someday they would be mine."

Peter was smiling and his eyes seemed to be tearing up. "What?" she said as she gave him a curious look. "Did *you* give them to her?"

"I did . . . the night before we said good bye."

"She never told me," she said and gave him a quick kiss on the cheek. "I think Mom would be very happy if she could be here now."

"I think so too," Peter replied.

Everyone danced until midnight. The out-of-town guests stayed the night. Brandy and Joey stayed the night as well. Before she went to bed, Brandy removed the earrings and set them on the shelf inside the room safe. That night she dreamed about her mom.

In the dream, she saw her mom's gravestone. The earrings were resting on top. She saw her mom's face and then she heard her mom's voice speak to her from above, from heaven. "Your happiness was always my final project. I'm at peace now," her mom said. Then the image was gone. Brandy woke up feeling relaxed and warm inside. Joey was next to her, kissing her gently on the lips. She told him she was happy, and he told her that he was happy to have her by his side. But, as he spoke, the risk they took by reuniting was in the back of his mind. He remembered the nightmare he had not too long ago, and the words of Ed Perez: "You and I will never be like normal people. Our past lives will always be with us. Watch your back amigo. *Hasta luego.*"

ACKNOWLEDGEMENTS

Editing a manuscript for style, grammar, punctuation, capitalization, and spelling can be a tedious job. I'm fortunate to know three people that had the mind set to do an excellent job of it. I wish to thank my wife, Jean Sundaram, who has an accounting background; my friend Bob Greiner, who has an analyst background; and my friend Gary Battel, aka The Weatherman, and former employee of NOAA, for the time and effort they put into it.

I want to thank my BETA readers: Col. Tom Genetti, Ret.; Mary H. Fox, Author; Tim Sosinski, retired architect and entrepreneur; and Anonymous for their valuable observations and suggestions.

I also want to thank Joe Hoolihan and the other members of the Savage Writers' Circle. Their critical evaluations and recommendations were very much appreciated. They made several suggestions on how to make the story a must read.

ABOUT THE AUTHOR

Peter Eisenhut is a graduate of Cornell University and the University of Rochester. His career experience includes employment by two multinational organizations, and as an independent consultant. He has expertise in process analysis and planning, as well as information and communications management. He is also an experienced writer and presenter. His mystery novels are inspired by his career experiences and his travels. *Final Project* follows his second novel, *The Boulder Creek Project* and his first novel, *The Pen Project*.

Peter lives in Columbia Maryland with his wife Jean. You can visit his website and blog at **www.petereisenhut-author.com**

Printed in the United States
by Baker & Taylor Publisher Services